SPECIA   **DERS**

TH ᴜⅬᵛᴇRˢCROFT FOUNDATION
(.3)

was established in 1972 to provide funds for research, diagnosis and treatment of eye diseases. Examples of major projects funded by the Ulverscroft Foundation are:-

- The Children's Eye Unit at Moorfields Eye Hospital, London
- The Ulverscroft Children's Eye Unit at Great Ormond Street Hospital for Sick Children
- Funding research into eye diseases and treatment at the Department of Ophthalmology, University of Leicester
- The Ulverscroft Vision Research Group, Institute of Child Health
- Twin operating theatres at the Western Ophthalmic Hospital, London
- The Chair of Ophthalmology at the Royal Australian College of Ophthalmologists

You can help further the work of the Foundation by making a donation or leaving a legacy. Every contribution is gratefully received. If you would like to help support the Foundation or require further information, please contact:

THE ULVERSCROFT FOUNDATION
The Green, Bradgate Road, Anstey
Leicester LE7 7FU, England
Tel: (0116) 236 4325

website: www.foundation.ulverscroft.com

Léan Cullinan grew up in a distinguished literary family and has been writing since childhood. She is a graduate of the MPhil in Creative Writing at Trinity College Dublin and sings in one of Ireland's finest choirs. An incurable textile nerd, she lives in Dublin with one husband and two sons.

Visit the author's website at:
www.leancullinan.com
Twitter: @leannich

THE LIVING

The Troubles may be officially over but, for the first generation to come of age in Ireland's flimsy peacetime, the ghosts of the past are all too close to home . . . Cate Houlihan is adrift in a life that doesn't feel her own, struggling with a new job at an eccentric publishing house and stifled by overbearing parents. When romance blossoms with the gorgeous, intelligent — and British — Matthew Taylor, it seems as if things might finally be going her way. But Cate's job brings her into contact with the country's Republican past. And the lines between this, her family, and her new relationship are beginning to blur . . .

LÉAN CULLINAN

THE LIVING

Complete and Unabridged

ULVERSCROFT
Leicester

First published in Great Britain in 2014 by
Atlantic Books Ltd
London

First Large Print Edition
published 2015
by arrangement with
Atlantic Books Ltd
London

The moral right of the author has been asserted

This novel is entirely a work of fiction. The names,
characters and incidents portrayed in it are the work
of the author's imagination. Any resemblance to
actual persons, living or dead, events or localities, is
entirely coincidental.

A catalogue record for this book is available
from the British Library.

ISBN 978–1–4448–2433–9

Published by
F. A. Thorpe (Publishing)
Anstey, Leicestershire

Set by Words & Graphics Ltd.
Anstey, Leicestershire
Printed and bound in Great Britain by
T. J. International Ltd., Padstow, Cornwall

This book is printed on acid-free paper

For Niall

This is what it feels like: I have been unzipped, yanked open with grubby fingers. They are rummaging through my contents. My heart clenches in the unlooked-for light. I'm unable to pull back from the search, pinned as I am to this chair.

In reality, of course, they have not gone so far as to pin me. No need. I am seated at a plain table of the institutional sort, one leg of which is slightly askew. When I lean on the surface with my bare forearms, it rocks, making my drink of water slosh in its plastic cup. My throat hurts. The room has been painted recently. It has that smooth, echoey smell and no dirt in the corners. Little runnels of emulsion have dripped and dried below the ledge of the high, barred window.

The questions come like waves, or like the statements and developments of a sonata — themes elaborated, contrasted, juxtaposed. I am a poor participant in this performance. I don't have adequate answers.

I feel sick. My mind spins wildly, spiralling out in all the nightmare directions. I look down at the tabletop and try to breathe

1

deeply. I finish my water. I have no idea why I'm here. Not really. I'm cold and sore and stupid, no doubt, and possibly in great danger. I'm trying not to follow the spiral that leads to the real pain of the night, the agony of discovering that I've been duped, led on, lied to, used as a pawn in this filthy game by someone I believed I could trust.

I'm trying not to think about the gun.

Part One

Holding the Line

I was deep in the dream that dogged me — endless variations on a theme: trying to find a place to have sex. This time it was at a party in a strange chaotic house, trailing from room to room, beds heaped with slippy coats, and I was half-undressed, cold and tense, and none of the doors would lock, and people kept peering in at the two of us through windows I hadn't noticed, and the boy I was with had spotty shoulders, and someone in the distance was singing trills . . .

When I opened my eyes I didn't immediately remember where I was. The window was too big and too close. Sunlight surged in around the edges of the curtains. I killed the alarm on my phone and sat up in this too-narrow bed as the day drifted into focus. The bed's owner, an ex of mine — although apparently not ex enough — was nowhere in evidence. For a minute I was still, enjoying the cool air on my naked back, taking long breaths and feeling my way around the hangover. I looked at my phone again: I'd had less than three hours' sleep. Probably still slightly drunk. I yawned, and there crept over me a sort of glossy alertness that I knew would let me down later on.

I heaved myself out of bed and dressed slowly, trying not to think too hard about the day ahead. This would be my first hangover at work since I'd started there. I breathed a fervent wish that no one would notice.

It dawned on me only as I fished in my handbag for a comb that the little rat must've left without saying goodbye. That was all askew, this being his place, not mine. Presumably, he felt Denise could entertain me well enough. I called that taking liberties. He'd never have done it while we were still going out.

I went slowly downstairs, feeling off balance, precarious. When I got to the kitchen I found Denise sitting at the table, painting her fingernails and reading something on her phone. She looked up. 'Oh, there you are. Come here, are you guys back together or what?' Always the diplomat. The Louth flavour was completely gone from her accent. *Our Dee from Ardee*, she'd been called when she and I had arrived up in Trinity College five years ago, all fresh-faced and ready for action. She'd worked hard to shed the monicker. To hear her now, you'd have sworn she was born and bred in Dublin 4.

I ventured a grin. 'No, we just . . . had a relapse. We probably shouldn't have.'

Denise had been going out with a nice tidy boy since third year. She had no patience with my messier approach. She lowered her chin in a combative sort of way, which for a dizzying second flashed her resemblance to her rat of a cousin. 'Well. Do you want tea?'

'Stay where you are — I'll make it.' I moved across to the counter and switched on the kettle.

Denise swiped at her screen, careful not to smudge her nails. I made tea in the big orange pot I'd given her for Christmas a few years ago. My hands were cold now, and my guts had begun to stir upsettingly. That bottle of take-out wine had been a mistake. So had drinking midweek in the first place — I should've held firmer.

'Have a yoghurt or something,' Denise said as I opened the fridge for milk.

I sat down and poured the tea.

Denise said, 'So, any scandal? You've got a real job now, haven't you? How's life, workin' for the Man?' She punctuated her last question with a theatrical wiggle.

'It's going pretty well.' I told her a bit about Bell Books, the tiny, old-fashioned publisher where I'd recently started working, and my attempts to crank its clunky, steam-powered website into the twenty-first century. I realized as I spoke that I really did like this job, which was a novel sensation. I'd temped for a year before getting it, and had been lucky to escape with my soul.

'Didn't what's-her-face think you should work in publishing? Career guidance woman?'

I recalled our career guidance teacher — bottle-end glasses, fluffy jumpers, permanently anxious expression. 'O'Connell? Yeah, I think she said that.'

'Well, there you are.'

Denise talked about her research group, her supervisor's deadpan sense of humour, the frustration of contaminated lab samples. She was trying to get hold of a fresh batch before some atomic deadline incomprehensible to me. As she talked I remembered her at the age of eight: so excited by life, bucktoothed and purposeful, so certain about her future. 'I'm going to be a scientist.' And here she was.

Not for the first time, I felt wistful for the student life, the freedom of it, the elastic pace. There was a distance between me and Denise now that had never been there before.

I stayed until it was clear I'd be late for work. 'What are you up to today, anyway?' I asked as I put on my jacket.

'I'm going in to college in a while. Oh, I'm meeting the lads tonight in town. O'Neill's, I think. If you felt like joining us?'

Joining us? What was that about? Did they think I'd become a different person? The only one of our gang who hadn't gone straight into a postgrad degree. I quelled my irritation and said I'd probably be along.

Outside, July was making a late bid to redeem itself. Clear sunshine and exactly enough breeze. Good augury, I thought, as I hurried out of Denise's estate and down the road towards the tram stop. The light, the liquid air, the crisp shadows, made even Dundrum look picturesque.

Despite the breeze, I quickly broke out in a sour, hungover sweat, dampening yesterday's shirt. I wasn't going to pull off today, was I? Even if I managed to keep it more or less together, they were bound to notice the smell. My mood darkened. Last night hadn't been worth this. Not even close.

A tram arrived soon after I reached the stop. I sat at the window, leaning my temple against the glass and hating everything. Stupid trees. Stupid birds. Stupid sky.

When I thought about the prospect of meeting the others in O'Neill's tonight, the energy drained from me still further. Oh . . . I could go for a bit, couldn't I? It would be good to see everyone. Catch up on all their news. They'd be talking about their research woes and swapping tall stories. Drinking till closing time, then back to Denise's house for more drink, leading seamlessly into the political ranting and rebel songs. That was the drill. I was tired of it.

I began to spot registration numbers to sing, a habit I'd picked up from my first proper boyfriend in college. Each number represented a note of the scale, with zero being a rest. Ignoring year and county, the game was to find a number corresponding to a tune. It passed the time.

A white hatchback at Windy Arbour had 11566, which was almost 'Twinkle, Twinkle, Little Star', but not quite.

Not quite didn't count. You had to play by the rules. Stupid numbers.

⋆　⋆　⋆

At least let me slip into work without George noticing. Bell Books was on the top floor of a big, shabby Victorian house in Rathmines. George, who owned the lot, lived in the basement, and the middle floor had for decades been occupied by a dressmaker, now deceased. I opened the cast-iron gate, wincing at its screaming hinges, and walked up the garden path past the wicked old tree that overshadowed it. George's office window looked on to the front garden. Maybe he'd be away at a meeting, or something. Fingers crossed.

I crept up the uncarpeted stairs, but I was out of luck: before I rounded the return I heard George's guffaw booming from the open door of the main office. His voice carried clearly down the stairwell. 'Of course, our friend was having none of it, and muggins here — standing there like a big eejit — and did he say one word to your man? Not at all!'

Another man gave the response — 'Not at all! Nottattall!' His voice was a peculiar combination of breathy and shrill.

When I entered the office I found George talking to a man I hadn't seen before. They stood in the middle of the room, and seemed to occupy the entire space. Paula, the editor, was at her desk by the window, working on some proofs.

Our visitor was not as tall as George, but nearly twice as wide. His head sat squarely on massive, sloping shoulders. He was dressed in cords and tweed, with a pale check shirt buttoned up tightly under his chin. Fine, dark hair covered the top of his freckled scalp and made a little frill at his collar.

George wiped a tear of mirth from the corner of one eye with a thumb knuckle. The gesture flowed into a gracious acknowledgement of my arrival. 'Ah, here she is, our new recruit.'

The stranger beamed at me.

'Hello,' I said. As George seemed to expect me to go on, I added, 'I'm Cate Houlihan.'

'John Lawless,' said the man, extending a well-upholstered hand for me to shake.

'Pro-*fessor* John Lawless, no less,' corrected George, 'of UCD. The professor here is going to write us a preface for one of our forthcoming books.' He turned to Lawless with a meaningful look. 'John, this is Fintan Sullivan's niece, would you believe.'

John Lawless opened his mouth, widened his eyes and drew his head slowly back in an exaggerated pantomime of comprehension. 'Ah, yes,' he said, and I thought I detected a hint of a Northern accent. 'You have the look of your uncle, all right.'

I decided Lawless must be one of Uncle Fintan's friends from that unlikely dreamtime before my memory, *his radical youth* — like George, in fact, who had offered me this job, sight unseen, on the strength of the association. They probably all knew each other back in the day. I tried to picture the three of them together — my neat little uncle in his jacket and tie, dwarfed by these bulky men.

Lawless nodded in confirmation of his assessment. 'You'd be Nora's daughter, so.' He turned back to George. 'The offspring of the Countess herself, is it? You'd better watch your back, now, George, with a child of Nora Sullivan's at large. She'll be rising through the ranks in no time at all. Look to your laurels, I'd say, ha?'

'Oh, sure, I know, sure,' said George. 'Cate'll be running the show before we know where we are.'

I went to my desk. Apparently my late arrival was going to be overlooked. As my computer woke up I tried to reconcile my idea of Mum with this fresh view of her. 'The Countess'? I couldn't see it, frankly.

George said, 'Come on, so, we'll get down to business. I have Eddie's first draft here.' The two men moved towards the inner office.

'Any word on the revision?' asked Lawless.

'Ah, no. We're still waiting on him to find a way to get it to me. He won't trust the e-mail or the post. Old habits die hard, says you.'

Lawless left in the mid-morning, and George interrupted Paula for a report on her doings. In the middle of their discussion — final text of The Irish Horse just in, revised design spec sent to the typesetter, image proofs overdue — George looked at the time and announced that he was late for his meeting. He bundled some papers and a laptop into a new-looking case, swapped his jumper for a greenish tweed jacket, and whirled out the door.

I heard his footsteps on the stairs stop suddenly, then return. His grey mane popped round the edge of the door. 'Paula, I nearly forgot. Eddie's book.'

'Oh, yeah?' Paula wrinkled her face into a sceptical mask.

'Your man in London wants sight of the full manuscript before he'll talk to us.'

'And?'

George came all the way back into the room. 'And . . . John agrees with me — it's weak — it's full of Eddie's usual bullshit. I've basically told him to rewrite it. I don't want to show it to your man as it is. What do you think?'

'Lookit, George, how is this even a question? You have to show it to him. He's not going to make an offer until he sees what he's buying.'

George made a dismissive sound and shook his head.

Paula pressed on. 'He's a publisher, for god's sake, he knows what a first draft looks like. It might be a bit raggedy, but it's all there. Wouldn't you want to see it, if it was you? You would of course. This is totally normal, George.'

'Arrah, it's annoying, is what it is. It's sensitive stuff. We need some guarantees.'

'It's just bad timing, is all. Any idea when we'll have the new version?'

'Haven't a clue. Sure you know the way Eddie is. We know not the day nor the hour.'

'Well, what about . . . Could we put off talking to your man until we have the revision?'

George considered this. 'Not really. He's ready to turn tail, I'd say. I want to get the contract signed, sealed and delivered. It's a case of strike while the iron is hot.'

'Then you're going to have to show him the bloody thing, George.'

George turned on his heel, clutched his hair, then spoke to the ceiling. 'OK. If he rings, tell him it's in the post.'

'It will be,' said Paula, unsmiling. 'Go to your meeting.' I admired how Paula stood up to George. They'd worked together for years, and she had no reverence for him.

George left again, and an ecclesiastical silence descended upon the office. Paula hunched and frowned over her work, sucking coffee at intervals from an insulated mug. I opened up the database for the new Bell Books website and continued copying information across.

Most of the firm's recent output had titles like *Castles of Ireland*, *Coastal Walks in Ireland*, *The Secret Life of the Irish*

Lighthouse. I'd seen them on the shelves: thick, heavily illustrated volumes with hard covers and dust jackets — the worthy sort of book you might find in Uncle Fintan and Auntie Rosemary's house in Swords. Besides these, there were several series of State and semi-State publications — policy papers, research reports and other institutional utterances. George called this 'the bread-and-butter work', and I'd picked up the impression that it might have been given to Bell Books as a favour.

There was also a rather more intriguing category, which hadn't been added to in some years. It included titles like *Thatcher's Gulag*, *This Is My Country*, *Red Hand of Murder* and *Heroes of H-Block*. Most of them were out of print now. As a teenager, when everything was clear and there were no grey areas, I would've devoured them. I'd half-wondered about getting hold of some of them for Micheál, my brother — he seemed to be even more steeped in all this stuff than I'd been at his age.

Yes, I liked this job. I loved that George had named the company after a detail in an old legend: the story of Mad Sweeney, undone by the tolling of a church bell. The atmosphere in this quiet, messy office was unlike any I'd encountered before. There was little of the activity I was used to from temping: the flurries of coming and going, the constant phone calls, the dance of drafts and deadlines. Work here was methodical, slow and thorough. It reminded me of the library in college, but during the more peaceful parts of the year, not the frenzy of exam time. I'd thrived in that industrious calm, researching my essays, reading in spacious circles around my courses — and further, often spending entire afternoons browsing through the shelves of the Stacks.

After several weeks at Bell Books, I'd grown adept at navigating the office land-scape — the network drive, stationery, e-mail templates and phone enquiries — and I enjoyed George's confidence in me with regard to the new website. George was irascible, but warm and articulate, and he clearly cared a lot about his work. He had a trick of looking at you sideways through those narrowed eyes, sizing you up, making mental notes — then opening out into a disarming smile.

'How are you getting on, there, you OK?' Paula rose from her desk.

'Grand, yeah.'

'I've to go down to the post office now, before George gets back and changes his mind. If Martin Bright's office phones from

London about the MacDevitt project, tell them the manuscript is on its way.' She disappeared into George's office, to emerge a few minutes later carrying a large envelope and wearing a sour expression. 'I think Eddie's the only author we've had this century who won't use e-mail. I ask you. In this day and age.'

'Is he a bit eccentric?'

'Fuckin' throwback, excuse my French.' And with that, she left.

*   *   *

July rolled into August, the limpid evenings just beginning to deepen at the edges, with perhaps a faint impatience to get on to autumn. The weather continued fine, and I continued to like my job. My parents and Mícheál went on their annual holiday in Kerry; I consolidated my recent tradition of declining to join them there.

On a Thursday evening at the end of the month, I headed into town for the first choir rehearsal of the season. I arrived a few minutes early and went to join some of the others by the piano. Tom Silke, impeccable as always in a waistcoat and tie, turned to greet me. 'Well, *a Chaitlín*, and how are we this clement evening?' Tom was one of very few people from whom I'd tolerate my given name. He leaned in close. 'Come here to me, did you see our new tenor?'

I looked around but noticed nobody unfamiliar.

'Oh, is he not here? He must be in the jacks. He's an absolute dish, if you like them a bit grainy.'

'Fresh blood, is it?' It was rare enough in Dublin choral circles, particularly on the tenor line.

'Yes, indeed,' said Tom. 'Mizz Duffy has come up trumps. Our lightning conductor. Connections in all directions. Don't ask me how she got hold of him.'

The choir began to cohere; I took my usual seat among the altos. The door to the corridor squealed, and a stranger edged into the room. He was quite tall, slim but not skinny, and he had curly dark hair and large, deep-set eyes. I put him in his late twenties, maybe even thirty. He carried himself well — straight-necked, square-shouldered, grace-ful as he walked towards the empty chair beside Tom. He hadn't shaved. I could hear Tom's voice in my head: *if you like them a bit grainy*.

Diane Duffy, our faultlessly coiffed con-ductor, raised her hands for quiet. 'Welcome everybody, welcome back! OK, I'd like to start . . . ' She waited for the simmer of talk to subside. 'I'd like to start with a very warm welcome to Matthew Taylor. Wave to the nice people, Matthew.'

Heads swivelled to acknowledge the new-comer, who said, 'Hello.'

'Matthew's here to help with that little tenor famine we were having,' Diane went on. 'He'll be joining us for our Belfast gig in November, anyway, and I hope for the Christmas concert as well. Matthew, thanks for coming on board — I hope you enjoy yourself.'

'I'm sure I will, thanks,' Matthew said. He sounded English. I decided I wouldn't hold it against him.

'Speaking of Belfast,' Diane went on, 'I hope everyone got the e-mail about that. Here's the sign-up sheet. Pass it round, and cross out your name if you definitely can't be there.' She handed the list to one of the sopranos. 'Now, they want a twenty-minute set from us, the usual old favourites, plus we'll be joining with two other choirs to perform a newly commissioned work — of which more later. This is a big opportunity for Carmina Urbana, and we'd obviously all like to do a superb job, yes? OK, good.'

The sign-up sheet reached me with no names crossed out; I passed it on.

Diane was still speaking. 'And I'm also putting the finishing touches to our Christmas concert programme. It will feature, by popular request, *Chichester Psalms*, which if you don't know it is by Leonard Bernstein and is absolutely delicious.'

An appreciative murmur ran round the room.

Diane turned away to the piano and thumped out a major chord, then faced the room again, hands poised, commanding. 'Now, on a very gentle *ooo*.' She pointed at each section and gave the notes. 'Listening for tuning and blend, then altos drop a semitone on my cue — three, four . . . '

We settled into our warm-up exercises, then worked through a Mendelssohn *Benedictus*. I noticed Matthew Taylor's voice behind me on the tenor line — full and strong, but light. It sounded like a trained voice. He was better than Tom, I realized, and much better than any of the other tenors.

During the break I drifted over to where the two of them were talking.

'Allow me to present Cate Houlihan, the *sine qua non* of the alto line,' intoned Tom. 'Matthew went to Cambridge, it turns out. He seems to have picked up one or two singing tips there.'

A shy dimple appeared on Matthew's cheek. 'I was just asking Tom about these concerts that are coming up.'

Tom took the cue. 'Yes, well, we've got this gig up North in November — vee prestigious although musically bankrupt, one suspects — and then I think our proper concert is in the second week of December.'

'Our *proper* concert,' Matthew repeated. 'I see how it is. I take it Belfast will be improper?'

'That's entirely up to you, dear boy — I'm not responsible for your conduct.' Tom was caricaturing himself.

'What brings you to Dublin?' I asked Matthew.

He was a PhD student, he explained, come to do some research in the UCD history department. He'd been in Dublin for just a few weeks. He'd visited on a family holiday several years ago, but he couldn't remember much. He liked it, so far.

'UCD,' sniffed Tom. 'Well, you weren't to know.'

Matthew looked a little alarmed.

'Tom lectures in Trinity,' I told him.

'And my father before me!' said Tom.

Matthew gave a slight bow. 'I'll bear it in mind.'

Diane called the choir to order. 'Little treat for you now.' She had a stack of music, which she distributed in bundles to be passed along. 'It's our peace anthem for Belfast!'

I looked at my copy: *A Song of Ireland* was

printed across the top. Over to the right, the composer's name.

'Trevor Daintree?' Tom rumbled behind me. 'Never heard of him.'

We started with a relatively easy passage from around the middle of the piece, in which the men held long, mild discords on open vowels while the women ambled above them in thirds and fourths. After that, though, the harmonies became less obvious, the Latin text twisted itself around our tongues, and we became mired in the complex rhythms.

'Is there a particular reason,' Tom mused, 'why this Trevor Daintree person was not drowned at birth?'

Diane laughed with the rest of us. 'We're not really feeling the love, are we? Maybe it'll grow on us. OK, once more from bar one-eighty-three, and then we'll do some nice Bernstein.'

★ ★ ★

The little pub round the corner, where we always went after rehearsal, was hot and full of breath. The television was on, tuned to some match. Ollie, the barman, knew us well. He raised his hand in greeting as we trooped in, and spotted Matthew. 'What's this, a new victim?'

We ordered drinks. Matthew had a

Guinness, earning much macho backslapping from the others. 'I drink it in England too,' he said, 'but it's really not the same.'

In the jostle for seats, I ended up beside him. Or was it that he ended up beside me? That was an appealing thought. He smiled as we sat down, as though to acknowledge our prior acquaintance. His mouth was finely contoured, with a perfectly crisp boundary where the dusky pink of his lips ended and the white skin began.

'So,' he said, 'what do you do when you're not singing?'

'In those rare moments, you mean? I work for a publisher.'

'Oh?' His elegant eyebrows registered interest. 'I was a publisher's reader for a few years, before I bit the bullet and re-entered academia. What house do you work for?'

House seemed an impossibly elevated term for George's outfit. 'You won't have heard of it. It's tiny. It's called Bell Books.'

He flexed the corners of his eyes. 'Hmmm. I think I might have, actually. Do you publish mainly Irish interest?'

I couldn't help smiling. 'All Irish publishers publish mainly Irish interest,' I told him gently.

He looked slightly embarrassed. I watched the tiny ridges on his lower lip, how they caught the light. His ear, too, was particularly lovely — a dainty pink swirl that hugged the side of his head, framed bewitchingly by dark curls. He said, 'But no, I'm sure I have come across you before. Bell Books. You don't do fiction, do you?'

'No, it's all government reports, touristy books, history, that sort of thing.'

'Ah, that's it. I think my supervisor is writing a preface for one of your books.'

'Is your supervisor John Lawless?'

'Yes, that's right, he was telling me about it last week.' Matthew seemed unconcerned by the coincidence, which was a good one, I felt, even by Irish standards. He went on, 'What's the author's name again?'

'Eddie MacDevitt,' I said, and immediately got the feeling that perhaps I shouldn't have. 'But I'm not — I don't — I'm not working on that project. I don't really work on the books themselves.'

'Don't you?'

'I just do the website, and correspondence and stuff.' It was my turn to be embarrassed. Suddenly, my job seemed meaningless and dull.

'That could be fun,' said Matthew. 'What's Eddie MacDevitt like as a correspondent?'

He was so keen, I wished I had something exciting to tell him. 'I don't know,' I said. 'My boss is handling the whole thing himself.'

'I see,' he said. I tried to fight the conviction that I'd somehow blown my chance at a first impression.

We turned our attention to the general conversation. Val Dunne, a fellow alto, was unhappy. 'Wait — what? They want our actual *names*?' She was addressing Joan Richardson, the hearty Englishwoman who acted as benign dictator of the choir committee and stiffened the musical sinews of the soprano line.

Joan said, 'Yes, that's right, we have to send a complete list to Belfast next week. Names, contact details, dates of birth, the lot.'

'Dates of birth? You're joking!'

'No, it's all seriously official.'

Val wasn't giving up. 'So you're saying, some random fuckers up in Belfast are going to have my name and address and phone number and e-mail and fucking *shoe size*?'

'But, Val, they're not random fuckers.' The obscenity sounded peculiar in Joan's mouth. 'It's the Civil Service. They're responsible people. This is a high-profile event. They need to know who's going to be there, that's all.' Her tone was cajoling now. 'Yes, all right, they're going a bit overboard with the red tape, but you know how bureaucrats are.'

Val sat back and scowled at her shiny red fingernails. 'Well, I don't see how having my mobile number is going to help them, is all.'

'I'm sorry,' said Joan. 'It's a condition of our doing the gig.' She looked deflated. She and Val were housemates — perhaps she was worrying about stony silence in their shared spaces.

I left soon after that and went for my bus. Waiting at the stop, I sang the registration numbers of a few passing vehicles. Just as I spotted my bus turning the corner, a large dark saloon car manoeuvred out of a nearby parking spot and rolled slowly away from me. I read its number: 52845. Tricky. Was there something there? *52845*: I whistled it under my breath . . .

Aha! It was the opening of *Chichester Psalms*, which we'd been rehearsing earlier. How gratifying that I was now in a position to make this catch. I wouldn't have known it two hours ago. A complete phrase too — very rare. It boded well for the coming season, I decided. I bounced up and down as I hailed the slowing bus, and grinned. I felt oddly as though I'd accomplished something.

★ ★ ★

Back in my flat I made a cup of tea and sat at the table in the living room looking out at the soft darkness. Through the window I could

27

see the top branches of the young ash tree that grew on the pavement opposite. They hadn't been visible earlier in the year. They waved at me, and I waved gently back.

On reflection, I wasn't too worried about having made a bad first impression with Matthew. It had been OK. Anyway, he was the one who'd gone all nerdy about my job. I wondered fleetingly if he was thinking about me too — a squishy thought, and one that required prompt management. I'd better find something to bring me back down to earth.

I switched on the radio as I tidied up. There was an interview with some dried-up academic about recent outbreaks of trouble in the North. Dissident Republicans rearing their scaly heads again. A couple of weapon stashes, a punishment beating, a bomb plot mercifully foiled. Dr Expert described in careful, polysyllabic detail how these ongoing paramilitary activities could ultimately, if unchecked, precipitate an unthinkable return to historical instabilities. Both interviewer and interviewee spoke with assured middle-class Dublin accents, the rounded intonation of entitlement and benign dispassion. The sound evoked the flavour of home. School-days, back a decade or more. Homework in front of me on the dining table. Radio voices floating in from the kitchen. Head down as

28

Mum and Dad argued about the same old, same old news: *Republican ceasefire — would it hold?*

'Nora, they got what they came for, and they need to do the decent thing now — lay down their arms and not be acting the maggot.'

'They're not acting the maggot, Paddy. This wasn't what they came for. This was never about bureaucracy. You know that as well as I do. This is about beliefs. This is about history. This is about *blood*.'

* * *

Nothing could possibly have appealed to me less that Sunday than a trip to Ardee. There were so many arguments against it, starting with enforced interaction with my family and going right through to the fact that my car (which wasn't really mine) was having one of its periodic crises. I wished I'd stood up to Mum when she'd rung. But Sunday lunch with Uncle Fintan and Auntie Rosemary was nearly as immutable as Mass itself. From time to time, it simply had to be endured.

It might not be so terrible — I hadn't seen Uncle F in ages. Then again, Mum had been hassling me to talk to him about my rent, which he'd set at a nominal rate when I'd

29

moved in here. I sat in my living room, gulping down coffee and thinking of my uncle, his bemusement at the prosperity that his little investment in the eighties had brought. Even now, no negative equity for him.

Out in the street, I encountered my downstairs neighbours, Sheila and Aidan. Their smart black hatchback stood agape. Sheila turned from the car as I emerged, and walked back towards the house, carrying a small potted bush in one hand and some garden tools in the other: a matching spade and fork, a trowel hanging from her finger by a leather loop. More plants stood on the footpath where they'd been unloaded from the car.

'Hiya, Cate,' said Sheila. The tools were gleaming new, unsullied by soil or stone.

Aidan was wrestling a plastic-wrapped futon mattress out of the car. He lifted his chin in greeting. 'How's it going?' He looked groomed, as always, in pristine jeans and a pale green shirt.

'Here, let me give you a hand,' I heard myself say. I took hold of the slippery package at its nearest corner and tugged at it.

Aidan murmured and shook his head, but I stuck to my guns. I could feel the strain in my shoulder muscles. Why was I persisting? We heaved the thing on to the footpath as Sheila came back.

'Thanks,' she said. 'My folks are coming for a visit next week, so we're trying to make the place look a bit respectable.'

'Ah, hence the plants and everything.' I nodded.

'I know! We actually asked Mr Sullivan ages ago and he said we could plant whatever we liked out the back, but then do you think we did anything about it? So now we've just got a few bits and pieces and we're going to stick them in and see what happens.' She spoke rapidly, in an unceasing stream. 'Is he well, anyway?'

'Uncle Fintan? Yeah, I think he's in good form.'

'Oh, that's good. He was off to Spain on his holidays when we saw him last. He was due a holiday, I'd say.' Sheila shook her head sadly. 'I thought he was looking awful tired.'

'Ah, yeah,' I agreed. I was beginning to edge away.

'And how's the new job? Going well?'

The last time we'd spoken had been the morning of my first day at Bell Books. 'It's going great,' I said.

'Well, that's good,' said Sheila.

'Listen, I'd better ... ' I raised a valedictory hand and began to move towards my car, which was parked across the narrow street.

31

As I walked, the engine of a car parked a little way down the road hummed to life. I looked at it, and felt a tiny thrill of recognition as I realized that it had the same registration number as the one I'd seen a few days ago: 52845, the opening phrase of *Chichester Psalms*. Funny how Dublin seemed so big, yet you ended up crossing the same people's paths all the time. Was this the same car? I couldn't remember the make or year of the one I'd seen before, so I couldn't tell for sure.

'Spooky,' I said to the ash tree as I fished for my keys.

It was shortly after I took the Ardee exit off the M1 that my car decided to stage its big huff. Suddenly and inexorably, it slowed, ignoring my frantic pumping of the accelerator. I was lucky to be able to indicate, brake and pull over before the momentum dissipated altogether. I switched off the engine and sat in silence, gathering my resources.

When I felt ready, I phoned the house. Dad answered — just home from Mass, grudgingly willing to head back out and help me.

'OK, bye, Dad, thanks a million.' I felt like a fifteen-year-old who'd missed the last bus. Mortified. Beholden.

My accent, too, had slipped back into its old patterns: the Louth lilt bleeding easily through the Trinity College patina that I'd taken such care to build up. Cate from Ardee. Such a comedy hometown — you could never admit to it without some Dublin fucker exclaiming 'Arrrrdeeee!' in what he fondly imagined to be a Louth accent.

But you couldn't lie about it either. Someone would always know.

Dad pulled up across the road and motioned for me to wind down my window. 'Leave that car where it is — I'll get the young fella from Lanigans to pick it up in the morning.'

Back at the house, I followed Dad into the hall just as Mum came out of the kitchen, arms outstretched. 'Caitlin! It's lovely to see you, pet. Come on in — we're all set.'

'Hi, Mum.' I gave her a brief hug and avoided eye contact. Why wasn't she having a go at me?

'Look who's here!' Mum exclaimed, unnecessarily, as we went into the dining room. Uncle Fintan, Auntie Rosemary and my brother Mícheál were seated at the table, under starter's orders. Mum took two quick steps towards Uncle Fintan and said in a pantomime whisper, 'Is she up to date with the rent? Is she?'

I flinched. 'Mum!' This was a bit much, even in the circumstances.

Uncle Fintan gave his soft laugh. 'Oh, yes, Nora, she's. Sure isn't she a model tenant?'

His voice was gentle and slightly blurred, still carrying that distinct Castlebar accent that he shared with Mum. I'd always loved his trick of breaking off before he finished a sentence. He spoke with a slow expansiveness, his vowels like clear pools of water. He beamed at me, and suddenly I was included in the joke.

Chair legs barked on the wooden floor as everyone settled themselves at the table; heads bowed in appropriate humility as Dad mumbled 'Bless-us-oh-Lord'. I found myself mouthing 'Amen'.

I was sitting beside Auntie Rosemary, who sprang up as soon as grace was said to help Mum serve the soup.

Uncle Fintan was his usual yielding, nervous self, his eyes tracking his wife as she moved around the room. She wore a double string of glass beads that oscillated and clicked as she stretched to put the bowls on the table. Her arms were nut-brown from her holiday.

'Tha — thank you, that's,' said Uncle Fintan as Mum gave him his soup. Dad ate noisily, rumbled approval. Mícheál, gangly and shiny-faced, stared at his placemat and tapped the tabletop with his spoon while he waited to be served.

Was he *sulking*?

The soup was too salty, just as Dad liked it. Roast pork followed, with mounds of mashed potato, limp baby vegetables, and a shallow jug of viscous, cooling gravy.

Conversation, at first, was confined to praise of the food.

Mum tutted as she tucked into her mash. 'This needs more pepper.' She frowned at the table, where no pepper was in evidence, then turned to Mícheál. 'Would you get the pepper for me, love?'

Mícheál rolled his eyes, hauled himself to his feet, stumped over to the hatch, reached into the kitchen for the pepper-grinder, slouched back to the table, and set the pepper down beside Mum with a little thump, like a chess piece, before resuming his seat. I squirmed on his behalf — the whole performance had been so pathetically immature.

Mum let out a tiny, outraged *Ah!* and bounced back in her chair as though she'd been hit. 'Mícheál Houlihan, I'm surprised at you!'

Mícheál studied his clasped hands.

'What's this, now?' Dad wanted to know.

Mum sighed and said, 'Is this about the flag?'

'What about the flag? What flag?' Dad asked.

Mum smirked in a way that would have made me feel murderous if I'd been in Mícheál's place. 'It's his tricolour,' she explained. 'Apparently it got dirty after the match yesterday.'

'PJ threw his boot at me!' Mícheál burst out. 'It hit me on the arm, and then my bag was open and it fell in. And now my tri-colour's got mud on it, and it's dishonoured, and we have to burn it! We have to!' His eyes were wide, and his cheeks had turned a deep plummy pink.

'Don't be so ridiculous, Mícheál, we do not!' Mum lifted her hands in conciliation. 'We'll handwash it — we'll show it every care and respect — it'll be as good as new.'

'It won't be, Mam, it's dishonoured. We have to burn it. They told us at Irish college.' Mícheál finished triumphant — he had played his best card.

Ah, Irish college. Three weeks of cultural re-education in a rural idyll. Lustful teens chewing sausages and playing endless card games, all through the medium of the melodious Irish language — not a word of English allowed, or you were sent home.

Mum drew herself up and said, 'The rule, as I recall, is that the flag must not drag on the ground.'

'It has a muddy bootmark on it!'

'Well.' Mum pursed her lips.

'Mam!' Mícheál appealed to Uncle Fintan. 'I'm right, amn't I?'

I was aware of Auntie Rosemary taking a deep breath beside me. All eyes turned to Uncle Fintan.

'Well, I.' His voice wobbled.

'We have to burn it!'

Uncle Fintan's glance flicked between Mícheál and Auntie Rosemary, then settled on his sister. 'Well, Nora, we wouldn't have, now. It wouldn't have been considered fitting for the flag to be muddied, when I was.' He breathed out, and looked for a moment as though he wanted to say more, but instead slumped back in his chair.

Auntie Rosemary delivered a disgusted snort.

'There'll be no *burning* of any *flag* in my *house*.' Dad pronounced his verdict. No appeal. 'And, Mícheál, you'll know another time not to leave it lying around. All right?'

Mícheál glared briefly at him.

Dad put one big hand on the table and leaned slightly towards Mícheál. 'All right?'

'Yeah.' Mícheál nodded, dropped his eyes. The spotlight turned on me.

'Well, now, and I hear you're working for a publisher. Is that right?' Auntie Rosemary's elbow grazed my rib; her perfume colonized the space between us.

'Oh!' Mum put on her stricken face. *Where did we go wrong*, it said, *that you tell us so little about your life?* Out loud, she asked, with a hint of sourness, 'What's this, another temp thing?'

I was used to her game. I wasn't giving in. 'Yeah, kind of.' I took a drink. 'But it might lead to something a bit more long-term.'

'Who is it you're working for?' Dad avoided being cast in Mum's drama when he could.

'It's a guy called — ' I began, then caught Uncle Fintan's frightened eye. *No trouble, please*, I read. He didn't want me to mention George Sweeney. When he'd put us in touch he'd asked me to keep his involvement under my hat. 'It's called Bell Books,' I mumbled. I wanted to keep talking, to cover up the glitch and to avoid being asked how I'd heard about the job. 'It's a contact from a temp job I had last year,' I said, not looking at Uncle Fintan, hoping I wouldn't get caught in the lie. 'I think my old boss's cousin used to work for them, or something.'

'Well, you'll enjoy that, I'd say,' Auntie Rosemary said, after a pause. 'Publishing's an exciting business.'

'Seems interesting enough, all right,' I said. I had to steer us into safer waters. I asked Dad how his back was, and Mum took the bait. She and Auntie Rosemary began dissecting the question of men who won't go to the doctor, and I was finally able to relax.

'I think I'd better go home, actually,' I said as we stood up from the table. 'I'm not feeling brilliant.'

Mum pursed her lips. 'Are you coming down with something?' she asked — *you don't*

38

look after yourself properly clearly audible in her tone. 'You're very pale-looking.'

'No, it's just a headache.' I remembered the broken-down car. 'Have you a bus timetable handy?'

'I'll run you up,' said Uncle Fintan, sounding slightly breathless at his own audacity.

'Don't be daft, Fintan!' Mum exclaimed. 'It's miles away!'

'If she's not feeling well, I think,' Uncle Fintan said, standing up and sidling towards the door. 'And I've one or two things to check in the. Stay where you are, Rosemary — I'll be back before you know it.'

I hurried to get my coat before the combined forces would change his mind.

A Corelli concerto grosso sprang to life as Uncle Fintan started the car, and we conversed gently about styles of Baroque performance. I loved that he and I shared this interest — my musical tastes were so far from those of my parents and brother. I'd grown up with gravelly Dubliners and Wolfe Tones ringing in my ears.

'Caitlín — or — it's Cate I should be.' Uncle Fintan looked straight ahead at the road. 'I wanted to thank you, earlier, for.'

'That's OK,' I said. 'How did Auntie Rosemary hear about my job, then? Did you not tell her?'

'No, I didn't at all — I was as surprised as you when she.'

'She has spies everywhere!'

He laughed. 'She sees your neighbour Sheila at the Simon Community soup runs — maybe she mentioned.'

We fell silent. I shifted in my seat, steeling myself.

'Listen, Uncle F, there's something I need to ask you.'

'Oh?'

'Mum's worrying about the rent. My rent. She thinks it's too low. Are we . . . are we still . . . ?'

'Oh, lord bless us and save us, what's she? I wouldn't dream! Ah, sure, listen, love, don't be worrying about it at all.'

'Thanks — I really appreciate it.'

We were silent again, then I heard him take in breath. 'Come here to me, I was going to ask you a.'

I waited. He said nothing. 'Oh?' I ventured.

'There's something I have, for. It's a package for George Sweeney, I've had it in the car for a little while, looking for the chance to, and I wonder, could you?'

'Give it to him? Sure, no problem.'

'Oh, marvellous, that'll save me.'

The traffic was light, and we reached Terenure in a little over an hour. Uncle

Fintan got out of the car and opened the boot. I couldn't help staring as he pulled up the felt that covered the boot's floor and extracted from under it a large white envelope swaddled in shiny brown tape.

'This is what I was,' he said, 'for George.' He replaced the felt carefully and closed the boot. He held the package out to me, but he didn't meet my eye.

I took the envelope. It was heavy, and it had 'SEOIRSE MAC SUIBHNE' handwritten on it in green ink. It took me a second or two to parse this as the Irish version of George's name. There were no stamps. 'Right you are, Uncle F,' I said. 'I'll give it to him tomorrow.'

'Give it straight into his hand, now, won't you?'

'I'll do that.'

'And tell him . . . tell him I was asking for him.' Uncle Fintan looked suddenly straight at me; a gleam of enthusiasm — almost of mischief — passed across his face.

'I will, of course. Will you have a cup of tea before you go?'

'Ah, no, I'd better get. Rosemary will be.' He was already edging towards the driver's door.

As I carried the package up the stairs to my flat I tried to imagine George and Uncle Fintan's friendship, how it might have worked. When I thought about it, actually, it made a strange kind of sense. George would be the star, of course, with Uncle Fintan as his soft-spoken sidekick.

★ ★ ★

I gave George the envelope first thing on Monday. He thanked me, then turned and brandished it at Paula. 'Lookit here, now! Oh ye of little faith!'

'I never said anything!' she returned.

'Here we go,' said George as he ripped open the envelope. He took out a thick sheaf of paper and gripped it with one hand so he could flip through it. 'One revised manuscript, all present and correct. Thank you very much, young Cate.'

I moved to my desk.

'Did you know it was coming today?' Paula asked George.

'I had my suspicions,' said George. 'I had a postcard last week, hinting it was on its way.'

'Did he say Cate would be bringing it?'

'He did not. Need to know basis, Paula, need to know.'

'And did he give you any way of contacting him? Is it even worth asking?'

'Ah, he has to be careful, still.'

Paula pointed a finger at me. 'And how did

42

you get hold of it?' Her curiosity seemed coloured with irritation.

'Em . . . my uncle gave it to me.'

'Oh, right,' she said. 'Of course. Fintan 'The Gentleman' Sullivan. Well,' — she turned back to George — 'enjoy.'

George emitted a satisfied chuckle and disappeared into his office with the manuscript.

I was stung by Paula's tone. 'I didn't know you knew Uncle Fintan.'

'Oh, yeah,' she said, nodding slowly and catching the side of her lip between her teeth. 'One time, I did know him. Quite well. Haven't seen him in years.' She'd been gazing at the air above my head, but now she looked straight at me. 'Is he well, anyway, this weather?'

'Yeah, he's fine,' I said, and dropped it.

The atmosphere at work intensified by several notches after the arrival of that manuscript. On many days, I barely spoke a word. George and Paula were glued to their desks, and communal tea breaks became a rarity. I busied myself with the new database, which I'd almost finished populating.

George called me into his office one day and asked, with a careless gesture that belied the fervour in his eyes, if I'd be interested in trying my hand at some copyediting. There were a couple of big jobs coming in, he said, and Paula could do with the help. I had a degree in English, didn't I? Knew my spellings? Cared about grammar? I assented, and Paula gave me some basic training that afternoon, running cleanup macros on a set of conference proceedings. She was spiky and distracted — clearly up to her elbows in *The Irish Horse* — and my beginner's errors did nothing to improve matters. After a few days I decided I'd had enough spoonfeeding and would work it out for myself.

One afternoon the phone rang, and a woman's bored voice said, 'I have a reverse-charge call for George Sweeney from Ernie McDevil in Spain. Will you accept the charges?'

Flustered, I put her on hold. 'Paula? Can we accept reverse charges?'

Paula looked up. 'Who is it?'

'I think she said . . . Ernie McDevil? That's obviously — '

'Spain?' Paula asked sharply. She sprang from her chair and made for George's door. 'Put it through,' she said to me as she rapped twice on the door and opened it.

I took the operator off hold. 'Yes, we'll accept the charges, thank you.' I heard George whoop in the inner office.

A man's voice said, 'Seoirse?'

'Putting you through.'

Paula came back to her desk and resumed her chair without looking at me.

I said, 'That was Eddie MacDevitt, wasn't it? Bit cheeky to reverse the charges.'

She hesitated visibly before saying, 'Cate, do you *know* Eddie MacDevitt?'

'What? No, of course I don't know him. Why would you think that?'

She shook her head and looked at the floor. 'I dunno. I thought maybe . . . you might.' After another pause, she said, 'Lookit, trust me, Cate, you should count yourself lucky if you're not involved with that mess. Stick to your fisheries conference, is my advice to you.'

The afternoon slid by, unpunctuated by any further phone calls from the underworld.

★   ★   ★

I came into town after work to meet Denise in the Stag's Head, but went first to get fish and chips from Burdock's, the tiny chipper round the corner from Christ Church Cathedral. I joined the queue and studied the backlit wall menu, weighing the attractions of cod and sole.

Someone else came in as I was paying. I picked up my food, opened the packet a little to let my cod cool, and turned to encounter

45

the pleasing shape of Matthew Taylor.

'Hello!' he exclaimed, with that swooping English inflection that made him sound so much more surprised than he could possibly be.

'Hi.' I stood there, wreathed in fishy steam, letting the little flurry of pleasure subside. He was grinning at me, his teeth slightly uneven, crowding at the front of his mouth.

He bought chips, and we made small talk as we walked together towards Dame Street. The moon was visible above the buildings, a pale sliver like a clipped fingernail in the airy sky.

'Bell Books has quite an interesting backlist, hasn't it?' said Matthew.

'Have you been looking at our website?'

'I had a bit of a snoop around.'

'Really? Why?'

That shy dimple I'd seen before. 'Well, it's my period, you see — recent Irish history, the Republican movement and so forth. You actually published quite a few of the sources I used for my MPhil research.'

I bit off the end of a chip. 'Well,' I said, 'not me — I only started working there this summer.'

'Is that right? What's George Sweeney like to work for?'

'He's OK,' I said. This was the first time we'd really spoken since the evening he'd arrived at choir. Why did I feel, again, as though I were messing it up? Fantasy-Matthew never asked me this kind of question. I was already anxious about how I'd extricate myself from our conversation in time to meet Denise. What on earth could I say about George? 'He's a bit of a workaholic, maybe?'

'Arrives early and stays late, you mean?'

'Well, not so much that, since he lives downstairs. But I don't think he ever really stops, you know? The company is his life. He's very driven. Which is kind of inspiring, and kind of annoying.'

'Yes, I could see that.'

We were past City Hall, and I couldn't see Denise welcoming Matthew into our evening plans. 'Which way are you . . . I'm . . . going to meet my friend.' I took a large bite of cod and felt young and stupid.

'Oh, yes,' said Matthew. 'My bus stop's this way.'

We parted at the corner of South Great George's Street, and I proceeded towards Dame Lane.

A passage from *Chichester Psalms* was running through my head — halfway through the second movement, a furious invasion of sound from the male voices after a serene and gorgeous soprano passage. We'd spent a lot of time on diction at last night's rehearsal, taking advantage of Tom's expertise as a biblical scholar.

Lamah rag'shu, lamah rag'shu goyim, lamah
   rag'shu . . .
Ul'umim yeh'gu, ul'umim yeh'gu rik?

Tom had drilled the men in their glottals and gutturals. Diane had made a point of reading out the translation: it was a text I recognized from Handel's *Messiah*.

Why do the nations rage
And the people imagine a vain thing?

Bernstein's music was fractured and spiky, loud and sinister and brash.

Yoshev bashamayim
Yis'hak, Adonai
Yil'ag lamo!

insisted the men —

He that sitteth in the heavens
Shall laugh, and the Lord
Shall have them in derision!

And then the women came floating in again with their dreamy melody from the beginning of the movement, with the text of the Twenty-third Psalm — 'the Lord is my shepherd' — and a singular marking — 'blissfully unaware of threat'.

★ ★ ★

I ducked into the Stag's Head just as it began to drizzle. Denise had nabbed a table in the corner and was nursing a pint of cider. She greeted me in a parody of her old Ardee accent: 'How's Hoolie?'

'Call me that again, Missus, and I'll put your face through the wall.'

'Can't be going denying your roots, now.' Denise reached up to ruffle my hair.

I dodged her, sniffing in feigned dudgeon. 'I'm going to get a drink.'

Standing waiting for my Guinness to settle, I glanced along the bar to see if I recognized anyone. Several unmistakable Trinity students, of the sort who had frequented this place since time immemorial. Earnest, bespectacled men with Byronic hairstyles. A woman in dreadlocks and a black cape. A couple of excellent beards.

Two middle-aged men in suits looked as though they'd come to the wrong place. They were both drinking orange juice, and beads of sweat sparkled on their foreheads. One of them had big-lensed, silver-rimmed glasses, just like Dad's.

I carried my drink back to our table.

Two pints down, we were joined by some more of the old gang, and the evening grew loud and hilarious. Denise and some of the others wanted to go dancing, but I declined and went to catch the bus.

The cold night air was a pleasant shock. Energized by time passed in good company, I sped along to Dame Street and on down towards Trinity. The pedestrian lights were with me, and I didn't break stride until I got to my bus stop outside the Provost's House. It had begun to drizzle, but my wait was not long. I sat upstairs on the bus and smiled out into the darkness.

I got off one stop early and went to the shop to get bread for the morning. As I stood waiting to pay, my attention was drawn to another customer. A man: I saw him in profile, silhouetted against the milk cabinet.

He was middle-aged, dressed in a grey suit, with glasses just like Dad's. I was suddenly certain he was one of the two men I'd seen earlier in the Stag's Head.

What — had he *followed* me? Was he some kind of stalker? My stomach tensed.

Don't be ridiculous. He must just live nearby.

I left the shop still anxious, paused a few steps down the road, took out my phone and pretended to be texting.

After a few moments the man came out and walked in the opposite direction from me. He got into the passenger seat of a car parked a little way down from the shop. I turned and began walking again, telling myself to leave it alone, not to be so stupid. I must have been aware of the car's engine starting up, because I knew exactly when to glance as it drove by.

A kick of adrenalin as the car passed me: it had that same *Chichester Psalms* registration number I'd seen before. Which — surely — meant that they *were* following me, this man and his unseen driver — that they'd quite possibly been following me for weeks. I tried to recall exactly where and when I'd seen the car before, but no memory would stay still for me. Even as I told myself not to make a mountain out of a molehill — that everything could be simply explained — my mind whirled and my tongue thickened with fear.

I hurried home, my heart hammering.

Part Two

Modulations

I put the man with the big-lensed spectacles out of my mind. There was absolutely nothing I could do about him. Sunday lunch in Ardee, meanwhile, was a necessary evil, since I wanted my car back. Dad drove it to collect me at the bus stop. 'Now,' he said, 'I got Lanigans to throw in an oil change for free, and I've given her a tankful of petrol.'

'Thanks, Dad.' I wished he wouldn't keep buying me petrol. It was an encroachment, a silent curtailment of my autonomy.

'Mind you don't let it run too low.'

Lunch followed the invariable pattern: Mum, Dad, Mícheál and me, Uncle Fintan and Auntie Rosemary, salty soup, roast lamb and three sodden veg, dessert, desultory conversation.

'Is it George Sweeney you're working for, now, Caitlín?' Dad asked suddenly as we tucked into our over-sugared fruit salad.

'It is, yeah,' I said. 'Why do you ask?'

'Piece about him in the paper.'

'Oh?'

'He's got a new book coming out that'll set the cat among the pigeons.' Dad looked at me

55

with unaccustomed eagerness. This must be the MacDevitt book. I wished I could tell him I had the inside scoop.

'Hold on till I find it, now,' Dad continued. 'Mícheál, would you ever get me yesterday's paper?'

Mícheál sighed and began to rise to his feet.

'Oh, it can wait till after lunch, can't it?' Mum's voice had a warning note; her lips were tight.

'Not at all!' pronounced Dad, and I saw a wicked twinkle in his eye. 'Mícheál doesn't mind. Get me the paper, would you?'

Mícheál, sullen, did so.

'Wait, now, till we see,' Dad said, making a show of juggling the big pages. Triumphant sigh. 'Here we are.'

The rest of us sat in silence as he read: '*Bell Books to detonate green timebomb* — ha. Timebomb is right. *George Sweeney of Bell Books has acquired the memoirs of Eddie MacDevitt, well-known Republican campaigner of the early 1970s.*'

Opposite me, Mum gave a tiny flinch. She closed her eyes for a second, then glanced over at Auntie Rosemary. The atmosphere tightened.

'*MacDevitt has been living abroad since 1974, address unknown* — best of his play;

there's a fair few dangerous men would like to get their hands on him.'

Out of the corner of my eye, I could see Uncle Fintan's head hunching slowly down into his shoulders, his body curling like a leaf. Auntie Rosemary had pressed a hand to her chest.

'*The book, which may be published as early as next spring, goes into unprecedented detail about the dealings of senior Irish and British government figures with the radical Republican organization Laochra na Saoirse, briefly active in the early 1970s, and will confirm numerous decades-old suspicions* — blah blah blah,' said Dad, taking no apparent notice of the effect the article was having on his kin. 'Well, of course it will — sure didn't the dogs in the street know what they were at?' He paused for just long enough to make it painfully obvious that nobody else was going to speak, then went on in tones of sonorous joviality, '*It is an open secret* — ha, 'secret' it says here — *that Sweeney himself, as Seoirse Mac Suibhne, was active in Republican circles* — '

I couldn't bear it any more. 'Dad,' I said. I looked over at Uncle Fintan, who chose this moment to upset his water glass over Auntie Rosemary's lap.

'Fintan!' Auntie Rosemary leapt up and

bent over to hold her dripping skirt away from her legs.

'Oh, I'm so sorry! I'm such a. Here, let me.' Uncle Fintan dabbed weakly at his wife, who was glaring at him with ill-concealed fury. He was ashen-faced.

Mum took Auntie Rosemary off to find dry clothes, and Dad sat silently behind the newspaper, apparently unperturbed. Uncle Fintan slumped in his chair, looking miserable.

'That sounds like a cool book,' Mícheál said to me. 'Will you be working on it?'

'Doubt it,' I said, and watched his face fall. He went off to do his homework.

When Auntie Rosemary came back downstairs she said shortly to Uncle Fintan that they would go, and he put up no resistance. Mum and I showed them out, giving hugs all round as though nothing peculiar had happened.

I followed Mum back into the dining room, where Dad still sat with the paper.

'You went too far, Paddy,' Mum said to him in a low voice.

He grunted. 'Ah, sure, she'll live. I was only having a bit of fun.'

★ ★ ★

58

At work the next day, George called communal elevenses, which he had not done for
weeks. I assumed he wanted to talk about the
article in the newspaper, but he said nothing
about it at first. We drank our tea and exchanged
superficial chat. George made a meal out of
his biscuit, chewing noisily and smacking his
lips. Paula mostly looked out the window.

'You'll have seen that article in the paper
about Eddie's book, so?' George said at last.
He shook his head solemnly. 'We can't have
that, you know. We have to keep her under
wraps until she's ready to go. Bloody
journalists.' He took another biscuit from the
pack. 'You haven't mentioned it to anyone,
have you?' His eyes flicked uncomfortably
between the two of us.

'No,' Paula said, her voice full of contempt.
''Cause I'm not stupid, George.'

'Ah, no, fair enough,' George said. 'And
what about you, Cate? Even a bare mention
could do it.'

'No,' I said, and weathered a little jolt as I
remembered telling Matthew about the book.
Could Matthew be a journalist? It was
possible, I supposed. But I'd given him no
detail — certainly none of what was in that
newspaper article. I said, 'I don't even know
what's in the book.'

'Eddie lives abroad for good reason,' said

George. 'We don't want anyone going after him.'

I looked at George, thinking *open secret . . . active in Republican circles*. I wondered what he'd got up to.

He laid one hand flat on the table. 'Now listen. Somebody might try to get you talking. They're full of tricks. And by the way, I saw a young fella snooping around here over the weekend, so don't think it's not happening. I want you to promise me. If anyone asks you about it, it's *no comment*, all right?'

We finished our tea and went back to the main office, where George hovered at Paula's desk. 'I've to go off in a minute and meet John Lawless about the MacDevitt preface, but tell me, how's our equine friend? Has he come back to you yet?'

'No, he hasn't,' said Paula to her computer keyboard. Her jaw was set.

'Might be worth giving him a nudge, no?'

'Oh, yeah,' said Paula, with open sarcasm. ''Cause you know I'm only dying for him to send back his queries so I can stop sitting on my arse here, twiddling my fecking thumbs, George.'

'Ah, now, there's no need to get upset, Paula, I was only asking.'

'Well,' said Paula, 'if you're finished asking, I've a lot to do.'

Despite the tensions, things were better that week. Paula showed me how to apply a consistent house style to the footnotes and bibliographies of the fisheries conference papers, and I found that I rather enjoyed untangling them.

★ ★ ★

Choir was picking up pace now: several weeks into the season we were beginning to hit our stride. Diane's programme for our Christmas concert was exquisite: Mendelssohn, Copland, Mahler, and of course the Bernstein, our centrepiece. We rehearsed these in parallel with the more popular pieces we'd be performing in Belfast. We socialized together too, and as September took hold, an invitation went round: our bass-line committee secretary and his soprano wife were warming their new flat.

The evening in question was stormy, and when I weighed up the relative merits of drunk-but-wet or sober-but-dry, there was no contest: I'd drive. I donned the long, emerald-green shift dress that I'd worn to last year's Trinity Ball, concealed, powdered, painted, and set off.

The flat was in Ballsbridge, at the top of a tall Victorian house. Donal, the host, let me in and welcomed me upstairs with as much pride as if he owned the whole house. Linda, his wife, met us at the door of the flat and showed me where to put my coat.

We'd sung at their wedding last April — a musical extravaganza in Linda's native County Kilkenny — but apart from that I didn't know the two of them very well. In the spare bedroom, I added my coat to an already impressive pile.

'Come on through,' said Linda, crossing the tiny hallway and gesturing for me to follow.

The sitting room was large, with a bite cut out of one corner for a kitchen. Music pulsed from an iPod dock in the corner. The room was already quite full of people, of whom maybe a third were from the choir. No Matthew. I checked out the new faces. Old habits die hard.

'Great flat — so central,' I said to Linda. I heard myself deliver the line, like someone years older and several notches more sophisticated.

'Well, this is it. Couldn't be better, really. Anyway, help yourself to drinks! Nibbles!' She waved me to a table on which bowls of snacks and a large selection of bottles were arrayed. I poured a glass of fizzy orange, which messed with my chronology again, making me feel simultaneously too old and too young.

Over by the fireplace I saw Tom and Diane. I started towards them, and Tom spotted me. 'The bould *Mizz* Houlihan herself! *Ave, Cate-o!*' he exclaimed, with a florid beam. He was at his most ebullient, clearly in all-out party mode. He put an arm round me. 'And how's my favourite alto?'

'You're such an uncle, Tom,' I said, giving him a gentle dig in the ribs and nodding a greeting at Diane.

'You hear that, Diane? Cate has me down as avuncular.'

'Course you are, Tom,' said Diane. 'You are the *quintessential* uncle.'

'I'm not, actually. My sister is a bit old for kids at this stage. I'm a father, mind you. Will that do?'

I did my best to mask my surprise, but Tom was plainly on to me. 'I am. I've two teenage sons. I don't see much of them these days.' He sighed brightly and squared his shoulders. 'Come here, you were saying,' he prompted Diane.

'Oh yes, well, I sent the list of names off to Belfast last week, and they've given us the go-ahead, so we're all set.'

'And tell me, our Mr Taylor is definitely doing that gig, isn't he?'

'He is indeed,' said Diane. 'No offence to your good self, Tom, but we need him!'

'Oh, I concur,' said Tom. He looked around. 'Where is he anyway?' He raised his glass. 'I'm allowing myself one ogle per drink.'

Diane giggled. 'Tom, you're shameless.'

'I am,' he agreed. 'Honestly, you'd think I was single, the way I go on.' He sighed. 'In any case, the gentleman in question appears regrettably straight.' He smirked at me. I gave him a glare.

The two of them began to talk about music. I couldn't listen. Matthew was *here* — somewhere in this flat. I finished my drink and excused myself, moving back out to the hallway like a tiger on the prowl. What I'd do when I found him, I wasn't quite sure.

There weren't many places he could be, and my first guess proved correct. A splinter group had formed in the quieter environs of the spare bedroom. Val was in a low chair by the bed, where Joan and a few other choir people had pushed the coats back to make space to sit. Matthew and Linda stood under the blazing light bulb, drinks in hand.

The women seemed to be discussing the flat. Matthew looked on, his face thoughtful, difficult to read. He looked . . .

He looked *fucking gorgeous*, in point of fact. I kept a grip on myself and made an inoffensive remark about this being the chill-out room.

'Yeah,' said Linda. 'It's a nice little room, isn't it? We might make it into a study, we were thinking.' She looked past me, to where Donal had just come in. 'Hello, Mr Breen.'

Donal had a bottle in each hand. 'Hello, there, Missus. Top-up for anyone?' He poured wine into the proffered glasses.

Linda said, 'The landlord keeps calling me Mrs Breen.' She added airquotes. 'I can't be doing with that at all. Donal thinks it's sweet.'

'Well, I do,' said Donal, mock-aggrieved.

'It's a load of shite,' said Linda. She took a long swallow of her wine. ''Mrs Donal Breen' — I mean, I love you and all, Donal, but for fuck's sake. I'm Linda Muldoon. It'd be like putting on a new face, or something. I couldn't do it.'

'Ah, you'd get used to it,' Donal said.

'Well, why don't you change yours then?'

'Because it's not — I'd be — I don't know, I just wouldn't.'

'Well, don't expect *me* to, then.' She turned to me. 'Would you?'

I hesitated. 'It hasn't arisen.'

'Yeah,' Linda said, draining her glass and holding it out for Donal to fill up. 'First catch your man.'

Talk turned to the Belfast gig. Mircea the

Romanian bass said, 'Yes, but what is the gig exactly? I mean, what is the event?'

Joan explained, 'It's a European peace summit — they've invited the Turks and the Greeks and the Cypriots, and I think a big name may put in an appearance. Not Clinton or Blair, I can't remember who they said it was. Anyway, we're singing at a sort of gala evening on the Saturday. They've got three choirs lined up to do that Daintree piece — London, Belfast and us — voices from all three communities, peace and harmony and all that jazz.' Joan paused for a drink of beer and looked down for a moment before going on. 'And by the way, to be blunt, they will probably run a background check on all of us. The audience is going to be full of government ministers and diplomats from all over the place.'

'Hang on, though,' put in Val. 'That doesn't make any sense. Why would they waste their time investigating Carmina Urbana when they can just use someone like the National Chamber Choir — people who do this kind of gig all the time and already have whatever clearance they need?'

'They could do that,' said Joan. She looked uncomfortable. 'But . . . '

'Oh!' said Val. 'It's the Diane connection, isn't it?'

'I suspect it is,' said Joan.

'What's the Diane connection?' asked Mircea.

Joan lowered her voice and leaned forward, glancing from face to face. 'It's not something she advertises, particularly, but Diane is the daughter of Jennifer Mallon, if you remember.'

I didn't. Or, wait, a faint memory stirred. A name to bring out when you needed to end an argument — ironclad, irrefutable. *Jennifer Mallon*: I could hear it in Mum's voice.

Beside me, Matthew spoke for the first time, 'Wasn't she . . . shot by a British soldier some time in the early eighties?' He'd spoken as softly as Joan had.

Joan nodded.

Val said, 'It was one of those totally awful, unnecessary tragedies — I remember hearing about it at school. She was driving her baby daughter to visit her dying husband in hospital — I know, you couldn't make it up — and she got caught in the wrong place at the wrong time. Young soldier panicked. Shot her and she crashed the car.'

Mircea said, 'Wow. And Diane was her baby?'

Joan nodded. 'The father died of cancer a few months later. Diane grew up with her aunt and uncle in Kildare, I think.'

Val said, 'So it's like this big symbolic deal to have Diane's choir singing at a peace event. I'd say the Brits are super-sensitive about it.' She looked awkwardly at Matthew.

'So we ought to be, by the sound of it,' he said.

There was a silence, broken by Val standing up. 'Joan, you'll have another of these lads?' She offered to take Joan's empty beer bottle.

'Very much so, my dear,' said Joan.

Linda flopped down on to Val's vacated chair and leaned over to talk to Joan and the others on the bed. Matthew and I remained standing. I could feel the heat of him, his beauty, snaking around me like a fog.

He turned towards me. 'Did I read something about your employer in the newspaper?'

Really, Matthew, you want to talk about work, *again*? Oh, well, better than nothing. I'd have to be careful not to overstep George's boundaries this time, though. I said, 'You mean the MacDevitt thing?'

'Yes, that's right. The Laochra na Saoirse memoir.'

I couldn't help smiling.

He hesitated. 'What? Did I say that wrong?'

'No, it was lovely,' I said. 'You have no idea how completely bizarre it is to hear Irish spoken in an English accent.'

'Well, how do you say it?'

I channelled my Leaving Cert Irish teacher and delivered the phrase in its full rolling, guttural glory. 'Actually,' I confessed, 'that's not how I say it. But it's how a native speaker would say it. More or less.'

'OK, and what did I say?'

We'd turned now to face each other, standing close enough that if I moved my hand carelessly it would brush his sleeve. 'It was more . . . *lake-ra na sair-sha*.' I caricatured him, exaggerating his crisp diction.

He sniffed. 'Fine, I'll just refer to them as the Heroes of Freedom, then, shall I?'

'Grand, so,' I said. 'But come here, how do you even know about them? I barely do. We didn't learn about them at school.'

'It's my field,' he said simply.

Val was back with Joan's beer. 'What's your field?' she asked. 'History, isn't it?'

I put a tiny bit more space between me and Matthew, in case she'd notice.

'That's right,' Matthew said. 'Republicanism, really. Tell me, Val, have you heard of Laochra na Saoirse?'

'Weren't they one of those People's Front of Judea-style factions in the seventies?'

'Exactly.'

Val said, 'Ha. *So* different from nowadays. We've really moved on.'

They chatted easily about politics, while I struggled against the feeling that they were the grown-ups and I was the child. I had nothing to add to their discussion.

'I'm going to see if anyone's dancing,' I said suddenly, and headed back to the sitting room.

Several people were, to some nineties Britpop thing — bouncing and twisting in the centre of the floor. I joined in for a while, then got myself some water and stood by the window. The lower sash was closed over the tops of several carrier bags containing beer, which had been left outside on the fire escape to keep them cool. Rain had collected in the plastic crevices, working its way in under the sash.

I danced some more after I finished my water, then stopped to rest again. Somebody put on Lady Gaga, and suddenly the dancers were a bristling throng, all leaping and posing and roaring along with the lyrics. I saw the group from the spare bedroom come streaming in, Val dragging a reluctant Matthew by the hand. They joined in on the outskirts with an improvised Gaga-esque dance, in which their attempts to cast Matthew as the Lady herself fell flat. He was not playing ball.

As the next song began Joan arrived beside me, puffing. 'Oh, good lord, I'm too old for this. Time for some sustenance.' She raised the window and bent over to retrieve another beer from her stash. Matthew emerged from the dancing mass and came towards us, a particle reaching escape velocity.

'You've got the right idea, Joan,' said Matthew, reaching out the window to get a beer of his own. 'You want one, Cate?' He was panting slightly, and the whisper of his breath was thrilling.

'No thanks,' I said, trying to keep my voice steady. 'I'm driving, I'm afraid.'

'Ah, yes, you are, aren't you?' said Joan. 'Now, feel free to say no, but would there be any chance of a lift home when you're going?'

'Sure,' I said, 'no problem.' I checked the time: it was nearly midnight. 'I'd be thinking of heading off fairly soon, actually — would that be all right?'

'Absolutely,' said Joan. She gave me a sympathetic look. 'It's not so much fun when everyone's pissed, is it? I'll just go and find out if Val wants to come too.'

Matthew and I went on watching the dancing. I got the impression he was working up to something. 'Look, um, again, feel free to say no . . . but is there any chance I could have a lift too?'

'Sure,' I said, my voice sounding squeaky and unprepared. I realized that I didn't know

71

where he lived (yet), and also that I'd drive him to Shankill or bloody Swords if he asked me to.

There was a brief pause, while Matthew registered the fact that I hadn't asked him where he was going before agreeing to take him there — I could see the realization move across his face like a searchlight — and then he said, 'Thanks. You're a star,' and blinked a few times. He took a long swallow from his can, and I watched his throat work as he threw his head back, the skin stretched across his smooth Adam's apple. I gazed at the point where the flesh curved and disappeared into its cave of dark fabric. My lips would fit that curve beautifully — the thought set off a cluster of sparks from my belly to my knees.

I said, 'I'll just go and see if Joan's ready.'

He lifted his drink. 'Fine, I'll finish this, then — see you in a minute.'

I picked my way between the dancers and found Joan in the hall with Tom. She had her coat half on and was still holding her drink. 'Nearly finished!'

'Don't worry,' I said. 'We have to wait for Matthew.'

This raised a few eyebrows. Tom let out a noise like a surprised siren. 'The bould Matthew, no less!' he said. 'I'll drink to that!' He proceeded to do so, clinking his bottle with a flourish against Joan's.

'It's not what you're thinking,' I said. 'He just asked for a lift, that's all.'

'So your intentions are entirely honourable, young lady,' said Tom gravely.

'Entirely.'

I went to the spare bedroom to retrieve my coat. Val was sitting in the low chair again, joint in hand, garlanded in sweet smoke. There were three or four others kneeling on the floor at her feet, like acolytes. I knew none of them.

When I got back Matthew was just emerging from the sitting room with Donal. Joan hastily drained her bottle. Tom turned to Matthew, and I could see he was on the point of embarking on an innuendo. I seized him for a goodbye hug, which took him off guard a little, bid goodbye to Donal, and hustled Joan and Matthew out the door.

Outside, the wind blew fine rain into our faces. I led the way round the corner to the car and unlocked it. Matthew and Joan came after me, arm in arm — Joan was the more unsteady on her feet. There was a brief dispute on the kerb about who should have the honour of ceding the front seat, which Matthew lost. Joan climbed into the back.

I tried not to let my eyes keep flicking to my passenger as I started the engine and pulled out from the kerb. 'Joan's first, I presume,' I said firmly, and nobody argued. We spoke very little on the way there, exchanging sparse comments about the party, the music, Donal and Linda's flat.

Joan and Val lived not too far from me, in a small terraced house in Rathgar. I stopped the car outside and kept the engine idling, watching until Joan found her keys. The hall, with its red walls and white woodwork, looked bright and warm. The light rippled through the wavy glass in the door as Joan closed it.

★   ★   ★

'Right, then,' I said, turning to Matthew. 'Where do you live?'

'Kilmacud,' he said, 'but — ' He tipped his head down slightly and pinched the tip of his nose, giving me a sideways look. The streetlight caught on a curl that had dropped down over his temple. 'But, well, I just thought, rather than make you drive all the way out there, maybe you might have a sofa or something I could sleep on, and then I could get a bus in the morning. Or something.'

I sat fizzing for a year or so. 'Yeah, sure,' I said at last. 'I have a sofa — you could — that would be great. Fine. OK.'

74

I started the engine again and performed an awkward turn between the rows of parked cars that lined Joan's street. When I'd got us moving again I said, 'Do you often invite yourself to stay the night with strange women, then?' I glanced across at Matthew as I stopped the car at the T-junction. His eyes were gleaming.

'Oh, rather,' he said. 'The stranger the better. I'm known for it. In fact, this is nothing. Sometimes I accost them in supermarkets.'

He raised one eyebrow. Our eyes locked, and suddenly I felt as if I'd been touched, hooked. A rope of meaning tautened between us. My mind formed the thought carefully: *He wants to kiss me.*

'So this is your traditional English reserve.' I turned on to the main street.

'Exactly. Well spotted.'

By the time I parked under the ash tree my belly was dancing a tarantella, and hordes of hopped-up spiders were running up and down my limbs. I was nearly sure I was right about Matthew, but nearly is nerve-wracking.

I let us into the house and held a finger to my mouth for silence as we went upstairs. 'So. Here we are,' I said as I opened my door. I stood aside to let Matthew in. 'One sofa, as advertised,' I went on. 'I'll get you blankets and stuff in a bit.'

It was odd to see him here. He stood in the middle of my sitting room, leaning on one foot, hands held slightly out from his body and his head tipped forward, as if the ceiling were too low. I afforded myself a long look as I took off my coat, from his dark blue jeans to his curly hair. He loped over to the window, covering the distance in three long strides, and looked out into the street. He stood to one side, looking slantwise.

'Very Victor Laszlo,' I said, quietly enough so that he didn't have to hear me if he didn't want to.

'Very what?'

'You know, Victor Laszlo? *Casablanca?* That scene in the hotel where he's looking out the window at the watchers in the street.' Matthew looked a bit puzzled, but didn't say anything. 'I don't have the Venetian blinds, mind you,' I continued, then stopped, suddenly self-conscious.

'I've never seen *Casablanca*,' he said. 'Is that dreadful?'

'I'm shocked — shocked!' I said. 'We'll have to do something about that. In the meantime, would you like some tea?' I moved towards the kitchen.

'Tea,' said Matthew firmly. 'Yes, please.'

In the kitchen I watched my hands as they lifted the kettle and grasped the tap. Matthew was at the kitchen door when I turned from the sink, leaning his face against the door jamb, four fingers curled round below, almost to the wall. It was such a tactile pose, it sent further tremors through my system. I took a gulp of air.

'Where's your bathroom?' Matthew said. His speaking voice was exquisite, soft and light, like feathers brushing my skin.

'Other door,' I said, gesturing with my free hand. 'Through the bedroom. Sorry about the mess.' I turned back to set the kettle going.

Having put out mugs and teabags and spoons, I went and arranged myself on the sofa, leaving plenty of room to one side. From the kitchen I could hear the small, deliberate whisper of the kettle as it began its long climb towards boiling point.

Matthew came back and sat down, right in the middle of the available space.

'So,' he said, 'have you managed to sneak a peek at that Republican memoir, then?'

Oh, for fuck's sake! Everyone, it seemed, wanted to hear all about how central I was to the production of this one bloody book. Dad, Mícheál, and now Matthew. How tragic to be such a disappointment to them. I swallowed my frustration with difficulty. 'I told you,' I said. 'I'm only a serf. George won't let me near that project.'

'So what does he let you near, then?'

'Well, actually, in fairness, I have started copyediting. I'm working on a set of proceedings from an indescribably glamorous conference about fisheries.'

'Gosh, how magical.'

I caught his eye, and we looked straight at each other for just a little longer than was strictly necessary.

'This George Sweeney's a bit of a control freak, then, is he?'

I allowed myself a disloyal laugh. 'You've met him, have you?'

'Not yet,' said Matthew, and we had another of those looks.

The kettle switch snapped off just then, sending me springing to make the tea.

'Milk and sugar?'

'Just milk, please.'

I tried to focus on the task at hand. Pour, stir, squeeze teabags and dump in sink, plop and cloud of milk, deep breath, careful walk back to the sofa. 'Sir's tea.'

'Thank you, Madam.' He smiled as he took his mug, a warm, open smile that bolstered my hopes.

As I sat down, Matthew said, 'He's quite the Irish nationalist himself, though, isn't he?'

'George? Um . . . yes, I suppose so.' Presumably he was, if the allegations in the newspaper had been true. 'You wouldn't really know from talking to him. Why do you ask?'

'I was wondering if he'd be worth interviewing for my research.'

'Oh, right,' I said. I did not want to talk about his research. 'Something about the Republican movement, isn't it?'

'Yes,' said Matthew. 'Basically, I've come to answer the Irish Question.'

'Oh?' I said, feeling more than a hint of annoyance now. 'And tell me, what is the answer to the Irish Question?'

'Blowed if I know. My supervisor says I'm such a lazy English wastrel I'll never solve the riddle. But the authorities — by whom I mean Sellar and Yeatman — are fairly clear that every time Gladstone came close to discovering the answer, the Irish secretly changed the Question.'

I frowned. 'What are you on about?'

'Sorry — historian joke. Never mind.' He took a sip of tea. 'It's a book.'

I decided to drop it, and tried to think of some other conversational direction to take. I drew a blank. 'So, what exactly are you researching?'

'Well, if you really want to know, at the moment I'm looking at the career of a civil servant who was sacked by Harold Wilson in 1976.' He spoke with exaggerated dullness.

'You make it sound so interesting,' I said, relaxing a little.

'Don't I just?'

I paused, then said deliberately, 'I could listen to you all night.'

Once again, we were looking straight at each other. Much more softly, he said, 'Then I intend to go on talking.'

But in fact, he fell silent.

From there, it was a smooth, delicious dance towards the moment when we drifted closer together on the sofa, the moment when we crossed the line and slid into each other's space, the moment when we got so close that our faces blurred — and then Matthew brought his hand up and rested his fingertips on my cheek as we kissed, gently at first, then more urgently, deep, searching kisses that made my body hum, planted a knot of clean, singing pleasure in my very centre.

Eventually, I stood up and whispered, 'Come on.' Matthew got up too and allowed me to lead him by the hand into the bedroom. I fervently thanked myself for having changed my sheets that week. 'I've decided,' I said, 'that it's far too much trouble to get out the spare blankets for you.'

'Oh really?' He raised an eyebrow.

'I'm afraid so,' I said. 'You'll just have to share my bed with me.'

There was a moment, a short time later, as I crossed the room to turn off the light, when everything seemed to teeter on an edge. I felt acutely aware of my nakedness, how my pasty body must look under the unkind bulb. With my hand on the switch I looked back towards the bed, to see Matthew propped on one elbow, head held back slightly, face solemn, looking intently at me.

In that moment I almost made a flippant remark to puncture the atmosphere, but something stopped me. Some niggling idea at the back of my mind that here was a junction, a choice between flippancy and seriousness.

Without letting go of Matthew's gaze I turned off the light, then groped my way back to the bed and the eager mysteries of his body.

★　★　★

Other times when I'd brought a man home to bed for the first time, I'd spent a sleepless night, dozing but always conscious of his presence, always slightly wary — of what I might do in my sleep, of what he might do if my vigilance slipped. This first night with Matthew, though, I slept soundly until ten o'clock in the morning. I woke to hear him moving around in the bathroom, and levered myself up on one elbow, blinking in the flood of sunlight that washed through the thin curtains. Matthew came back in, running his fingers through wild hair.

'Ah, there you are,' he said, mimicking an absent-minded aristocrat.

'Good morning, Mr Taylor.'

'You must be Ms Houlihan,' he said, with a little too much *ee* in the middle syllable. He climbed back into bed behind me and began to stroke my back, gently, slowly.

'Oh well, if you say so, I suppose I must . . . ' I turned to him, and we kissed — carefully at first, both conscious of the sharp taste of sleep in our mouths.

It was a long time before we got up. Finally, I couldn't ignore the twinges of hunger any more. I heaved myself ungracefully out of bed and shambled into the kitchen to put on the kettle and find some bread to toast. The floor was chilly under my feet. I leaned against the sink surround, letting the hard countertop press into my flesh.

'Wow,' said Matthew from the door. 'A naked breakfast service.' He was dressed in his jeans and shirt, his eyes sleepy. He put his arms round me and kissed my neck. I started buttering the toast, enjoying the feel of his clothes against my body, his lips on my skin.

There was a moment of giddiness — vertigo, almost — when I thought, how can this possibly be happening? How did we get here? Is Matthew Taylor *really* standing in my kitchen kissing me? Then I put the knife down and turned to kiss him back.

Breakfast shaded into brunch, after which we ambled into town through a sunny, breezy afternoon and ended up going to a film in the Savoy. It was a lavish Hollywood feel-good movie, much better than I expected. We bought popcorn and fizzy drinks, and Matthew sat with his arm round me for most of the film. When we emerged afterwards into the yellowing dusk I felt as if I'd been given a transfusion of energy.

It was windier than it had been, a damp, whipping wind that threatened to develop into rain. Matthew turned up the collar of his jacket and pinched the end of his nose. We walked down to the river hand in hand.

We stopped at the bridge. 'Madam,' said Matthew, 'you've been charming company.' He kissed me gently. 'I believe my bus stop is this way,' he said.

'Mine's just across here.'

'Right.' He fished in an inner pocket and produced his phone. 'I suppose we'd better do this bit, then. What's your number? I'll text you.'

I told him my number, and a few seconds later I read on my phone: 'This is me. 990'

'What's the nine hundred and ninety for?'

'Think about it,' he said.

'It's ten less than a thousand . . . which is . . . I don't know.'

'Go on, you're on the right track. Think Latin.'

I laughed aloud. 'Oh, my god, it's *XM*, right? Like a Roman numeral?'

'The woman is sharp!'

'The man is a big nerd!'

We kissed goodbye, and Matthew loped off towards the river, turning to wave at me before he'd gone thirty feet. I floated across to the bus stop and replied to his text as I waited: 'Look, I can be a nerd too! 90' I could still feel the ghost of his touch, taste his sweat, his kisses. I felt shiny and precious, like silver.

⋆ ⋆ ⋆

Summer was long gone: the urban greenery on my wonted routes grew russet-flushed, the light turned to liquid gold and the promise of chill brushed my face. As always, I loved it when branches whispered to me as I went by, and one or two leaves dried out and fell, a prelude to the devastation ahead. I hunted out last winter's hat and scarf, although it was not yet cold enough to wear them.

Matthew came round every few days. We

went on proper dates: saw plays and films, visited galleries, ate in restaurants, spent slow, delicious nights in my wide bed. He was funny, considerate — and had an antiquated streak that meant he ended up paying for both of us more often than not. He had a poise to him, a polished presentation that I found irresistible. He made a commendable carbonara — 'my party piece,' he said. His hands were always warm.

By mutual agreement we were discreet at choir, confining ourselves to friendly greetings and participation in the same conversations at the pub. It seemed important to establish the dynamic between us properly before exposing it to scrutiny.

I'd never felt so grown-up. Mostly, I'd gone out with men who didn't do dates — who preferred to wander into my world and stay there for a while, oscillating between bed and the sofa. Late-night DVDs over ice-cream or pizza from a box. Relationships saturated in the flickering light of the television screen. Matthew was different. He seemed whole, somehow — self-contained — drawn to me not out of some unarticulated need but by conscious choice. It was exhilarating, like nothing I'd experienced before. The straightforwardness of our interaction astonished me. I did not talk about my past, and nor did he.

With him, there was no need to go digging in the murk. I was used to twisty dramas, coded messages, labyrinthine desires — anything but the plain English we seemed to be able to use with one another.

Now and then I wondered what my younger self would have said about all this if she'd known. Teenaged Cate had held some rather intemperate opinions — she would have looked askance, to say the least, at a British boyfriend.

I went shopping with Matthew one Saturday afternoon and bought a beautiful vintage coat — red corduroy, with a big furry collar. Feeling bold, I wore it out of the shop, and we proceeded down Grafton Street, arm in arm.

A voice behind me shouted, 'Hey! Cattle!'

Instinctively, I jerked away from Matthew and spun round. Only one person called me that.

Mícheál was standing in the queue for the cash machine, laughing at me. 'Made you jump!'

'What are you doing here?'

'Me and PJ got tickets to the match.'

What match, I neither knew nor cared. I wanted to punch him in his ruddy-cheeked face. 'This ignorant little gobshite,' I explained to Matthew, 'is my idiot baby brother. And Mícheál, not that you deserve to be introduced to actual people as if you were a normal human being, this is my friend Matthew.'

'Pleased to meet you,' said Matthew.

'Hi, Matthew,' said Mícheál, making it sound like a challenge.

'Behave yourself,' I told him. 'And never call me that again, OK?'

'Ah, fuck off, I'm only messing. Is that a new coat, is it?'

'None of your business, gobshite.'

'It's nice.'

I took a deep breath. 'Well, thank you. Enjoy the rest of your day.' I could do heavy sarcasm too, it turned out. Gathering the shreds of my dignity about me, I ushered Matthew away.

We were barely out of Mícheál's line of sight when Matthew threw his arms round me and collapsed on my shoulder in a fit of giggles. 'Cate, that was priceless! You changed into a completely different person! Your accent, your tone — everything — it was amazing!'

I sniffed, trying to weather the embarrassment. Despite myself, I began to giggle, and soon the two of us were guffawing together. It was too absurd.

Later, at dinner, I said, 'We all change into different people when we're with family, though. It's like going back in time.'

'Maybe,' said Matthew.

Carmina Urbana continued to practise for the Christmas concert and the Belfast gig. Diane finished introducing us to the new music, and we settled into the familiar pattern of note-learning and polishing. The easier pieces fell into place quickly, so that they could be left for light relief at the end of a rehearsal. Our antipathy towards Trevor Daintree and *A Song of Ireland* did not abate.

Tom was absent one week, and at break time Joan stood up to tell us all that his father had died. A choir would be much appreciated for the funeral.

I got George's permission to take Monday morning off and offered Joan and Val a lift. I collected them in Rathgar, and as we neared Rathmines, Val spotted Mircea the Romanian bass, standing disconsolate at a bus stop in the drizzle. He climbed into the back seat beside Val.

'This will be my first time to a Catholic funeral,' Mircea said when we were moving again.

Joan explained to Mircea that it would be a Protestant funeral.

'Ah,' Mircea said, 'but I thought it was said Church of Ireland — is this not the same as the Catholic Church?'

The discussion that followed revealed Joan as quite an expert on the details of Catholic and Anglican worship. She also turned out to know where the Romanian Orthodox Church in Dublin hung out.

'I am atheist,' Mircea said, with a long *ah* sound. 'But don't tell my mother.'

The route into town was clogged, and it was already ten o'clock by the time I found a parking spot on South Frederick Street. We hurried through the Nassau Street entrance of Trinity, down the ramp and on past the old library towards the college chapel in Front Square. The drizzle had stopped now, and muted sunlight made the place look down-right idyllic — gracious old stone, city traffic receding, browning leaves on elephantine trees shimmying in the wind.

It felt strange to be back here. I'd hardly stepped on to the campus since I'd left. I would've been picking up my Master's degree around now, if I'd taken my place. If my parents' verdict had gone the other way. 'It'd be different if it was a *qualification* of some kind,' had been Dad's last word. Mum had said, 'You have to start thinking about the future.' I'd gathered that it was bad enough to have chosen Trinity in the first place, without getting notions about *more* study.

As I followed Joan and Val through the massive doors and up the stairs to the organ loft, I felt at home — at home with the dark wood and the dust, with the bright curving vaults above us, with the lovely bulbous acoustic that caught and magnified our voices.

I waved a greeting to Matthew, but we didn't get a chance to speak. Rehearsal was just beginning. We sang first through a selection of solid hymns, accompanied by a worried organist with thinning blond hair, whom Diane introduced to us as Stephen Bailey. I loved singing the traditional Church of Ireland hymns, with their squarish melodies and straightforward harmonies. They were so much more comforting than the weedy folk-group efforts of my youth. I'd sung in Trinity Chapel Choir for just two terms in my final year, but it had been the highlight of my week. The sparse dignity of the Anglican service, the measured tranquillity, the sense of intellectual engagement, were so different from the droning, smug Catholicism I'd grown up with.

Tom's father had apparently been a big fan of English Baroque, and we were to sing two anthems by Henry Purcell. We started with *Hear My Prayer*, which I hadn't sung before but others had. The music was in eight parts, twining and curling around each other to weave a delicate, shimmering fabric of sound.

'Lovely,' Diane said, after our first run-through. She tapped her tuning fork and listened. 'Tuning's good. We need to work on the diction. *Hear my prayer O Lord* — give me a clear *d* there, right on the downbeat — and then *and let my crying come unto thee* — we want a very exaggerated *and-a-let* there. *And-a-let*. And roll yours *r*s if you can — *crrrying*. It's a bit . . . *English*, I know . . . ' she faltered, and I heard Val beside me give a very tiny snort. 'But that's all right,' Diane went on, recovering. 'We have English people in the choir. Listen to how they do it.'

'You know,' Val muttered, 'it might actually be . . . *kind of OK* to sing Purcell in an English style.'

Diane said, 'All right, once more from the top.'

The service was efficient and dignified, the readers calm, the priest consoling. As the offertory gifts were brought up, we rose for the first Purcell piece. 'Thou knowest, Lord, the secrets of our hearts,' we sang. Tom gave a moving eulogy, which was among other things a meditation on changing times, a changing Ireland. His father had been born in 1923, just after the Civil War.

Afterwards, everybody went across Front Square to the Exam Hall, where tea and sandwiches were served. I went to find Tom, who received my condolences with a quiet solemnity that conjured a lump in my throat. Having shaken my hand, he excused himself and went to greet a tall, black-haired woman and two teenage boys whose abundant curls marked them out as his sons. I could see Matthew across the room talking to Donal and Linda. I exchanged brief and stilted words with Stephen, the organist, about the music we'd just performed. Joan and Val joined us just as Stephen was drawn aside by the vicar.

Val spoke quietly. 'So Stephen got a mention in the death notice, at least.'

'Oh?' Joan was pleased. 'As Tom's partner?'

'Yeah — well, not explicitly, I don't think. Survived by children Joyce and Thomas, grandchildren whatever their names are, and by Elizabeth Silke and Stephen Bailey, sort of thing.'

'I hope Elizabeth's being decent to Tom,' Joan said.

I felt like an eavesdropper.

I looked for Matthew again, but he was nowhere to be seen. As I scanned the room my pocket buzzed. He'd sent me a text: 'Sorry to disappear — I have to rush back to UCD. 990' I texted back: 'No probs. See you soon. 90'

I went back to my car alone and drove out

towards Rathmines. It took a couple of miles to admit it, but I was upset by Matthew's leaving like that. We hadn't exchanged a single word all morning. Would he not at least have crossed the room to say goodbye to me in person? Without meaning to, I began to slip into a little whirlpool of worry. He wasn't being honest with me, I angsted. He was so reserved, always, and I had no real feel for how much of that was cultural and how much of it was just him.

I stopped to pick up a sandwich for lunch before going back to work. I was in front of the deli counter, waiting my turn, when I recognized someone walking past the window: it was that man with the big-lensed glasses, like Dad's. I'd seen him that night in the Stag's Head, and later near my house, when he'd driven off in the car with the *Chichester Psalms* registration plate.

'Yes, please?' said the server at the deli counter.

'Hang on.' I ran out into the street.

What was I doing? How was it done? I looked wildly around, up and down the street, but saw neither the man nor the car. I felt like an idiot — I hadn't a clue where to start. I went along the row of shops a little way. The man was not in the launderette or the Chinese takeaway. He could have been in the hardware shop, but I had no intention of burrowing in there to look for him.

It might not even have been the same man. I'd barely glimpsed him. I might have accosted a perfectly innocent stranger and accused him of stalking me. That's if I'd even have the guts to accost him in the first place. Did he know I'd seen him? Would they — whoever they were — change their strategy now?

Lacking other options, and feeling very small, I went back to buy my sandwich.

★   ★   ★

I arrived at work to find the place in crisis: Paula and George were arguing loudly in the inner office. Paula accused George of having no head for business, being wilfully ignorant about the amount of work he was heaping on her desk, living in cloud-cuckoo land. George defended himself but was clearly on the back foot. I didn't dare disturb them.

Eventually, Paula declared that she had had enough and issued a thunderous resignation. George did his best to talk her out of it. She had four weeks of holidays due to her; he said he'd give her six if she'd take two now and come back to work. Two weeks, she said, was an insult. She'd take four now and three more at Christmas, thank you very much, and

George could like it or lump it. And she'd be keeping an eye out for other openings. She stalked back out to her desk, greeted me curtly, collected her things and left.

George and I had a planning meeting after he'd calmed down a bit. There were three books at proof stage, locked in to the printers' schedules, as well as the fisheries conference proceedings, which was already slipping behind, and another big illustrated job due in. We said nothing about Eddie MacDevitt, although I could feel him lurking in the silences.

It was my idea to take the company laptop home with me and work some overtime — I could at least do the routine copyediting and proofreading for him to check afterwards. George huffed and puffed a bit but agreed in the end that it was the best solution.

'Keep a note of the hours you do,' he said. 'I'm trusting you on this one.' His eyes were sharp as needles.

I did a couple of hours that evening, and George was pleased with the results. 'You might have the makings of an editor, all right,' he told me.

I mustered my courage. 'What about the MacDevitt book? Will we be starting work on that soon?'

George shook his head. 'I'll be taking care

of the MacDevitt book myself, Cate. It needs a bit more work than your average manuscript. Poor oul' Eddie is the salt of the earth, but words . . . not his strong suit, you could say.'

By midweek, it was clear that the stress was getting to George. He banged about in his office, growled down the phone, lurched out to meetings with his collar askew. He was fighting with his computer one afternoon when he lost it completely. I heard a yell of frustration, a thump, and then something that sounded like his chair falling over.

Into the silence, he said, 'Cate, could you come in here for a minute?'

I came in as he was righting the chair, and he gave me a distinctly sheepish look. He picked up from his desk a device about the size of a grill handle, black, with a few buttons and a cord connecting it to the back of the computer. 'I got a loan of this yoke from John Lawless, and I can't get it to work at all.' Now he looked helpless.

'What is it?'

'It's a scanner, would you believe. You're supposed to be able to scan in text. I keep getting what looks like the text, but I can't select it. It's as though it's a picture of the text, not the text itself. Does that make any sense to you?'

'Can I help?'

'God, I hope so. I haven't the time to go typing out Eddie's entire manuscript, as well as everything else.'

I thought about asking him why he didn't just scan it in on the photocopier, but I suspected that would make matters worse. George and the photocopier had a rocky relationship at the best of times. Instead I said, 'Let me have a look at it.' I came round and sat in George's chair, taking the scanner from him. He handed it to me as though it were made of eggshell, and gave a tiny whimper as I tried pressing some buttons. After a few moments, with his permission, I went online and found the manual. Changing scanning mode was predictably straight-forward, but George reacted as though I'd rewritten the laws of physics.

'Lord bless us and save us!' he exclaimed, as the first paragraph of Eddie MacDevitt's manuscript, in fully editable text, appeared on his screen.

'There you go.'

I stood up from his desk and was just about to leave his office when he coughed and said, 'Cate? I've a feeling you'd be a lot quicker at this than I would. What do you think?'

'Would you like me to do the scanning for you?'

The look he gave me was of pure relief.

I finished scanning the manuscript quite quickly, sitting in George's office while he used Paula's desk. He wouldn't risk putting it on to any machine other than his own. 'Not every word comes through perfectly,' I told him. 'It'll need to be checked.'

'Oh, listen,' he said, 'this is only step one. We've a long way to go.'

I smiled. He'd said *we*.

The next day he called me in again and showed me a second copy of the manuscript, thick with red marks. 'This is how I've been whiling away the long evenings,' he said. 'These edits all need to be keyed in.' He paused and looked up. 'Will you do that for me?' It was as though he were asking me a personal favour — as though he weren't my employer.

For a moment, I hesitated. Now that George was taking me into his confidence, perhaps I should take him into mine and tell him about the men in the dark car. But then he might change his mind. If the men in the car were about anything, they were about the Belfast gig, weren't they? That's what I'd decided. I didn't need to turn down this professional opportunity on the basis of a handful of quite possibly random encounters.

'Of course I will,' I said firmly.

I marched towards the bus stop that Friday evening, clasping the fat leather handles of the laptop's case, humming a passage from *Chichester Psalms* and feeling unusually pleased with myself. It was exciting, I found, to be doing a job I cared about. I detected none of the background resentment I'd always felt while temping, which I'd assumed was intrinsic to the working experience. Perhaps I was turning into some kind of *motivated professional*. How strange.

The evening was pleasant — just a hint of dusk on the fringes of the sky. Trees rustled in a fickle breeze, letting go of a few leaves every so often, delicately, like an exhalation. The leaves were already huddling in heaps against the kerb, stirred by little gusts.

I was still humming the Bernstein as I stood in the shower later on, soaping vigorously. Matthew and I were going to see a French film at the Irish Film Institute. A proper date, which might make up for the strangeness of this week. We'd barely spoken since the funeral. One phone call to arrange tonight, and that was all. He hadn't been at choir yesterday.

I dressed quickly and put some soup on the stove and bread in the toaster, then came back into the sitting room and set a place for myself at the table. The ash tree's black fingers quivered in the light from the street lamps, and I endured a rush of fear, a feeling almost like vertigo, that Matthew wouldn't come to the cinema, that he'd stand me up, that I was deluding myself about the importance of our connection. We hadn't had what people call The Talk. I'd decided to be comfortable with that, but just now doubt washed through me, leaving an unpleasant aftertaste.

What, after all, did I know about him? I was in uncharted territory — no points of reference, and other than Carmina Urbana, no friends in common to flesh out my picture of him. And he was so private — always staying at my flat, never inviting me back to his or taking the lifts I offered him, saying little about his personal life, his family, what he did when I wasn't there.

I got to the Irish Film Institute at five past eight and couldn't see him. I checked the bar, the shop. He wasn't usually late for things. In fact, he'd teased me about my own unpunctuality — and I'd noticed myself trying harder to be on time for him. Was this his idea of making a point?

I paced the lobby, trying to reason myself out of this angry impatience. It wasn't his fault, I told myself. The only reason I was reacting like this was because I'd been letting myself fret about our relationship. He'd be along in a minute.

Fifteen minutes later, my rationality was wearing thin, and the film was about to start. I texted him: 'Buying tix', and went to the desk to do so. Added to the impatience, and the guilt for feeling it, was now my irritation that I'd been the one to pay for our tickets. We'd fallen into some baldly chauvinistic habits, Matthew and I, and I didn't like it.

'Hello, there, sorry to keep you waiting,' he said, at my elbow. I turned a little too quickly; he must have seen the seething emotions on my face. 'What's the matter?'

'Mr Punctuality shrugs off his own lateness,' I said, feeling weak. He raised his eyebrows and stood still, staring me down. I wilted. 'Don't worry about it. It's no problem.'

'Good.' Brisk. We headed for the cinema door.

I weathered the sting as best I could. As we neared the door I said, 'What kept you, anyway?' I wondered why I couldn't leave it alone.

He gave a short sigh. 'I just got caught up in what I was doing. Doesn't that ever happen to you?'

'Sure,' I said.

'Oh, damn.' He took out his buzzing phone and looked at the screen. 'Sorry, I have to take this.'

I stood to one side and let the people behind us pass ahead. Matthew had stepped a few feet away and was stooping over his phone, blocking his other ear with his free hand. I couldn't see his face or hear what he was saying. Beyond the door, I could hear music.

At last Matthew came back. 'Got the tickets? Come on.' He guided me into the dimness of the auditorium.

'Who was that on the phone?' I whispered, as a trailer ended.

'No one of consequence,' he said. Conversation over. He leaned his head back against the plush seat and closed his eyes.

I watched him, wondering what he was feeling. I wanted to press a button, get a readout. Send in my spies. I searched out his hand, and he returned my conciliatory squeeze.

After the film Matthew seemed more himself, though still reserved. We had a glass of wine in the cinema bar and talked companionably enough about the film, about other French films we'd seen, about our favourite films. I relaxed gradually, realizing as I did just how tense I'd been all evening.

I put on my middle-aged voice. 'How was your day, dear?'

His face softened. 'Oh, the usual. You know: the lonely life of the scholar. Meeting with my supervisor. Cups of coffee in the arts block. Sincere intentions to go to the library, suppressed. What about you?'

'Pretty good, actually,' I said. I wanted to be open with him. Make a real connection. 'You know what? I am working on the MacDevitt memoir after all.'

He took a sip of wine and blinked at me lazily. 'Really? How did that come about?'

I told him about Paula's departure, George's ineptitude, my moment of glory with the hand-held scanner. He laughed at that. 'So what's the book like?'

'It's, oh, I don't know. It's a bit frustrating, to be honest. I mean, I've only done, like, two and a half chapters, but so far it's just a load of meandering anecdotes, in this really round-about style that doesn't ever say anything straight out. I don't know who'll read it, frankly.'

'Well, frankly, I probably will. It's pretty relevant to my research.' He leaned a little closer. 'I don't suppose you could slip me an advance copy?'

I shook my head. 'No way. Not a chance.'

'Oh well. Worth a try.'

I wished I hadn't mentioned MacDevitt. 'How's your research going, anyway?' I asked.

'Oh . . . so-so.'

'What is it you're trying to find out about that guy you told me about — the one who was sacked by Harold Wilson?'

'You remembered that?'

I shrugged. 'It stuck in my mind.'

'You really want to know?'

I nodded.

'All right, then, I'm trying to prove that this man was having unauthorized talks with Republican groups in the seventies, around the time the IRA mainland campaign was kicking off.'

Mainland. A flash of irritation, but I let it pass. 'Sounds exciting.'

He looked at me and paused before he spoke. 'Not really, I'm afraid. At least, I suppose it's exciting in the abstract, but in practice it's just a whole lot of tedious sifting through civil service archives looking for scraps of evidence. Which mostly isn't there. It's incredibly frustrating.'

'I take it you can't ask the man himself?'

'He died in 1999.' Matthew sighed. 'The only concrete thing I've got so far is an expenses claim with a train ticket to Blackpool, on a trip where he was only supposed to be going as far as Preston.'

'Preston,' I said. 'Blackpool. They sound like places from a book. Where is Blackpool?'

'You don't know where Blackpool is?' His tone was gently mocking.

I bristled. 'Well, why should I?'

'Well, I don't know — did you do

geography at school?'

'Yes, of course. I got an A in the Junior Cert, I'll have you know.'

'So, do you know where Nice is? Or Naples?'

'Yeah, more or less,' I conceded.

'But not Blackpool. What about, say, Birmingham? Or Bristol, where I'm from. Do you know where that is?' He seemed almost excited to be uncovering the extent of my ignorance.

'No.' I was sullen now. 'OK, look, we didn't do it. We skipped the chapter on British geography.'

'Seriously?'

'Yes. There wasn't time to cover the whole course, so the teacher decided to skip some of it. Perfectly normal. Did you learn Irish geography? Do you know where Castlebar is?'

'County Mayo. Sorry. But you're right. I didn't learn that at school.'

There was an awkward silence, broken by me, unbending, trying to rebuild the bridge. 'We went camping near Nice once. It was loads of fun — big campsites with scads of other Irish kids to play with.'

'We went to Brittany for a week when I was nine. It rained solidly, as I remember. We spent the entire week indoors playing cards. I think we went to the beach once, but it was horrible. We never went abroad as a family again.'

'Except to Dublin,' I said. 'Hello, independent state?'

Matthew looked blank.

'When we met you said you'd come here a few years ago on a family holiday.' I tried to keep my tone easy, hold back the tide of annoyance that boiled up from somewhere deep. So fucking typical English, that blind spot about Ireland. 'Foreign country since 1921, as it happens.'

'Cate.' Matthew spoke carefully. 'I'm studying Irish history. I have heard of the Treaty of Independence. I just forgot about the Dublin holiday. It's in a completely different category in my memory, because I was already an adult by then.' He reached over and laid a hand on my arm. 'All right?'

The tide ebbed, leaving me limp. 'Sorry,' I said. 'Yeah, I'm a bit touchy, I suppose. Years of habit. Family tradition. Whatever.'

'No kidding.' He laughed suddenly. 'I suppose I shouldn't mention all the visits to my mother's cousins in County Antrim, then?'

'What with the whole 'abroad' bit? No. You'd better not.' I took a drink, looked away, around the room, then turned back to him. 'Or actually, do. You went when you were a kid?' I was struck by the notion of Matthew as a little boy.

'That's right — we used to go nearly every

summer when I was in primary school. It was a farm, and the kids were around the same age as us. Loads of fun. Then later my sister and I went over on our own.'

Oh, so he had a sister? This felt too much like an interview. I waited for him to elaborate further, but he didn't.

'What were you like when you were a kid?' I asked, conceding again.

'What's any kid like? What were you like when you were a kid?'

'I suppose I was . . . shy. I read a lot. I was a good girl at school.'

So we talked about school. I ended up telling a string of anecdotes about things I'd almost forgotten — like the craze for collecting fancy notepaper and smelly rubbers. I'd been massively proud of my fancy notepaper collection, even if it was never as good as Denise's.

'You know, my dad might've made some of that,' Matthew put in. 'That's what he did — his company. He's retired now. He used to manufacture paper goods. Exercise books, envelopes, printer paper, all that sort of thing. The novelty stationery market was pretty lucrative.'

I told him about the sophisticated economy we'd developed around our notepaper collections: the trading, the hype, the fortunes made and lost. He said we were all insane.

I finished my wine before he did. I was about to suggest another when he drained his glass and made to stand up. 'Shall we go?'

Well, you don't leave me much choice, I thought, but I said nothing.

It was drizzling and chilly outside, with cruel little gusts that swiped at the edges of our clothes. We huddled along towards Dame Street, Matthew putting a stiff arm round my shoulders.

As we neared the taxi rank I said, 'So, will we go back to mine, then?'

Matthew caught my eye, then looked at his feet. 'Look, Cate, I'd better go home, OK?'

'Why?' My heart plummeted — and I sounded so whiny.

He sighed. 'I . . . look, I know I joke about it, but I really do need to get some work done over the weekend. My supervisor gave me a bit of a talking to this afternoon.'

I didn't know what to say. I had no idea how he'd react if I argued with him, asked him what work he expected to do tonight that couldn't be done tomorrow, told him we'd get up early, I'd make him breakfast. The barrier I'd felt before was firmly in place now. I stood and looked at him. How had I ever thought he was easy to communicate with?

'I'd like to come back, Cate, you know I

would, but I can't, not tonight,' Matthew said, and put a hand up to my face. I wanted to brush it away. I couldn't stand him knowing how put out I was. I felt unmasked, at his mercy.

I wasn't going to stand for that. Defiance flared in me. Fuck him, then, if he didn't want what I was offering. 'Fine,' I said. 'Give me a ring when you're less busy.'

'I will.'

We kissed goodbye. The rain continued to fall. Matthew went off to get his bus, and I stayed in the taxi queue, feeling deflated, thinking about going home alone to my tidy flat.

★ ★ ★

Next morning, Aidan from downstairs knocked at my door to say that he and Sheila were off for three weeks' holiday in China, and would I mind picking up their post. I was glad I'd dressed before he'd rung the bell.

I arsed around the flat all morning, anxious and indecisive. Eventually, very late, I got it together sufficiently to cook myself some lunch.

While I was cooking I had the radio on, keen to fill my thoughts with something other than Matthew's abrupt departure last night.

The news story of the day was an announcement by Unionist parties that they would consider withdrawing from the Northern Irish Assembly unless dissident Republican groups made it clear that they were ceasing operations. Level-voiced experts examined the issue from every angle. I could imagine my parents and Mícheál listening in Ardee, airing their heartfelt opinions on this latest evidence of Unionist obduracy, but I couldn't kindle in myself any of the outrage that would have been second nature in my teens.

I switched the radio off.

My phone glared at me from the dining table as I ate. I glared back. Matthew's number danced through my head, singing itself, mocking me. I couldn't ring. He'd tell me to go away.

We'd agreed that he was to ring me. That was important.

Maybe I could drive out to Kilmacud first, and then ring. Say I just happened to be passing, thought I'd call in — if he'd tell me exactly where his house was. I hadn't even got his address yet. I cursed my lack of guts.

I picked up the phone and dialled the number quickly, before I could change my mind.

'Hi, this is Matthew. I can't take — ' I killed it. There was no way I was leaving a message.

I threw myself into the armchair and rang Denise instead, for the first time in weeks.

'Hello?' She sounded sleepy.

'Hi, it's me. Cate.'

'Cate! How are you? Sorry, I didn't recognize your voice there.'

'Did I get you out of bed?'

'A bit, yeah. What time is it?'

'Nearly half three.'

'You're fucking kidding me. God, I'm such a slob.'

We swapped stories: my job, Denise's social life, her doctorate. Her parents had been up from Ardee for the week. She and John-Paul were planning a weekend away. I told her about Paula's grand exit at Bell Books, did an impression of George's reaction. I said nothing about the MacDevitt book. I was regretting having mentioned it to Matthew last night, given George's sensitivity about it, the reluctant trust he was placing in me.

'So what else is new?' Denise asked through a yawn.

I hesitated. 'Well, I'm kind of seeing someone.'

'Really?' Eager now. 'Tell me more. Who is he?'

'New boy in the choir.' I filled in some details; Denise made appreciative noises at appropriate intervals. It was good to talk to her.

She said the gang were meeting for drinks in Dundrum later on, and did I want to come. I'd love to.

★ ★ ★

I hadn't been out with the college gang in weeks. I was nearly afraid I'd have forgotten how to talk to them. I sat on the bus to Dundrum, watching raindrops slant across the misted windows. We rattled through the night, and suddenly I wanted to be home in my bed, curled up under the covers, warm and silent. But I'd told Denise I'd be there.

I thanked the driver as I got out. He was a black African, but his 'Have a good night, love' was pure Dublin. The rain had eased off, and the wind seemed to have died down. It felt almost mild, in that wild October way.

I'd just have one or two drinks and then go home.

I reached the pub door, its stained glass panels glowing golden from the light inside. As I pushed it open, sound washed over me, the bubbling noise of a hundred conversations. The air was thick and warm.

Over at the bar I saw the ever-comely Fenian Mick, a grin on his face and his red curls bouncing. He waved a greeting. 'Cate, *abú*! How're'ya?' As I reached him he was gathering pints into his big hands.

'Wait a minute and I'll help you carry those down,' I said, then turned and miraculously caught the attention of the barwoman. Gin and tonic, I decided, would be the drink of the evening. Just not too many of them.

'So what's the craic?' Fenian Mick asked. He nudged me. 'Come here, Dee says you've a new man.'

'God, news travels fast. Yeah, I suppose I have.'

I paid for my drink and picked up the remainder of Fenian Mick's order, and we wove our way to the back of the lounge where the others were sitting. Denise was there with John-Paul, and Pat and Elaine and Noreen and Liddy. A ragged cheer went up when they spotted me, followed by a lull as I helped distribute the round of drinks. The conversation picked up speed again, a tumbling parade of in-jokes, puns and one-liners, weaving and circling around a mercurial sequence of topics. I synched easily with it. I might not go to the pub with the gang so often these days, but I was apparently still fluent.

I was sitting beside Elaine, who after a while asked how I was. I told her about work — again omitting to mention MacDevitt — noticing that I was using the same phrases I'd used on the phone to Denise earlier. It was funny to think of myself, out in the big world, explaining what it was like to someone who hadn't yet ventured there.

I noticed Fenian Mick turning to listen to us. When I did my take-off of George he said, 'Sounds like my dad,' and I felt as if I'd stepped too close to him. He'd been very kind about the crush I'd had on him in college, though he hadn't felt the same way. He was one of the good guys.

I took another sip of my drink. The ice had all but melted, and the remaining liquid was tart and tepid.

'So, who's this new fella, then, Cate?' Noreen said, leaning across from Elaine's other side and tapping me on the forearm.

As though a light-switch had been flicked, I had an audience. Fenian Mick, Elaine and Noreen were looking straight at me, and the others had noticed too. 'Matthew?' I said, and something caught in my throat; I had to stop to clear it. 'He's lovely,' I went on, coming out of the cough, tossing off the verdict before I could hesitate, search for the right words.

'Dee says he's a Brit,' Noreen said, a little slurrily.

'Well, yeah, he's from Bristol.'

'I can't imagine you going with a Brit,' said Noreen.

There was a tiny, howling silence, then Fenian Mick said, 'Trinity made her soft,' and they all laughed. 'And why not, sure, if she wants him?' A memory swam into focus: Fenian Mick and Noreen having a massive rant about Queen Elizabeth's visit to Trinity. They'd wanted to organize a protest, but it never came off.

Fenian Mick slapped the table with the flat of his hand. 'Now, come on, Cate, give us the low-down. Name, rank, serial number. All that craic.'

'Well, OK, he's called Matthew, as I said, and he's a new tenor in Carmina Urbana — '

'Oho! A choirboy? Say no more,' said Elaine.

'And he's a postgrad in UCD.'

'Ah, he must be all right, so,' said Noreen. 'Matthew what? Would we know him? What's he doing?'

'Taylor,' I said. 'History.'

'Who's his supervisor?'

'Professor Lawless.'

'Lawless? Are you serious?' Fenian Mick guffawed. 'Well, whatever about *you*, Cate, I can't see John Lawless getting into bed with a Brit — he's a total 'RA-head. God, I'd love to be a fly on the wall at those meetings.'

'He's not *writing* on Republicanism, though, is he?' Elaine asked.

I hesitated. I knew how it would sound to them — how unlikely they'd be to accept the notion that a Brit could have anything useful to contribute on the topic.

'You should've brought him along tonight,' said Noreen, 'so we could all have a gawk at him.'

'Check him out, you mean?' I felt uncomfortable now at the thought of what they'd all make of Matthew. Or he of them, come to that.

'Ah, no, you know what I mean,' Noreen said.

'I didn't think of asking him,' I said. 'We're not really at that stage yet.' I could feel myself closing in, a flower in the dark.

'Well, how long have you been seeing him?' Noreen wasn't letting it go.

'I don't know,' I said. 'A few weeks, just.' It was exactly five weeks tonight, I was well aware. Noreen made a dubious face, took another swig of her pint.

I said, 'I think he'd be a bit overwhelmed if I just brought him here and plonked him down in the middle of you lot, all at once.'

'Ah, that's shite,' said Noreen. She looked away, her lip curled in disgust.

'Look,' said Denise, 'the man's entitled to be a bit scared of meeting a bunch of hooligans like us.'

'Exactly,' I said. 'Thank you.'

'But he has to be willing to meet your friends,' Noreen insisted.

'There's time for that,' said Denise. 'The key questions for the moment are: is he straight, does he wash, does he ring when he says he will?'

'All of the above, as far as I can tell,' I said, regaining my poise to some extent.

'Well, that's a good start,' said Denise.

'Going on past form, you mean?' I caught her eye, and we giggled. The messy darkness seemed to recede a little.

'Who's for more drink?' asked Fenian Mick, rising. I handed him the money for another G&T.

Four drinks later, I stood on the footpath opposite the pub, shivering, hugging my coat around me. The rain was at bay, although the surface of the street gleamed with wetness like a beach after a wave.

I was none too steady: the world heaved and flickered unless I kept a close eye on it. John-Paul had said I'd easily pick up a taxi on the road. The others were staying put until they were thrown out, then probably walking back to Denise's with a carry-out. I didn't regret not joining them. I was ready for my bed. As I'd got drunker I'd felt less and less part of the evening, more exposed, eroded.

I watched a car pull out of the pub car park and pause at the kerb, though there was no other car moving on the street that I could see. It rolled slowly out on to the road and lumbered along a little way to stop outside a late-night shop. I turned my head just in time to hail a taxi that was speeding to catch the lights.

The driver was young, distracted, listening to dance music. 'Do you mind?' he asked, gesturing towards the radio, and I told him he was grand, no problem. We didn't converse as we waited at the traffic lights. The driver whistled through his teeth, accompanying the repetitive riff of the music.

As we began to move again I looked out the window at the car sitting outside the brightly lit shop. I had a wild suspicion about it. The car had its head- and tail-lights on, and a man sat in the driver's seat, smoking. As we passed I caught the glint from his glasses. I snatched a look at the licence plate: 52845. I'd been right.

We drove on. I shifted in my seat so I could just see a bit of the road behind us in the wing mirror. There was a vehicle behind us now, all right, but the power of its headlights meant that there was no chance of glimpsing the number. It looked like the same car. Maybe I should tell the driver that I thought this car was following me, ask his advice. Maybe he'd turn out to be an expert at losing a following vehicle, weaving and turning, steering wheel wrenched from side to side and tyres squealing, the dance music turned up high for a soundtrack.

He'd think I was mad.

It had started to rain again.

I let the taxi go at the end of my road. I looked round as it drove off, but saw no dark car pulling up nearby. I hugged my coat around me and started to walk down the narrow cul-de-sac.

The car was sitting outside my house with its headlights on. My heart jumped, and for a second I thought I might throw up. I had to keep walking. To hesitate would be to suggest that I was somehow in the wrong. 'It's just routine,' I said aloud, and heard the distortion of alcohol in my voice. 'Oh, god, I am too drunk for this,' I whispered.

The pavement was like a tightrope. I looked down at my feet in their runners, left, right, left, right, watched as drops of rain fell on the fabric and were absorbed. The car was motionless, dazzling. I'd need to go awfully close to it to get to my front door. Point-blank range.

I couldn't think of any reason why they'd want to shoot me, but once I'd had the idea, it was hard to shake. My jaw clenched, and tears began to come. I looked down at my feet again: they were still moving.

No friendly light in any of the windows of my house. Aidan and Sheila were on their way to China. As I got nearer I readied my key. I was picturing the car door opening, a big man surging out, grappling me as I tried to reach home. I'd scream, I thought. I'd scream loud enough to bring the neighbours out into the street. I'd break his silver-rimmed glasses.

I was there. My key slid into the lock, and I looked round, hardly believing that nobody had tried to stop me. The car had slid back a length and was indicating to move off. I couldn't see who was inside. As I watched, the headlights flashed one painful throb into my eyes, and the car rolled smoothly away.

I let myself into the house, closed the door and sank to the floor of the hall.

★ ★ ★

I said nothing to anyone about the car outside my house. I woke up on Sunday, indeed, feeling certain that I'd blown the whole thing out of proportion — it was all in my head, my cruelly thudding head.

Rehearsal the following Thursday was

frustrating. Having dispatched our better-known pieces, we honked and squeaked our way through *A Song of Ireland*, completely failing to get a sense of the overall shape of it. The basses dragged; the sopranos struggled with tuning. We slogged through the pompous finale, then Diane, who had kept her cool with evident difficulty for much of the evening, said, 'All right, I don't think we'll get anything more useful done tonight. Let's go to the pub.'

I'd barely spoken to Matthew since our parting after the film on Friday. No chatty little text messages, no bridge of understanding. Lying in bed alone one night I'd cooked up a joyless little drama, wherein he, tiring of my company, was looking for excuses to back out. We had nothing in common; he was cleverer than me, more attractive. I wasn't what he wanted. Maybe he even had a girlfriend back in England. Such things were not unheard of.

When he fell into step beside me as we walked out into the street, I was surprised. He left some space between us, and I felt the distance like a canyon with a wintry wind sweeping down it. I turned to look at him, saying nothing. The others all seemed to have gone ahead.

As we neared the corner, Matthew caught

at my sleeve and pulled me towards the railings. We stopped and kissed fiercely, at first touching only with our lips, but then relenting, holding, hugging, warming each other.

Matthew said into my ear, 'I'm sorry I haven't been . . . I've been stupidly busy.'

'It's OK.'

He stroked my hair, and I drew back to look at him. 'We're like a pair of illicit lovers,' I said.

He shrugged. 'Well . . . '

'Do you mind the others knowing?'

'I thought you might,' he said, the dimple on his right cheek deep with a half-smile. I didn't believe him.

I said, 'I think it's sort of inevitable, unless we're a lot more . . . '

'Careful — ' said Matthew.

'Secretive,' I said.

We did some more kissing.

'I don't have a problem with them knowing,' I said, savouring the bright new knowledge that there really was something for them to know about.

'Fair enough,' said Matthew. 'But I don't want to make a thing of it, if you know what I mean.'

'What about . . . ' I paused, 'public displays . . . ?'

'Hmmm,' said Matthew, kissing my forehead in a thoughtful way. 'I don't really want to be too blatant about it. Not yet.' He drew back and looked at me, eyes serious. 'Is that all right?'

'That's fine,' I said. 'Sort of an open secret, then?'

'Exactly.'

'Right you are.'

'Story of my life,' he murmured as we turned to walk on towards the pub.

Inside, the others were settling themselves round a cluster of tables, piling coats in a corner, declaring their orders to the ones who were going up to the bar. I made for a table where Joan and Tom were just sitting down. Matthew tapped me on the shoulder and asked what I wanted.

'Pint of Guinness, thanks.' I sat down to face the other two, who eyed me with mischievous interrogation.

'Well, look who has a new friend,' said Joan.

'What?' I said, trying desperately not to blush.

'That was a tap on the shoulder, if I'm not much mistaken,' said Tom.

'Indeed it was,' said Joan.

'Proprietorial, one might almost say,' said Tom.

'Rubbish,' I said, unable to keep my wide grin in check. I busied myself with taking off my coat and stashing my bag under the table.

'Have it your way,' said Joan, disdainful.

Matthew returned with pints for the two of us, just as Val and Anja the Austrian soprano joined our table. They were deep in a debate of some kind.

I couldn't put my finger on exactly what annoyed me about Anja. She was the picture of perky zeal. You could imagine her practising her English syntax, memorizing lists of idioms. 'But that is exactly what I say,' she insisted as she and Val sat down. She appealed to the table at large. 'If you are going into public life or you are becoming a celebrity, you must give up your right to privacy. People are going to look up to you for your leadership, and they have the right to know what sort of person you are.'

'But no, that's nonsense,' said Val. 'You can't just make a blanket rule like that.'

'They have a right to know about anything that might affect your ability to do your job,' Tom said. 'Apart from that, it doesn't matter what you're like in private.'

'But what if you are a criminal?' Anja seemed really incensed.

'Well, that's what Tom is saying,' said Joan. 'If you're a criminal, that would affect your job. And if the public had any sense, they wouldn't vote the crooks back into office.'

Val said, 'And celebrities don't have any power anyway, so who cares what they do?'

'They have no political power, maybe,' said Anja. 'But they certainly can have influence on people's behaviour.'

'I don't think they can, really,' Matthew said mildly. 'I think they sometimes give people an excuse — '

'Oh, we're talking round in circles here,' said Val, setting her glass on the table with a slight thump. 'The bottom line is, you can't enjoy a life lived under scrutiny the whole time. Nobody has a right to follow you around and spy on you. As long as you're doing no harm, you have a right to your secrets.'

I looked over at Matthew and saw his mouth twitch minutely.

'But how can anybody tell if you are doing harm or not until they found out more about you?' Anja persisted. 'I think people really want to know who they are dealing with. It matters to them.'

'Doesn't matter to me,' Val said, causing Anja to let out an exasperated sigh. I recalled Val's outrage at her contact details being sent to Belfast. She was playing devil's advocate.

Matthew took out his phone and frowned

at the screen, then began to text.

Anja said, 'No, but obviously it matters to lots of people, or the media that report it wouldn't survive.' She took another drink. 'Anyway, it's entertainment. What is wrong with that?'

Tom said, 'Most of it is engineered by the PR people, anyway.'

'Yes, exactly — they like it,' said Anja happily, and downed the rest of her drink.

I turned to see Matthew bending to pick up his coat — cursed my weakness when the sight sent a bolt of adrenalin through me. Fear is not the appropriate response here, I told myself. Matthew stood up, unfolding himself smoothly from the low bar stool. I wanted to lay hold of him and drag him home to bed.

'You off, Matthew?' Joan said.

'Yeah, sorry,' said Matthew. 'I've got to go and meet somebody.'

'See you soon, then,' I managed to say. He waved to the crowd of them, and was gone.

I looked back down, hoping nobody would speak to me for a minute or two. Matthew had left without finishing his pint.

Two hours later I was well on my way. I was in a fine mood — thoughts of Matthew's departure had receded to a manageable distance, and I was successfully ignoring the fact that

I'd have to get up for work in the morning.

I was having a heart-to-heart with Val. I barely knew Val: quiet and difficult-looking, with her dark spiky hair, her nose-ring and her blood-red fingernails. She finished rolling a cigarette, took another sip of her pint.

'I take it you don't smoke?' She turned the bag of tobacco towards me.

'No thanks.'

'I knew you wouldn't. I was only testing you. I'd be a soprano only for these, I swear.'

'Jaysus, keep smoking,' I said, and we roared laughing.

'I give up every New Year. Lasted nearly eight months this time round.'

'Well,' I said, 'keep at it.'

'We all have our vices,' said Val. She leaned in closer. 'Isn't that right, Cate?'

I wondered what she was getting at.

'What's yours? Go on, mine are obvious.'

I took a drink and looked into my glass, swirling the dark stout around, dissolving the foam patterns that clung to the sides. I thought about my inability to draw boundaries, the way my defences seemed so very breachable, my foundations so unsure. 'Impossible men, I suppose,' I said, and hoped Val wouldn't ask me to say any more.

'Is that all?' Val said. 'Well, that's easily cured.' She stood up and patted my arm as she edged past en route to her nicotine hit outside.

* * *

Matthew and I were in Bewley's, drinking tea and being awkward with each other. He seemed preoccupied, and I wasn't up to pressing him. I looked out the window at the rainy Saturday afternoon that was already beginning to darken. We'd been to the cinema, to see an all-too-forgettable romantic comedy, and we'd sat too close to the front. My neck was still stiff; the film had not been worth it.

I was trapped in the cycle of unanswerable questions — about him, about how much he liked me, about who he was, really, under-neath it all. I so badly wanted to find out.

'Penny for them,' he said suddenly.

I looked down at the table and came to a little decision I'd been mulling over. 'I found something you might be interested in,' I said.

'Oh, yes?'

'It's in the MacDevitt book.'

Matthew picked up his teaspoon and slowly stirred his half-empty mug. 'Go on.'

With some effort, I set aside my qualms about George and his obsession with confiden-tiality. I wanted to help Matthew. 'You know the way you're researching that train ticket that went to Blackpool instead of Preston?' I looked up to see him staring at me. 'Well, there's a description in Eddie's book of a meeting with a British official, in Blackpool.'

'Really?' His eyes were wide, his expression open and soft.

'Yeah. He doesn't actually name the guy, but it could be . . . maybe?'

Matthew reached over and gripped my hand. 'Cate, I'm not joking, you have to get me a copy of that manuscript. Can you e-mail it to me?'

'Ooh, look at you and your academic fervour.'

'Tip of the iceberg, my dear. But seriously, can you e-mail me the file?'

I shook my head. 'George would kill me if he found out.'

'How would he find out?'

I wished I'd said nothing. 'Listen, it'll be published in a few months. You can see it then.'

'Oh come on, Cate, now that you've told me, I have to know what's there. I've been hunting for almost a year, and I haven't found a thing. This could be completely central to my thesis. Look, I'm not going to talk to any journalists, for goodness' sake.'

'I know you're not.'

'Just a little e-mail? For me?' He was

hamming it up, batting his eyelashes, inclining his head like a supplicant puppy.

'Listen, George is so careful about this book that he gets me to use *his* computer to work on it. He'd never let me e-mail it. I'll ask him if I can print out that section and show it to you before the book comes out.'

'No, no, no, it's so simple, you just copy and paste the description of the meeting into an e-mail to me, and click Send. Thirty seconds. Job done.'

'Matthew, I've told you, I can't. You'll just have to wait.'

'Oh, have it your own way,' he said. He still looked happy.

We finished our tea and made our way out on to Westmoreland Street. Matthew put his arm across my shoulders — I felt the heat of his palm through the fabric of my red coat. Outside in the yellow-grey dusk, a fine freezing drizzle fell; it clearly had no intention of letting up.

'I'm sick of this,' Matthew said, peering dolefully up at the sky. 'I want to move to Florida.'

'With the hurricanes and the crocodiles?'

'Alligators, I think you'll find.'

'Actually, you big pedant, I think *you'll* find there are both crocodiles and alligators in Florida.' I poked him in the chest. 'So, what next? Are you going home?'

'Yes, home,' Matthew said, with a note of regret. 'I've got loads of reading to do.'

'I'll drive you,' I said suddenly, and stood by to study his reaction.

His eyebrows rose; his fingers came up to pinch the tip of his nose.

'Come on, it's raining,' I pressed. 'You don't want to catch your death. Honestly. It's no bother.'

He glanced up at the sky again. 'That would be really great,' he said. 'Thanks.'

We crowded in under my umbrella and splashed our way to the car.

Matthew was quiet on the way out to Kilmacud. He fiddled with the radio, choosing the classical music station, which was playing a Baroque organ piece that fluted and spiralled very soothingly. My attention strayed a little as we glided down the dual carriageway, lulled by the swishing of tyres, the squeak of windscreen wipers, the kaleidoscope of headlights, tail-lights, street-lights, remembering the feeling I always used to get being driven through dark and rain by my parents — a sense of calm within chaos, of passing safely through.

'That was our turn,' Matthew said. 'Sorry, I should have warned you earlier. You can take the next one.'

We crawled up through Stillorgan and on to Kilmacud. Matthew directed me into an estate whose streets were paved in ridged sections of corrugated concrete. We made two or three turns — enough for me to wonder how easily I'd find my way out again — and finally pulled up outside a two-storey house with a pebble-dashed front and a bushy laurel hedge. The bright green leaves looked fake.

'So this is Castle Matthew.' I spoke just a little too loudly. 'Are you upstairs or downstairs?'

'Up.'

'Like me.'

There was a pause, during which Matthew looked out at the house and made no move to go.

'You left your light on,' I said. I put my hand to the back of his neck, gently scratched at the soft nest of hair that grew there. He allowed himself to be drawn, leaned over and kissed me.

When he drew back he unbuckled his seatbelt and said, 'I'd better let you go.'

'Oh, I have time for a cup of tea,' I said, and immediately realized I shouldn't have. The sinking feeling in my stomach was almost painful.

Matthew took a swift breath, held it, then said, 'Look, Cate, I'm sorry, but I'm afraid I really don't. I've got so much to do. I'd better make a start.'

I nodded, closing my eyes in acquiescence.

'I'll see you tomorrow, OK? When I've squared my conscience by doing some work for a change.' Matthew reached over for another kiss, his fingers on my cheek. He seemed genuinely regretful, at least. He squeezed my hand, opened the car door and hurried towards the shelter of the porch. He waved, and I pulled away from the kerb. I wanted to wait until I could see him in the lighted room, but I knew I mustn't. I made a three-point turn and rolled slowly back towards the mouth of the estate.

★   ★   ★

On Tuesday, George brought me along to a meeting to take minutes. He was bidding for work on a new series of excavation reports from the National Museum, and he wanted to support their belief that Bell Books was a bigger outfit than it was. He drove us into the city centre.

'I wish Paula wasn't away,' he said. 'I'm nervous leaving the office empty. I saw that young fella snooping around again over the weekend.'

I nodded.

'By the way, I've told this crowd you're my PA — is that all right?' He said *Pee Yay* carefully, as though it were a foreign word.

'That's fine, George,' I said. We were both uncomfortable. George looked as though he'd slept in the suit he was wearing. I was in the one Mum had bought me to celebrate the end of my Finals.

'I want you to make a note of everything I say, OK?' George went on. 'I think they're going to give us the work all right, but they'll try and squeeze us on the schedule, and there's a few points I want to make clear.'

He found a parking space on the south side of Stephen's Green, and we walked through the departing garden, dead leaves rasping around our ankles and a stony sky above. My suit was lightweight, and the skirt exposed my stockinged legs to the slicing wind.

The meeting was uneventful. I tapped away on the laptop, committing all that was said to its pearly screen. We left just before noon and made our way back to George's car. It had started to drizzle. George held my umbrella over the two of us, and we hurried along, keen to end the uncomfortable intimacy necessitated by this arrangement.

Through the park again. It was raining more earnestly now. I began to suspect that there was a hole in my shoe. The laptop was heavy, and I was leaning awkwardly to stay underneath the umbrella. Despite the chill and the rain, I was sweating.

George was fussing about our schedule, trying to see how we'd fit in this new work if we got it. 'How's that fisheries thing coming along?'

'Fine, but I'm still chasing McCarthy.'

'She hasn't sent it back yet?'

'She keeps pushing it out another few days. I think she's waiting for some updated numbers from the Department. And Jackman has sent me three revised versions so far.'

'Bloody authors! Our job'd be much easier without them.'

I gave a dutiful laugh.

We emerged through the black iron gates of the park on to the broad granite footpath, and I happened to glance to my left at a dark car parked a few spaces down from George's. Two men sat in it, one with glasses just like Dad's. I started and stumbled, checking as I straightened up — and sure enough, there was the *Chichester Psalms* registration. The back of my mouth tightened, and a shot of fear suffused my gut — even as I swore inwardly at myself for being so ridiculous.

'All right, there, Cate?'

'Fine — sorry.' I drew back, brushed my hair from my face.

We made it to the car. George zapped the locks, and we huddled in out of the wet. He frowned at me.

'I'm fine,' I said. 'I'll be fine.' My heart pounded. I told myself not to be so silly, that there was nothing to worry about, but I couldn't make myself listen.

'You're as white as a sheet, Cate, if you don't mind my saying,' George said. 'If you'd like to tell me what the matter is, I'm happy to help.' He gave me his sideways look.

I stayed quiet.

'Fair enough, so,' said George, gently. He started the engine and eased out into a gap in the traffic.

'I'm imagining things,' I said. My breath caught. 'It's stupid, but I keep seeing this car around the place, in all sorts of different places . . . ' I trailed off. It sounded even stupider out loud than in my head.

'So you're wondering if you're being followed?'

'Well, wondering is too strong a word.' I felt myself blush, turned my head away. We pulled up at the lights. The wipers squealed across the windscreen.

'Who'd have a reason to follow you?' George's tone surprised me. It seemed that he was actually considering the idea.

'I don't know. It's a crazy notion. It can't

be true.' I wished I hadn't allowed the conversation to take this turn.

'You never know,' said George. 'Are you sure it's the same car?'

I explained about the number, the tune.

George chuckled. 'Lord above, that's a new one on me. I guarantee you they won't have thought of that one.'

'It's just a silly coincidence,' I said, still trying to keep my voice steady. 'I feel stupid even telling you about it.'

'Well, there are worse things than feeling stupid.'

We drove a little way in silence.

'So you have no idea who it might be?'

I looked across at him; he turned his head briefly and caught my eye. He seemed about to speak again, but he waited for me instead.

'My choir has a gig up North next month.' I told him about the list of names we'd had to send in, the extreme formality attending the whole affair. Oddly, telling the story made me start to relax.

'And have you seen whether it's the same people, or different?' George was interested.

'I think I've seen one of them in a few places.'

'Two men, is it?'

'I think so.'

'Irish?'

'They look it, I suppose.'

'Well,' said George, rubbing his chin, 'I suppose . . . there's an outside chance it could be paramilitaries — our side or theirs — but they'd have got you by now if they wanted you. It's more than likely our crowd, keeping an eye out.' He snorted. 'With their usual finesse.'

I sat quiet, contemplating the ease with which George had spoken of my being wanted by paramilitaries.

'Or, you know, it could have nothing at all to do with your concert in Belfast, and everything to do with Eddie's book.'

'You think so?'

George looked across at me. 'Have you come to the part about your uncle yet?'

'No . . . what about him?'

'Oh, it's not much, now, but I'd say our friends in the dark-coloured car know very well that there's a connection between Eddie and Fintan. They might think you're a good bet to tell them where Eddie's living.'

'But I have no idea where Eddie's living.'

'Exactly.' George looked smug. 'And you won't, either. Don't worry. It's like a little graduation, Cate. Congratulations, you have your very own Special Branch man. Take good care of him, and he'll give you years of faithful service.'

I laughed in spite of myself. 'What are you on about?'

'Oh, there's stories I could tell,' he said. 'Ah, it's all a bit of nonsense, honestly. You're in no danger from them. Don't worry about it.'

I yawned carefully. 'I'll try not to,' I said. 'It's probably just routine.'

We were stopped at a red light. George gave me another searching look. 'It probably is,' he said.

As we drove on, the subject closed, I turned over in my mind that phrase George had used: 'our side or theirs'. *Our* side. Or *theirs*. It was at once so familiar and so strange.

★ ★ ★

George dropped me back to the office and headed straight out again for a lunch meeting. I allowed myself a little interval of uselessness before opening my notes from this morning. I began to read through them, editing here and there to make sure they'd be comprehensible to George.

The doorbell rang, and I picked up the intercom handset. 'Bell Books?' I said — so practised now.

'Hello, Cate.'

I hesitated. 'Matthew?'

'That's right.' After a pause, he said, 'Can I come in?'

'Uh . . . yeah . . . come on up. Top floor.' Any professional tone I might have aspired to was gone now. I buzzed him in. A few moments later I heard his steps on the stairs and opened the door to welcome him.

He was grinning his most captivating grin, against which there could be no defence. I allowed him to enfold me in a ridiculous embrace. What was he doing here? I broke gently away from him and closed the office door. 'Social call?' I said.

He had the grace to look a tiny bit embarrassed. 'Sort of,' he said, and looked down at my feet.

'You're here about the Blackpool thing, aren't you?'

He closed his eyes, screwed up his face and said, 'Yes.'

'You complete nerd! I can't believe you couldn't wait.'

'Sorry.' He smiled, like a timid animal. 'So . . . is there any chance I could . . . ?'

I was transfixed by the solidity of him, his physical presence, the sheer unlikeliness of something so beautiful existing in a place of work. It was like that first night in my flat, when he had seemed more real, somehow, than his surroundings.

He pinched the tip of his nose and looked at me.

'OK, look,' I said, 'five minutes, and you never mention this to anybody.'

'Cate,' he said, 'you are a dazzling star in the firmament of scholarly research. You are . . . a blue giant, or something.'

'Thank you, nerd boy,' I said. I led him into George's office, feeling like a cat burglar. I may actually have tiptoed.

George's computer woke up with the MacDevitt file on screen. I'd been at his desk working on it before we left this morning. I searched for 'Blackpool' and highlighted the first paragraph of the short passage I'd told Matthew about.

'Here you go.' I vacated the chair, and Matthew sat down.

'Bullseye,' he breathed.

There was silence for a minute or two while he read the text. I looked out of George's window at the tree in the front garden. A scattering of obstinate leaves clung on here and there.

'Fantastic,' murmured Matthew behind me. I turned to see that he'd clicked away from the MacDevitt file and plugged a memory stick into the side of the keyboard. As I came back to the desk he dragged the file across to the memory stick's icon and let go.

The computer went *doink*.

'Wait — did you just take a copy of the whole thing?'

He looked round at me, face serene. 'Yes. It's much quicker.' At my shocked expression he went on, 'What? You want me to create a new file, copy across just those few paragraphs, save the file, put it on the memory stick, then go back and delete my file from the hard drive, then go in and delete it from the Trash?'

'I suppose,' I said, frowning. I had no logical argument to counter with. And I needed him out of this office, right now.

He ejected the memory stick and put it in his pocket. 'Come for lunch?'

I was breathing hard. I put my hands on his chest and pushed him towards the door. 'Matthew, I need you to realize, if George found out what you'd just done, he'd fire me. He'd genuinely fire me.'

Matthew put a hand on my arm. 'Relax, he's not going to find out.'

'You have to promise me. You can't tell anyone about this.'

'Look, as you said, it's going to be published in a few months anyway, isn't it?'

We came out into the main office, and another thought struck me. 'I'm still input-ting the edits! That's not even close to the final version. You can't quote from it

142

anywhere, ever. Matthew, please just delete everything except those paragraphs about Blackpool. Please. You have to promise me.'

He was looking concerned now. He reached out his hand again, but didn't touch me. 'Cate, it's fine. Honestly, it really is fine. You are not going to lose your job. I am not going to quote from an unedited manuscript. I just needed to see it, that's all.' He drew his hand across his chin. 'And now I have, and I am so grateful, Cate. You have no idea.'

It was at this point that George came into the office.

Blood pounded in my head, and my knees felt weak. I looked down at my hand, which had shot out and gripped Matthew's wrist like a manacle.

George had apparently made his entrance intending to address me at my desk. 'There are some idiots in this town who need to realize we're not living in the dark ages!' he announced. The conviction in his voice dropped off sharply as he noticed that I was not where he expected me to be. He fell silent altogether when he saw Matthew.

'Hi, George,' I croaked, and feigned a coughing fit, hoping it would explain my red face and crooked stance. Matthew, either playing along or believing my charade, patted me firmly on the back.

George came all the way into the middle of the room. 'I see we have company?' His tone was none too friendly. I sensed his embarrassment at having fluffed his entry in front of a stranger.

Matthew stopped patting me and extended a hand. 'Hi, I'm Matthew Taylor, I'm a friend of Cate's. She was just showing me the office before we go out to lunch.' His attempt at soothing cut no ice with George, who shook his hand briefly, with ill grace.

'Charmed, I'm sure,' George muttered. He regarded Matthew through half-closed eyes. 'You've an awful familiar look about you,' he said, and it sounded as though he was exaggerating the rural flavour to his accent in deliberate contrast with Matthew's trim English. 'Have I seen you around somewhere recently?'

Matthew said mildly, 'I'm afraid I don't know.'

George fixed him with a gimlet stare, then seemed to concede and turned instead to me. 'Don't be too late back from lunch, now. I'll want those minutes from this morning before the end of the day.'

'No problem.'

George stumped into his office and shut the door.

Matthew treated me to lunch at a restaurant in Rathmines, and when I got back

144

George was waiting for me.

'Where's your friend from?' he asked.

I didn't think it was any of his business, but I said, 'He's English.'

'Well, I gathered *that*. What's he doing here?'

'He's studying with Professor Lawless, actually.' I didn't like George's tone.

'Is that what he told you? I think I've seen him snooping around here before, you know.'

'That's . . . not very likely,' I said, keeping my temper with difficulty. 'Why would he snoop around?'

'Did he say anything about Eddie's book?'

'No, he didn't!' I exclaimed, without thinking. So that was my story now. I'd need to make sure Matthew didn't tell Lawless anything that would incriminate me. Tangled web is right.

George growled and retreated to his office. I was cross with him, his knee-jerk suspicion, his old-school distrust of an Englishman. I wished I could explain to him how out of touch he was.

★   ★   ★

There was something wrong in Ardee. It was partly that it was Sunday dinner, rather than lunch, but that wasn't all. I arrived well after six, expecting to be in the doghouse for

145

turning up late, but Mum bustled out into the hall as I came in, uttering bland, perfumed greetings and offering a cheek before retreating to the kitchen. Uncle Fintan was in the sitting room, sitting apologetically in Mum's armchair, dabbing at a streaming nose as I made muffled conversation with Dad and Mícheál.

I bore it for a few minutes, then went to help Mum get the meal ready. The habitual dance of preparation — serving dishes, cutlery, table mats, wineglasses, salt shakers and butter curls — was calming, at least. As the two of us moved deftly through the routine I put my finger on what was different.

'Where's Auntie Rosemary?' I asked.

'What, love?' Mum straightened from the oven, holding a laden tray of roast potatoes in two ancient, scorched mitts. A lock of hair hung lank over her glistening forehead.

I repeated myself.

'Oh. She's not well,' Mum said.

'Did Uncle Fintan come on his own?' That was uncharacteristic, to say the least.

Mum turned to me, her face stony, and took a breath to speak. There was a silence. 'Here, can you take the soup through, and I'll get this lot sorted out.' She nodded lopsidedly at the counter, where the bowls of soup stood ready.

Dinner was tomato soup and chicken casserole with potatoes and vegetables; Viennetta for dessert. Mild bickering between Dad and Mícheál. Mum dutifully reining in the conversation, bringing everyone's attention back to the food on our plates. Uncle Fintan receiving with studied humility a generous second helping of casserole, the last few potatoes.

'How's work going this weather, Cate?' Dad asked.

I hesitated, hearing Mum breathe in. 'Grand, yeah,' I said. 'Not much going on.'

'Are you working on that book Dad was talking about?' Mícheál asked — but Mum was ready for him.

'Get the ice-cream out, Mícheál,' she said. 'It'll be rock-hard.' She glanced at Uncle Fintan. There was to be no talk about Eddie MacDevitt's book.

Mícheál kicked at the door jamb as he went out to the chest freezer in the pantry.

The grown-ups put away two bottles of wine between them. I stuck to orange juice, feeling a grudging solidarity with Mícheál, who was scowling his way through his meal. I knew how he felt. Being in this house knocked years off me.

The sense of solidarity turned out not to be mutual. 'Hey, do you still have that Brit boyfriend?' Mícheál asked me as we passed round the dessert plates.

'What?'

'Cattle has a Brit boyfriend,' he said again, just to make sure everyone heard.

'Shut *up*,' I gritted, incurring a look from Mum.

Uncle Fintan looked up. 'And how do you know that, Mícheál?'

Mícheál was leering at me now, enjoying my downfall. 'I met him the day I went to the match with PJ. He talked like a Brit.'

'How long ago was that?' What was Uncle Fintan playing at, cross-examining Mícheál like this?

'Ah, a few weeks ago,' said Mícheál. He winked at me. 'Sure, maybe you've broken up by now, have you?'

'Well, and how's your love-life?' I challenged him. 'Are you still trailing around after PJ's big sister like a flatulent bullock?'

'Don't be rude to your brother, Caitlín,' said Dad, with a warning edge.

Mum changed the subject.

Later, as we were filling the dishwasher, Mum said, with exaggerated nonchalance, 'So, what about this young man, then?'

I closed my eyes and let out a breath. 'Nothing much to tell, really.'

'Well, are you seeing him?' Her consonants were just a little fuzzy around the edges.

'I am, yeah,' I said, turning away to scrape off a plate into the compost bin.

'And where's he from, exactly?' Mum might have thought she was making casual conversation, but I knew better.

I let out a short sigh. 'He's from Bristol, Mum.'

'Oh,' she said. 'Very nice.'

I left early, unwilling to navigate the complexities any longer. Mum walked out into the porch with me.

'Will you be all right, now, driving back up on your own?'

'Mum, they gave me a licence. It wasn't a clerical error, like.'

She put an arm round my shoulders and leaned in, sharing her wine-breath. 'Caitlín,' she said, 'be careful. You know what I'm saying? Be careful.'

I hugged her perfunctorily and almost ran out the gate. Her warning had not been about driving home. I couldn't decide whether she'd meant 'use contraception' or 'don't go with a Brit'. I couldn't decide which possibility was more obnoxious.

★ ★ ★

I rolled into my street to find my usual parking spot under the ash tree waiting for

149

me. I was distracted, tired — I felt as if I had drunk wine with my dinner after all. It was odd, wasn't it, how Uncle Fintan had drunk as much as Mum and Dad. Far too much to drive. He must be staying the night in Ardee. Which meant that Auntie Rosemary was not so much sick as hostile. I recalled her fury the day Dad had read out the article about Eddie's book — Uncle Fintan spilling his water to avert a discussion that must have taken place later on.

I locked the car and thought further back, to the day Uncle Fintan gave me Eddie's manuscript for George. 'Tell him I was asking for him,' he'd said, with a little puff of glee like a child getting away with mischief. It had seemed ordinary — a delivery by one old friend to another. I hadn't realized what a transgression it was.

It wasn't comfortable, this insight into the compromises of my uncle's marriage. Squirming a little, I opened the front door, groped for the timer switch on the landing light and trudged upstairs to my flat. I hung up my coat in the dark and walked into the sitting room, which was dimly lit by the streetlight. On the table the Bell Books laptop sat open like a shell, displaying its screensaver image, a shifting shape of brightly coloured lines, flowing unfussily within the confines of the small screen.

I turned on the light. Why hadn't I mentioned the laptop at dinner? It would have earned me a heap of credit with Mum — a company laptop, practically the hallmark of a *real job*.

I was conscious of a dim unease as I prized my shoes off and went into the kitchen to put on the kettle. I needed to calm down. Perhaps there'd be a late film on — something mindless. But as I turned back to the sitting room, the sense of wrongness hit me like a rubber bullet.

The laptop.

The screensaver.

Fuck.

What did that mean? Did it mean what I thought it meant?

The surge of adrenalin took me unawares, jolting me forward towards the table. As I reached it, the screensaver shut off, the laptop settling into its sleep mode with a satisfied little murmur. I stopped short of touching it, and instead stood motionless, caught in the tangle of possibilities.

Slowly, I turned and scanned the room. My bedroom door was ajar by about six inches. I tried to remember how I had left it. Open, I thought, but I wasn't sure.

It was one thing to be followed in the street; it was quite another to imagine a stranger in my flat.

I walked quietly towards the bedroom, but halfway there, the shock of a black doorway at the edge of my vision made me jump. My stomach lurched, and I let out a little yelp. Oh. I'd forgotten to close the door to my flat. The timer on the hall light had expired. I breathed, then went to close the door. From the kitchen came the small sound of the kettle clicking off.

In the silence left by the ending of the kettle's hiss, I heard a sound so ordinary that for a few seconds I did not appreciate its implication: downstairs, barely audible, the reedy whine of the front door, the soft swish of the insulation as the latch clicked shut.

Fear rose like fire all around me. I felt short of breath. I could hear the rushing of blood, feel the thump of my heart.

Without pausing to think, I hurried to the sitting-room window, pressing my cheek to the wall and peering out. I could discern nobody clearly, but from the movements visible I constructed at least one stealthy figure picking its way through the shadows. I dragged the curtains shut, fingers shaking.

Leaden-footed, I stumbled back to the table. I didn't know where to begin. Again, I scanned the room. Nothing other than the laptop appeared to have been disturbed.

Some loose change in a saucer on the coffee table was still there. No drawers pulled out; no unexplained disarrangement.

I listened at my bedroom door for almost a minute before reaching in and turning on the light. Nothing. I eased the door open and went in.

Everything seemed normal. The urge to curl up in bed and sleep until this all blew over was almost irresistible. I steeled myself and turned back to the sitting room.

The door to the entrance hall of my flat was still open, a yawning breach in my ramparts. I went and shut it, quickly, decisively, as though to convince myself that the action would make me safe. The situation felt unreal, dreamlike. My knees were trembling; my hands and feet were very cold.

I forced myself to go back to the bedroom and check the cupboards and drawers, the bathroom and (feeling a little silly now — which brought a strange relief) under the bed.

Nobody there, of course. No apparent disturbance in this room at all. My silver and amethyst necklace and earrings, a twenty-first birthday present from Mum and Dad, were safe in their box at the back of my bedside drawer.

I could phone the Gardaí. I'd never done that before — had no idea what it would be like. Would I have to answer questions? Accompany them to the station? Would they be annoyed with me for bothering them when nothing had been taken? Probably. I had no reason, in fact, to suspect that anything at all had happened. A mouse (ugh) had run across the laptop keyboard. The closing door I'd heard had been in another house. All I had was an ill-defined suspicion about people following me — people possibly still out in the street.

The Guards would think I was mad. They could do nothing anyway. Dust for fingerprints? Probably not even that. And what if it was the Special Branch who had broken in? How would that play out?

I could phone my parents. Dad would scoff; Mum would fret — and want to get landlord Uncle Fintan involved. And the Guards. Anyway, they'd all drunk far too much wine to be any use.

I wished Sheila and Aidan were downstairs. They weren't due back until next week.

I fished out my phone and dialled Matthew's number. Straight to voicemail — I let out a yell of frustration. *Bastard!* I paced the sitting room. I was trembling again. In shock, I supposed. I was starting to unravel, whip away into a mist of disorganized thoughts and unchecked emotions. I had to keep a grip.

Denise's phone went to voicemail too; her landline was engaged. I redialled over and over again, but there was no getting through.

Then I remembered phone tapping.

Panic, now, eddying in my gut.

I stood jiggling on my toes, needing a plan — any plan. I had to go somewhere, talk to someone. I started to phone my parents after all, but cancelled before the call went through. By now, I knew I couldn't pretend to be calm. There'd be a scene. I couldn't stand it. I'd go out, get in the car, drive over to Matthew's and make him let me in. I'd take the laptop with me, just in case —

Fuck. They'd be watching the house, of course.

So I couldn't go out the front door. Couldn't get to the car. I had visions of being set upon by grim men with vicious strength of purpose. Stifled; bundled into the back of a dark car with a tuneful registration number. Taken away for questioning. I didn't much care whether the people concerned were working within or without the law.

But I couldn't stay. I'd have to find some other way out. The flat roof of Sheila and Aidan's kitchen. The wall at the end of the yard. The narrow laneway at the back of these houses.

My heart raced; my breath came quick and

shallow. I packed the laptop in its black case, cursing how heavy it was and hoping I wouldn't damage it. When I was wrapped up — again — in coat, hat, scarf, gloves, with my handbag slung across my body and the laptop case in my hand, I stood in the sitting room and took a last look round. An idea struck me, and I switched on the television, then went into the bedroom and opened the window. The sash would lift by just enough to allow me out.

The flat roof was about two feet below my windowsill. I leaned out and put the laptop case down before bundling myself gracelessly through the narrow gap. It wasn't raining now, but the dark grey tarpaper surface of the roof was still wet from earlier. I pushed the sash back down as far as I could. It was harder than I expected to pick my way across the roof in the dark, feet crunching on the rough surface. I was anxious about my footing and — unable to see much — genuinely inconvenienced by the laptop. I reached the edge without mishap and considered my next move.

I must either make my way along the wall that divided this garden from the neighbours', or climb down into the garden and then somehow scale the end wall into the lane. I leaned out to assess the possibilities for climbing down by the kitchen window. Felt dizzy, drew back, took some deep breaths. Blood rushed in my ears.

Two gardens down, a dog started barking. If anyone came out and saw me, things could get very complicated. I had to move on quickly. My legs were like jelly, and a knot of adrenalin soured in my stomach.

OK, the wall. It was a continuation of the house wall, about a foot and a half down from the roof on which I stood. The top of it was curved, and it was alarmingly narrow. Very cautiously, I placed a foot on it and tested my weight. Sweat pricked out all over my skin, and I managed to leave the roof. I inched sideways along the wall with painful care — all of twenty feet. It felt like miles. At least there was no vegetation to slip on. The dog's barking subsided, to my enormous relief, making the noise of nearby traffic seem louder. When I reached the junction with the end wall I felt like cheering. I let out a long sigh, noticing only then that I'd been holding my breath. My mouth was dry, and I could taste my dinner on the back of my tongue.

I sat on the end wall and peered down into the lane. My eyes were used to the darkness by now, and I looked for easy ways down. There didn't seem to be anything handy. I'd have to jump. The wall wasn't very high.

First I took off my scarf and tied the end around the handles of the laptop case. The night breeze came chill across my sweat-damp throat. By leaning right down, gripping the rough concrete top of the wall with a gloved hand, I was able to place the case safely on the ground. Then I manoeuvred myself round so that I was facing the house, balanced on my hands. A siren from a few streets away rang through my head.

It was only as I dropped down on to the leaf-carpeted surface of the lane that it occurred to me that the television would be on all night. I hoped it wouldn't disturb the neighbours.

It took me a moment in the silent lane to collect myself. I put my scarf back on, after brushing off the leaves it had picked up on the ground. The rich, tangy smell of leaf mould rose around me. My breath sounded loud, and I could just see the ghostly puff of it on the air. I was astonished that I'd actually done it.

I picked up the laptop and started walking.

★ ★ ★

The worst bit, in the event, was getting to the end of the lane. I knew that it was a haunt for young drinkers, and there was a fine selection of traffic cones and shopping trolleys along its length, as well as the usual litter. A bricked-up gateway, set slightly back, reeked of stale piss. I walked along on the balls of my feet, stomach fluttering, clutching the laptop with an iron grip.

I met nobody. As I headed out into the better-lit street I relaxed and began to walk with more confidence.

It was colder than I'd thought, and damp, even if not raining. My senses were sharp: I could hear every car from a long way away, and I felt aware of everything on the street. I almost began to enjoy myself, in a detached sort of way.

Before long I hailed a taxi and gave the driver Matthew's address. I didn't phone him again, in case he tried to talk me out of coming. When we got to the house my heart sank to see that every window was dark. I took my time opening the garden gate and walking up the path. He'd better be there.

He wasn't there. Behind me, I heard the taxi driver turning his car. 'Here!' he called. 'Are you OK waiting on your own?'

'I'm grand, yeah,' I said, waving my phone. 'He's on his way.' A ball of cold fear sat in my chest.

'Fair enough, so,' said the taxi driver. He dawdled a bit but eventually moved away.

I phoned Matthew now, with no success. It

was after eleven — surely he'd be back soon. I had no idea what his habits were. I looked up at the sky — pale clouds spread out like a down quilt, lit by the city glow. There was nowhere else I could go. I hunkered down on the doorstep.

'Cate!'

I jolted out of a half-dream and jumped to my feet. I was shivering and aching from being still for so long in the cold.

Matthew was hurrying up the path, his long coat flapping. 'What the hell are you doing here?' He spoke roughly.

'I'm sorry — I . . . ' My voice came out in a scared little whine. 'My flat was broken into.'

He stopped short. 'Blimey. What happened?'

'I don't know. They just . . . they didn't take anything. I think they were looking for — oh, I know this sounds weird — but something on the laptop. My laptop from work.'

He frowned. 'Really?'

'I know. It's ridiculous. But I think . . . some people have been following me around for the past few weeks.'

'Following you around? Are you sure?'

'I think so. I don't know.'

'Did you phone the police?'

I was wrapped in a fog of confusion. Everything was wrong. 'No, I didn't. You see, I think it might actually be the Special Branch following me.'

Matthew took this in silently, looking down. 'Is that the laptop there?'

'Yeah.'

He gave a short sigh. 'OK, you'd better come in.'

'Thanks,' I said. I moved towards him, and he put an arm round me as he got out his keys.

'I can't believe I'm finally getting to see your flat,' I ventured.

'You are, at that.'

'Penetrating the inner sanctum.'

'Is that how you see it?' His tone was cool. I'd struck a wrong note.

'You're a very private person,' I said gently.

'Meaning a secretive bastard, I presume,' said Matthew. He turned away from me to close the door.

'No, come on, don't be like that. I just mean private. I know so much less about you than you do about me.'

'Well, you don't ask me very much.'

We began to climb the stairs. I didn't attempt to explain how it felt whenever I did ask about his inner life, his memories, his beliefs — as if there were a moat round him, and I shouting across it, unable to hear the answers.

The hallway of Matthew's flat had originally been the landing of the house. He indicated kitchen and bathroom at either end of it, then led the way into the sitting room. I followed, feeling frail and shaky.

Matthew visibly pulled himself together. 'So. Welcome.' He gestured vaguely. 'Tea?'

'Yes, please.'

I put down the laptop and took stock of my surroundings. The walls were painted a grating shade of yellow; the carpet was grey-blue, with tracks of wear curving through it. A fat, old, sagging sofa dominated the room, in front of which stood a coffee table with nothing on it but heat rings. Opposite, a television sat on a wooden chair, a DVD player balanced on its head. In the corner across from the door, a small pine-effect dining table with legs of tubular steel was clearly Matthew's desk. A black anglepoise lamp was clamped to its edge, and the surface area that was not occupied by an elderly computer was covered with papers and books. A slightly wonky swivel-chair did duty as a coat stand. Several cardboard boxes took up most of the space under the desk. There were no bookshelves — indeed, apart from a small cupboard with peeling veneer, which crouched behind the door, no obvious storage space at all. The overall effect was seedy, bleak, unloved.

Sounds of pouring and stirring came from the kitchen. I put my coat and bags on the chair, then crossed over to the window to close the curtains, which had a floral print and didn't quite meet in the middle.

'Here we are,' Matthew said from the door.

We sat on the sofa and sipped our tea. Matthew had added sugar to mine, for which I was grateful. I went on shaking long after I'd thawed.

'I'm having a weird evening,' I said.

'You poor thing,' said Matthew. 'Why don't you tell me all about it?'

So I did. I started from my first sighting of the dark car, back in August that night after choir. When I told Matthew what had made me notice the registration plate, he exclaimed, 'Ha! It had a tune in its number plate. Naturally!'

'Yes. It was a particularly good catch, too.' I sang it for him: 'Five two eight four five. Opening of *Chichester Psalms*.'

'So they pick the one car you're bound to spot. What are the chances?'

'I'd have saved myself a lot of worry if I hadn't been playing the game that day.'

When I finished my story, he said, 'And your hypothesis is that this is the Special Branch doing a background check for Belfast, yes?'

'Well, I thought so, but then George said it might be to do with the MacDevitt book . . . ' I trailed off, remembering what George had said about Uncle Fintan knowing Eddie MacDevitt — and the trouble Eddie's book was apparently causing between him and Auntie Rosemary.

'Somebody already knows all about the MacDevitt book, though, don't they, because they wrote that article in the newspaper.'

'Yes, but George said another time that Eddie lives abroad for good reason — and Dad said there are dangerous men who'd like to get hold of him. Maybe they think the laptop might have his address.'

'They'd just steal it, though. To me, this sounds more like the Special Branch.'

'I don't know. It feels pretty extreme. I mean, is the Special Branch allowed to break into my flat without a warrant?' I shook my head. 'Why am I even asking you?'

'You forget, my dear: I study this stuff. As far as I know, they aren't. But what makes you think they didn't have a warrant? They'd get one, if they thought there was something specific to find. Particularly if they consider you a security risk.'

'But that's bollocks! There's no way I'm a security risk. That's insane.'

Matthew said nothing.

I played with the edge of a hole in the sofa cover. 'Does it feel strange, having me here?'

'Yes, it does, rather. Not entirely sure why.' His tone was clipped, as though he were thinking about something else.

'Like I said, you're private.' I hoped he'd react better to the epithet this time round.

'Perceptive Cate.'

'Don't worry, I'm not nosy,' I said. I caught his eye and had to look down.

'Oh yes you are,' he said, and his voice was tender now, teasing. I put my tea down on the table, and he put his on the floor. When we kissed it was with surprising passion — there was a fierceness, a yearning that I had not felt from him before. He clutched at my hair, pulling me closer, plunging into my mouth, biting at my lips. My entering his territory had meant a lot, I realized. It made a difference. I kissed back with equal fervour, a pulse of pleasure beginning to spread in my belly.

'All right then, if you put it like that,' I said happily, when we paused for breath.

'Well, I'm glad that's settled,' Matthew said. He smiled slowly. 'Now, tell me, did you have a look at the laptop, see if you could find anything?'

'What? No . . . ' I shook my head, feeling hopeless, stupid. Obviously, that was what I should have done first of all.

'Then let's have a look, shall we?'

I stared at him. My stomach was fluttering at the thought that there might actually be something to find. That would be altogether too concrete for my taste. 'I don't know.'

'Just a quick peek,' Matthew said. 'It can't do any harm.' Was there a tinge of excitement in his voice?

'But we don't know where to start,' I said. 'It'd just be a game — there's no point.'

'Cate, this doesn't sound like a game.' He put his hand on the back of my neck. The dry warmth of his fingers was so reassuring, so exquisitely ordinary, that I could feel my shoulders relaxing under his touch. 'It could be important. I might be able to help.'

'Fancy yourself as an amateur sleuth?'

'Maybe a bit.'

I stood up reluctantly and got the computer, opening it on the coffee table. Matthew dragged the table closer to the sofa, and I went through the start-up procedure. I looked in a few folders, reading filenames, finding no clues. Although some of the documents were unfamiliar to me, everything seemed entirely unremarkable.

A thought struck me, and I called up the list of recently used documents in the word-processing program. Nothing I didn't recognize. I couldn't tell whether the order was different from before. I opened some files at random, but soon realized that this was futile.

I was aware of Matthew beside me, his fists gently clenched on bouncing knees. I turned to look at him. 'You really want to have a go, don't you?'

He nodded vigorously. 'Oh, yes, please.'

I sat back and let him take over.

Within seconds, I was lost. Nothing Matthew did remotely resembled my ineffectual pawing at the keyboard. He had multiple windows open, each delivering drips or waterfalls of orderly cyphers in white on black, which he examined before keying in further arcana. 'You know your stuff,' I remarked.

'My sister's a computer security expert. I've picked up a few things over the years.'

He resumed his purposeful tapping, muttering unintelligibly to himself. I finished my tea, waggled my feet, yawned, stared at the bare walls, the cracked ceiling. After a while I said, 'Well, Sherlock? Find anything?'

'I'm not sure. They might have installed some kind of scanning software . . . '

I felt as if he were speaking from a long way away. I said nothing, just sat and looked blankly at him.

'But the thing is, that could easily have been done remotely, while the machine was connected to the net — you use this for e-mail, don't you?'

I nodded.

'So they wouldn't have needed to get into your flat. They must have had some other reason. Something on the hard drive.' He turned back to the keyboard, lower lip protruding in thought.

I put my hand on his arm. 'Matthew, this is too bizarre. This is — I'm sorry, I just can't believe this is happening. I can't believe you're being so calm about it.'

He blinked, came back to me. 'Sorry. This must be awful for you. I read too many thrillers, I expect.'

He was so upbeat, I wanted to shock him, shake him, hit him, wake him up somehow to the enormity of what was going on. 'This is just not even on my map,' I said. 'I can't believe you know about this stuff.' Exhaustion rolled in from all sides, making my head spin, my sight flicker.

'I know almost nothing,' Matthew said. 'Just enough to be dangerous.'

'Stop it,' I said, and dissolved in tears. My throat ached with shame, but I couldn't help it.

Matthew's arms were round me, holding me close, rocking back and forth, whispering, 'Shhh, shhh, it's OK, don't worry about it. We'll sort it out. Cate, I'm so sorry, I shouldn't have been flippant. You must be feeling terrible.'

'Yes,' I said, between gulps of air, 'I'm feeling terrible, and I'm feeling stupid. And none of this is happening. It's all just crazy.'

Matthew reached out and shut the lid of the laptop. 'How about something to eat?'

'That would be nice,' I managed, in a craven whine.

'Shall I cook a frozen pizza?'

'Yes, please.'

Matthew went to the kitchen, and I heard him moving about. I was wrung out, squashed, cracked. I worried about him seeing me in this needy state. He would surely run now, I decided. He liked his privacy too much, his distance.

He put his head round the door. 'Ham and mushroom or pepperoni?'

I had to pull myself together, present a coherent face. 'Ham and mushroom, please.' I breathed deeply, tried to relax.

'Deed's done,' he said a moment later, and went to put on some music — a tranquil jazz singer. He turned off the central light, and we sat in the dim glow of the averted anglepoise with our arms round each other. We said very little. When the pizza was ready, Matthew cleared the laptop and its case off the coffee table. I sat, inert, while he brought the food and glasses of water in from the kitchen. He disappeared again and came back with a white candle in a metal holder. He found matches in the mess on his desk, and lit the candle with a flourish.

'There,' he said. 'Candlelit supper. Can't say fairer than that.'

We ate our pizza, which tasted far better than it deserved to. We kissed quite a lot between slices, and talked about nothing in particular.

'You know, you really are exceptionally pretty,' Matthew said at one point.

'In candlelight,' I said, fishing hard.

'Yes, also in candlelight.'

'Well, you're not the worst yourself.'

'Good. I must say, it's encouraging to hear that I'm not the worst.'

'Yes,' I said. 'But don't let it swell your handsome head.'

'Cruel woman.'

'Come here.'

We began to undress each other there on the sofa, and soon, in silent agreement, we got up and made our way to the bedroom. We didn't turn on the light. I had the impression of an open wardrobe door, a chair piled with clothes.

We crawled into bed and were soon naked, clutching at each other, moving together with grace and meaning.

Later, we lay facing the window, Matthew's long arms encircling me. I was still anxious and wakeful, despite my exhaustion. The image of his avid face as he hacked away at the laptop wouldn't leave my head. It was late — nearly two o'clock — but I knew I was a fair distance from sleep.

'I have to go to work in the morning,' I said. With the laptop, I mentally added. And tell George what happened. Which presumably means the end of my little home-based copyediting career.

'You sure?' Matthew murmured.

'Hmmm.'

'You could take the day off.'

'I . . . maybe. I don't know.'

'Come on. You may never have an excuse this good again.'

I reached a hand behind me to stroke his downy thigh. 'I'll tell you one thing. I really don't want to go back to my flat tonight.'

'Stay with me, then.'

'All right.'

I lay in the dark with my eyes open and my stomach clenched, wishing it were that simple.

Part Three

A Song of Ireland

I talked myself into going to work the next day, which was a mistake. George was furious because the printers had accidentally flipped an illustration in *The Irish Horse*, and nobody had noticed the error until the books had been bound and delivered. He loomed around for much of the morning, looking stormy. I heard him banging up and down his office, shuffling paper and cursing. Shouting into the phone — 'It's *very* noticeable! There's a bloody sign up on the wall behind the horse. You can *see* it. The text is clearly backwards!'

He appeared at the door, teeth bared. 'Have you Paula's mobile number?'

'Sure,' I said, hastily reaching for the office address book. I scribbled Paula's number on a sticky note, which George snatched from my hand. He bolted back into his office, slamming the door.

The details of the night before hovered around me like a flock of terrible black birds, skimming and swooping and landing without warning. I was upset with Matthew. He'd been business-like at breakfast, all terse and mechanical, as though the well of comfort we'd found together last night had run dry. There was no suggestion that I stay again tonight. He did his best, but I sensed that he wanted me out of his space. The portcullis was firmly down. We kissed goodbye like a pair of actors on a stage.

All morning I pretended to work. I could barely focus. At lunchtime I went down to the newsagent for a sandwich. As I walked back, my mind was fixed on the doors — the front door of my house and the door of my flat. I couldn't recall noticing anything odd about them when I got home from Ardee. Which meant these people might have keys. (They might be in there right now.)

There was nothing for it: I was going to have to talk to Uncle Fintan. I pulled out my phone and quickened my pace.

'Hello?' said Uncle Fintan, in his careful way.

'Hi, Uncle F, it's Cate. Have you got a minute?'

'Of course, Cate, I.'

'Listen, something happened last night. I think someone got into the flat when I wasn't there.'

'Oh, lord bless us and save us. When you weren't there. Was anything?'

'Well, no, I don't think so. But this is the

thing. I don't think the lock was broken. I think they might have keys.'

There was silence, and then Uncle Fintan said very gently, 'And if the lock wasn't broken, and nothing was taken, do you mind my asking, how do you?'

'I just . . . ' I faltered. What an idiot I was. I hadn't thought this through. I hadn't prepared myself to tell him the whole story — not by a long chalk. I was nearly back at the office; I stopped and leaned against a cold gatepost. 'OK,' I said. 'This is going to sound a bit wacky.' I told him I thought I was being watched. I told him what I'd found when I got home last night — the open laptop, the click of the front door.

'And what were they after, do you think?' Uncle Fintan's voice had an unusual energy — it sounded almost like fear.

'I don't know — something on the laptop?'

'Eddie's book, I suppose. Was it on there?'

'No.'

'Any contact details for him?'

'No, not as far as I know.'

'Good. And did you sleep in the flat last night?'

'No, I . . . stayed with a friend.'

'All right, so,' said Uncle Fintan, revving down to his normal speed. 'I'll get a locksmith over this afternoon. It shouldn't take too long. I'll meet you at the house when you come home.'

'Thanks a million,' I said. It was entirely inadequate to express my relief.

'Ah, sure, it's no trouble at all, Caitlín. You can always.'

I thanked him again and went back to work.

And with that, my courage was spent. I tried to muster the wherewithal to tell George what had happened, but I failed. When the day finally came to an end I just tucked the laptop under my desk and hoped he wouldn't ask about it. Hoped whoever I was hiding it from wouldn't break into the office to carry on where they'd left off.

Uncle Fintan phoned as I was standing at the bus stop in the sodium dark, eyes peeled for the *Chichester Psalms* car. He said, 'I'm at the house now and I have your new keys. Is it . . . are you?'

'I'm on my way.'

The journey home was nerve-wracking — both the juddering bus and the walk at the other end. I did my best to check every car that went past me. When I got to my house I nearly tried to open the door with my defunct key, but remembered in time to ring the bell. After a moment I heard movement inside, footsteps approaching the door. There was a pause, which I guessed meant that Uncle Fintan was looking at me through the spy hole. Then I heard the rattle of the chain, and the door opened at last. After I came in, Uncle Fintan carefully slid the chain back into place.

We went upstairs, and I made us tea. 'Will you stay and have something to eat?' I asked.

'Thank you, that would be.'

'Great,' I said. I made us a Spanish omelette with peppers and peas, and we listened to Schubert while we ate.

'Cate, you said earlier you thought someone was?'

I gave an inward sigh. I'd relaxed quite a bit, and I didn't relish the thought of discussing my worries again. 'It's just this car I keep seeing around the place. George reckons the Special Branch. He practically gave me a medal.'

Uncle Fintan didn't ask for more. After we'd cleared up the dinner things, he said, 'Actually, Cate, I might sleep on your sofa tonight, if you don't mind.'

'Well . . . sure.' Was this out of concern for my safety or to avoid a cold welcome in Swords?

Without overture I was assailed by a wave of exhaustion, as though the tension of the last two days had caused something essential to snap, leaving me limp and useless. I sorted out sheets and blankets for Uncle Fintan and went to bed.

I didn't feel much better in the morning. I'd kicked off the covers during the night, and I woke cold and stiff. I dressed quickly. It was early, but when I crept out to the sitting room I found Uncle Fintan already awake. I pulled the curtains and let in what daylight there was.

My attention was drawn to a car parked across the road a few houses down. A large, dark saloon; I couldn't see the number plate. I closed my eyes, feeling the anxiety start to build up again. And the tune in my head: *five two eight four five* . . .

'Is everything?'

'Yeah, I'm fine.'

Uncle Fintan came over and drew me gently to one side, away from the window. 'Is it the car?' He stood at an angle, looking out into the street.

I said, 'It's about three down, over on the other side. But I don't know if it's them.'

I indulged a brief fantasy of marching out there and confronting them, demanding to know what it was they wanted — what they thought I knew. What would they do then? They'd hardly gun me down in the street, would they? Perhaps I'd be arrested. Uncle Fintan would so enjoy bailing me out.

By the time I left for work the dark car had gone.

* * *

I was much better able to engage with my work today. George had cheered up, having come to a satisfactory arrangement with the errant printers, and I was almost ready to send the fisheries book to the typesetter. My head was full of quotas, spawning seasons and the consistent notation of Latin species names; when my phone buzzed it made me jump.

A text from Matthew: 'How's it going? Sorry I haven't been in touch. Supervisor is heaping work on my head. 990'

So he was sorry, was he? I texted back: 'That's all right. I haven't been in touch either, and I'm not sorry at all.'

'Cruel Cate:-)'

'Vicious, I am.' Indeed, I felt pretty vicious. It wouldn't have killed him to check how I was.

There was silence for a little while, and then another buzz: 'Room in your schedule for an evening with me, or will you be too busy being vicious?'

'Think I can squeeze you in between drug deal this afternoon and regular Tuesday night dog fight. Come round to mine and we'll cook dinner? I'll abduct a small child; we can have it with 3 veg.' Oh, I liked this idiom. I could keep it up all day.

'Sounds good to me. Can I bring anything? PS: I applaud your use of semicolons. 990'

That softened me a little. 'Just ur 133t slicing skillz; I'll get provisions. 90'

'There were no small children to be had,' I explained when Matthew arrived at my flat. 'Not even for ready money.' We made our carbonara instead, elbowing each other around the tiny kitchen.

We ate sitting opposite each other, drinking the wine that Matthew had brought and talking about nothing. We were skirting, both of us. I didn't want this interval of ease to end.

'Have you seen that car again?' he asked eventually.

'I don't know. There was a car parked across the road this morning. But I didn't see its number plate.'

'You didn't check it?'

'No, I could not be arsed.' I groaned loudly. 'I am so fucking bored of the car.'

Matthew frowned. 'And no more disturbances in the flat?'

'No.' I chewed on a nest of pasta, enjoying the salty zing of the bacon.

Matthew said, 'How long have you been living here? Did you move in when you started at uni?'

I shook my head. 'God, no. Two solid years of hellish commuting back and forth to Ardee. Uncle Fintan rescued me. Mum and Dad weren't pleased at all, to begin with.'

'Why not? You were an adult — you needed a bit of independence.'

'Yes, that was precisely their problem with it. I still went home every weekend until I graduated.'

'Gosh.'

'It's kind of normal here. You left home to go to university, didn't you?'

'Yes, I went to Cambridge when I was eighteen.'

'And what was that like?'

'Oh, you know. Kind of normal, as you say.' He looked off into the distance. I thought I could feel the portcullis quiver, the ropes groaning in the effort to hold it open. 'New city, away from my family. Nobody knew me. It was great. I used to tell the most outrageous fibs about myself. I went a bit mad, to be honest.'

'Mad how?'

'I don't know.' A note of frustration had entered his voice, as if he found it tedious to spell out these trivialities. 'I drank too much and didn't go to my classes, if you must know. I was predicted to get a First, but I only just scraped through my first-year exams.'

'Really?' I couldn't conceal my surprise. 'You big rebel.' I pointed a finger at him. He frowned. It was not quite right.

'Big idiot, more like. My father wasn't best pleased. I got used to stony silences at the dinner table that summer.'

'Ha. We didn't have those. We had torrents of hostile cheerfulness.'

'Now, that surprises me,' said Matthew, with a small twist of his head. 'I'd got the impression that your home life was fairly . . . untroubled.'

'Bland hell,' I said. 'Every now and then a crisis, but always miles under the surface. My parents weren't the sort to confide in us kids.'

'Seen and not heard?'

'No, not as Victorian as that. I think they just have a very rigid sense of what children can handle. They'd never discuss grown-up stuff with us. It just wouldn't occur to them that you could.'

I was remembering Sunday lunches with my grandparents and all the aunts and uncles and cousins on Dad's side. We were the youngest of the cousins. The children would be put sitting round the kitchen table, with the plastic-handled cutlery and the old, dishwasher-bleached plates and glasses, while the adults had linen and china and silver in the dining room. Mícheál and I were usually made to lay the tables; I'd bags the dining room, for the pleasure of handling the best things. The cousins were loud and overbearing, violent and derisive with each other, contemptuous of people and places they had seen. I tended to keep quiet and hope the conversation wouldn't touch upon me.

'What are you thinking about?'

'Sunday lunches.' I gave a theatrical shudder.

He reached across to stroke my cheek. 'It's OK, sweetness,' he said, saccharine-toned. 'All better now.' The warmth of his fingers moving across my skin was electrifying.

After dinner, we curled up together on the sofa and escaped into the stylized elegance of *The Third Man*. I hadn't watched it in years. Matthew stayed the night, but despite the superficial ease of our interaction, despite the physical closeness, I couldn't relax. Though he'd been smiley and tactile all evening, somehow it felt like a deliberate decision on his part, rather than spontaneous desire.

I couldn't sleep. I lay in the dark, in the grip of this weird sense that the room (the idea, the history of the room) was disintegrating around me. The bed where I lay with

Matthew could bear no relation to the bed where I had lain with others before him — and none of these spaces could have anything to do with the scene of my frantic, ludicrous escape the other night. Nor could those past selves be incorporated into the self that lay here tonight. A crowd of people, all Cate, battered on the door, the windows, but must be firmly resisted: curtains closed, bolts shot home. Tonight's self felt paper-thin — or worse, as if a breath of air, a draught even, would send her flying in swirls of ashen flakes.

Damn. I'd made myself cry. Torn between wanting Matthew to notice and hoping he wouldn't, I let two or three tears slide down my cheek and into the pillow, unwilling to move to wipe them away. I fought to keep my breathing regular — then blew my cover by sniffing.

'You OK?' Matthew's voice was thick with sleep.

'Yeah, I'm fine.'

'You sure?' He brought his hand up and laid it on my shoulder, breaking the hold I had over myself. For the second time in as many days I turned to him sobbing, burying my face in his chest, feeling like a caricature, a crude figure cut out of newspaper. Matthew held me, stroked my back, murmuring

'Shhhh' and 'It's all right', and I could feel his embarrassment as if it were my own.

'I'm sorry,' I said at last, when I could trust my voice again.

'It's OK.'

We were strangers, suddenly, alarmed to find ourselves in bed together, naked, in a tableau of intimacy that was belied by our awkwardness, our wooden expressions.

We were silent for another while, then Matthew said, 'Anything I can help with?' He sounded like a shop assistant.

I sniffed again, and thought about what to say. I wanted to puncture his calm; I didn't want to make myself vulnerable to his indifference.

'Are you afraid they'll come back again?' he asked.

'Kind of,' I said. 'But . . . that's not it.'

'Seriously, Cate, if there's anything worrying you, anything on your mind . . . maybe I can help.'

'Oh, it's complicated.' I had no will for this.

'I can do complicated,' Matthew said. 'They taught me how at university.' A reassuring note of interest in his voice.

I rallied myself. Maybe we could have a conversation after all. Maybe. Don't rush it.

Then I meant to say, 'I can't really describe it,' but what I said was, 'I just don't feel real.'

My words hung in the air.

'You don't feel real,' Matthew repeated, wooden again.

'I don't know. I was lying here, thinking, and I felt as if I were disappearing — or dispersing, maybe — as if nothing I did had any weight in the world. I'm just a shadow falling on thin paper.'

'I see what you mean,' Matthew said — then sensing me begin to recoil, added, 'no, I mean, you're right: it is complicated.'

'And you,' I found myself saying. 'You're not real either.'

We let this assertion infuse. My heart beat hard, and my legs began to throb — fight or flight. I'd gone too far. Now was not the time. I drew breath to speak, to retract, but then Matthew said, 'In what way?'

Onward, then, and hang the cost. I spoke quickly: 'I barely know you. We're so intimate in some ways, and I sometimes feel there's a — a real understanding there, and yet at the same time we're so distant. Sometimes I feel as if I'm meeting you for the first time. We joke about how private you are, but it's more than that. You . . . you. I don't know. You're so reserved. You vouchsafe so little of yourself.'

He murmured, 'Vouchsafe.'

'Sometimes, I ask you something simple, like what you did today, or what your life at school was like, and I feel like I'm giving you the third degree. It's never just an easy exchange of information. It's as if . . . I'm out in the cold, trying to peek through the cracks in your curtains. Picking through your dustbins.'

He laughed, but kindly. 'Come on, Cate, that's stalker talk.'

'I know,' I said. 'OK, it's not really like that.' I forced a laugh of my own. 'I don't go through your bins. Often.' But I felt miserable.

'Go back to the bit about disappearing,' Matthew said. Still calm, still interested — *and still evading like hell*. The habit must be absolutely ingrained.

I shook my head. 'It's just that I have no handle on my life at the moment, what I'm doing, what I want to be doing. I get up in the morning and go to work, and I come home and watch television, or read, or see you, or go to choir, and at the weekends I go out, go shopping, see a film, visit my family, and it all seems, just, flimsy. Like mist. And I'm floating along through everything, not thinking. Not engaged. Just empty. And it's been like this for ages. And I'm so tired of it.'

'So . . . you *want* to disappear?' Matthew said.

'Yes,' I said. 'No. I don't. It's a frightening feeling. I want to wake up and be real again, really in this world. I'm sorry — I shouldn't be spouting on about this to you.'

'Why not?'

'Thank you for listening.'

Later, I awoke in the velvet dark from a dream filled with worry. I was alone. There was no sound from the bathroom. I slipped out of bed and padded to the half-open door. Matthew was standing by the sitting-room window, at an angle, looking out into the street.

*　*　*

The worry persisted through the next few days, reified by a headache that wouldn't leave. I neither phoned Matthew nor heard from him. It was all unravelling. There was no comfort. He was lost. I was resigned.

Thursday rolled round again, and Carmina Urbana convened for a miserable rehearsal. *A Song of Ireland*, that jewel among peace anthems, continued to cause strife, with Daintree's impenetrable rhythms and gratuitous discords tripping us up every few phrases. Tom discovered a footnote explaining that the text had been written in English and translated into Latin, which he pronounced crass and pretentious.

Diane was in bossy mode, the ice and brass in her personality to the fore. 'This gig is *nine* days away,' she reminded us tartly, 'and the piece is barely presentable. At this rate we're going to let ourselves down badly. Nobody wants that.' We'd been too arrogant at the start. Her remonstrations, of course, made us sing no better. Our tuning deserted us entirely.

'All right,' she said at last, shaking her head. 'Learn your notes, OK? Just learn them. I don't know how I can be any clearer. Seriously. I want to start putting some sort of shape on this, not to embarrass ourselves.' She sighed, squared her shoulders and gave us a stiff smile. 'Right. Bernstein.'

The choir palpably relaxed.

After the break Diane handed out a piece for our set in Belfast, a new arrangement of 'Danny Boy'.

Tom groaned, 'Aw, Miss, do we have to?'

'It's a special request,' said Diane.

'But won't the Northern choir be annoyed if we nab their most famous song?'

'It's all about the peace and tolerance,' Diane explained. 'Seems they thought it would be good for us to sing music from each other's traditions. All right' — she gave the notes — 'from the top.'

Matthew sang the melody, with consummate skill and dignity, while the rest of us provided a sludgy backdrop of *Ooh* and *Aah*. Diane barely conducted us at all, as we hummed and crooned under Matthew's solo. His voice was smooth and lustrous with a pleasing depth of texture.

I grew tenser and tenser as we went on. I wanted to jump out of my seat and run away — Matthew's voice was too much: it came at me, surrounding and smothering, piercing and flaying. I missed my cue to join in the rousing finale, and limped along to the end, out of tune and harsh. The harmonies were trickier than they looked.

After we finished the read-through, Tom made a show of clearing a phlegmy throat and spitting. 'The things we do to maintain diplomatic relations! No offence to your good self, Matthew,' he added. 'You made the best of it.'

'That's right, Tom,' said Diane. 'We'll wow them. They'll love us.'

'It is so ridiculous,' I heard Anja say to her neighbour. 'This is not a man's song at all. People don't think about these things.'

At last the rehearsal came to an end. I helped put back a chair or two, keeping half an eye on Matthew to see would he come over to talk to me. We hadn't said a word to each other all evening.

I was standing near his coat, so we met as he came to put it on.

'All right, Cate?'

We made our way towards the door.

'You coming for a drink?' I asked, as we crossed the little hallway.

'Not tonight,' Matthew said. 'I'm for my bed, in fact.' He held the outer door open for me.

'Not for mine, then?' I said when we were both standing in the street.

'What?'

'For your bed? Not for mine?'

Blank look.

'I'm propositioning you,' I explained.

'Oh. Bit slow on the uptake, there.' He put a hand on my shoulder, looked at the ground. 'No, I'm sorry. I can't. Not tonight. I've got a busy day tomorrow. I'll see you soon, though, all right?'

'Yeah,' I said. A quick kiss, and Matthew headed off towards his bus stop.

I wanted to run after him and punch him in the gut. I hated to think that he might be just another of my mistakes.

       ★   ★   ★

I went to the pub with the others and regretted it. The conversation turned to the accommodation arrangements in the hotel in Belfast. Donal had made a list of who would be sharing with whom. I was dismayed to find that I was down to share with Anja, and Matthew with Tom. I did my best to conceal my agitation. It was awful. I could hardly concentrate on what people were saying.

I finished my pint quickly and took my leave.

A text message as I stood at the bus stop read: 'Wish I could've come home with you tonight. Talk soon. 990' I gripped the phone in both hands, squeezed my eyes shut.

And lo, he phoned the next day while I was at work.

'Listen,' I said, heart pounding, 'how are we going to sort out the room thing? Do you want to just let Donal know privately — ' I stopped, hearing an intake of breath on Matthew's end of the line.

'We, ah . . . OK, we might just leave it, what do you think? It'd be a bit blatant, wouldn't it?'

'Blatant?' My voice was chill.

'You know, if we're not supposed to be fully out in the open yet.' He was trying to sound offhand. Failing.

I felt my chest constrict, my throat swell. 'Well, I sort of thought we could do it discreetly.'

'Oh, come on, Cate, everyone would know.'

'Would that be such a disaster?' I didn't bother disguising my upset. I stood at the office window, staring out at the gloomy garden, willing George to stay put at his desk inside.

'Oh, look, I didn't mean — I just think . . . '

'You don't want people to know.'

'Yet. I don't want people to know *yet*.'

'Why not?' I was speaking now in a fierce whisper. 'Am I on probation or something? Because if so — '

'No, no, that's not it at all!'

I could hear him breathing on the other end of the line. I kept quiet.

'Cate? Can we talk about this later? Face to face, I mean.'

We arranged to meet in town. I went back to my desk feeling mixed, shuffled. The voice of reason — meet Matthew, talk about it, find out what's really bothering him — was drowned out by the voice of craven fear. *He doesn't want to admit we're going out. He's having a fling. No strings.*

We met at Trinity front gate at half past six and walked up Dame Street. People milled everywhere. I didn't know where we were going, and the thought of asking Matthew felt unbearable.

I lagged behind as we passed the Central Bank, thinking that we might turn right into Temple Bar. He looked back at me, scraping me open with his eyes, and took my hand.

'IFI bar?' he said. I remembered the

evening — it seemed an aeon ago — when we'd sat there dancing around a real conversation, drinking wine and being awkward with each other.

I nodded.

When we got to the IFI a film had just started: there was plenty of room in the bar. We found a table out in the airier space of the lobby, and Matthew went to get us drinks. I looked around, let the babble of talk soothe me, watched waves of people wash around the space, looking at posters, moving towards the ticket booth. The main doors swung in and out slowly, rarely at rest, as people arrived and left, setting the swirl of bodies in motion again at each turn.

I saw nobody I knew, for which I was truly thankful.

Matthew came back with two pints of Guinness, and in silence we saluted each other and began to drink. He seemed ill at ease, looking quickly around and sitting very straight in his chair. His fingers drummed absently on the tabletop. I found myself smiling, shaking my head at the absurdly staged feel of the evening.

'What?' Matthew said, and I caught his eye and he began to smile too.

'Just,' I said. We laughed together, and I relaxed a little.

'Belfast,' Matthew said. 'Look, I'm sorry I was so stupid on the phone earlier.' He reached over and squeezed my hand.

'So what's the problem?'

He said nothing. I waited. Eventually, he took back his hand. 'It's not really a problem. I'm just being . . . stupid. Of course I want us to share a room.'

I took a long sip, holding his gaze, daring him to utter the 'but' that hovered behind his eyes. 'So let's,' I said.

He sighed. 'OK. Let's. We'll work something out.'

'There's something you're not telling me,' I said suddenly, not knowing until I spoke that I would have the nerve to say it out loud.

My heart lurched as I looked at him. He was floored, cornered, eyes darting left, then back to stare at me — and then the barrier clanged shut and he frowned. Smiled warily. 'What do you mean?'

I couldn't speak. I drank some more, put my glass down, took a deep breath. 'Just that,' I said. 'There's something really big you're not telling me.'

'You're imagining things,' Matthew said, and the knot in my stomach tightened. I looked away from him, blinking hard. *Liar, liar, liar*.

'OK,' I said, when I was able. 'If you say so.'

He sighed heavily, reached into his pocket and brought out his buzzing phone. 'Sorry, I'd better take this.' He stood up and walked a little distance away from me, as was his habit.

I considered picking up my bag and coat and just storming out of there — turning my phone off, going home, packing a bag, heading for the airport, disappearing. Standby. Anywhere. Just for the weekend. Just to scare him. I'd have to come back, I knew, for Bell Books, for Carmina Urbana, for my family. But it would be good to shake him up.

By the time he came back I was calmer.

'I'm sorry, Cate. I'm not very good at this.'

'No,' I replied, sour-mouthed. 'Surprisingly bad.'

He looked embarrassed. 'Surprising,' he said. He reached for his pint again, and I took up mine. At a gesture from him, we clinked glasses. I said nothing. He said, 'To sorting things out.'

'Look,' I said. 'I think maybe we'd better go. I mean . . . ' I was blushing. Matthew looked taken aback — but made no effort to contradict me. 'I don't know,' I said. 'I don't want to sit here with you, with everyone around, trying to make normal conversation.'

'Right,' he said, exploratory.

I wanted him to say, let's go back to your flat and talk about it. He didn't. I said, 'So maybe

I'll just finish my drink and leave you to it.'

I was astonished. This wasn't like me at all. My insides felt as if they were shaking apart, but the outer shell seemed to be holding. My demeanour seemed, from my end at least, to be calm and collected. I stood up, pint in hand.

Matthew was silent.

'We can talk over the weekend, maybe,' I said, and he looked up at me.

'Yeah. That would be good.'

'Give me a ring, then,' I said, my throat filling with tension. I drained my glass and set it back on the table firmly. Gathered my coat and bag.

'I will,' said Matthew.

★ ★ ★

He didn't ring.

On Tuesday we had an extra rehearsal for Belfast. The peace anthem showed improvement, but overall we did not sound good. Val was absent from the alto line, which knocked much of the stuffing out of us, and there were only four basses.

Diane was on edge, inevitably: tight-lipped, stiff, her conducting gestures jagged and strained. We soldiered through our pieces with little verve. There was nothing to relieve the tension. Everything felt restless, rootless. I slumped in my seat like an empty sack.

'I don't think we're going to get much more done this evening,' Diane said eventually. 'See you on Thursday.'

It was Tuesday. It was strange.

I left without catching Matthew's eye. It was cold outside, but dry and clear. I took deep breaths, letting my nostrils sting, my cheeks tingle. I might almost walk home. Make myself a mug of hot chocolate and curl up in bed with a book.

I was striding along when I heard footsteps behind me. I glanced back to see Matthew hurrying to catch me up, his face worried.

'Hello there,' I said, and I could see he was surprised at my liveliness.

'Hi. What's the story?' He sounded tentative.

'Not much,' I said. 'I'm heading home now.' The weight of our last conversation descended like a hailstorm. My little bubble of false cheer dissipated in the night.

'Are you *walking*?' Matthew asked, and suddenly the lunacy of the idea was clear.

'No,' I said. 'I'll get a bus along here.' I didn't invite him to come home with me. I wasn't sure how that exchange went.

He fell into step with me, put an arm heavily across my shoulders. I didn't look at him. I was battling myself.

'I rang Donal,' he said suddenly. 'I said

we'd be sharing in Belfast. A double room.'

I stopped dead. 'Wow. What did he say?'

'Well, he slagged me a bit, and said he'd see what he could do. I reckon it'll be fine.'

I took a long breath. 'So we're out?'

'We're out.'

After a bit, he asked, 'Do you have plans now?'

'Not especially,' I said, with an inward sigh. 'We should probably talk. Come back to the flat, and we'll have hot chocolate and crisps. Comfort food.'

'OK, woman of weird tastes. I'll try anything once.'

We got to the bus stop and stood in each other's arms, letting the silence settle around us. When the bus arrived I took a window seat, stared out at the clear, streetlit night, Matthew's hand loosely clasped on my knee. The roar of the engine was comforting. It felt as if the silence meant peace, not a failure to communicate. I was sorry when we reached our stop.

We bought crisps in the late-night shop. As we came out again Matthew put his arm round me. 'All right, stay calm,' he said evenly. 'Dark car at one o'clock, five two eight four five. Is that the one?'

I snatched a glance, and nodded. I was glad of his support, but as we walked on I found that my reaction was nothing like as strong as before. I recalled what George had said: if these people wanted me, they'd have got me by now. I felt lighter, looser.

We continued up my silent street, and I let us into the flat.

All seemed to be as I'd left it, and I realized as I registered this that, of course, I'd been checking ever since the break-in.

Matthew fussed with lighting while I made hot chocolate. I brought the two mugs out to the sitting room, and we sat on the sofa.

The chocolate was comforting. My fingers were still thawing; I held them around the mug. Matthew opened my bag of crisps. The salt contrasted pleasingly with the sweet chocolate — a taste of childhood: party food. I alternated between the two.

'Meticulous Cate.'

'Yeah.' I looked around at the disordered room. 'Very.'

He leaned over and kissed me, then drew back, hesitated. 'I . . . I felt bad, the other night.'

'Is that why you didn't phone me at the weekend?' I asked, rather taken aback by my own sharpness.

'I thought you were going to phone me!' He seemed genuinely surprised. 'I didn't realize — I'm sorry.'

'It's not set in stone or anything,' I said, still peevish. 'You could have phoned.'

'I would have, but I thought . . . I didn't

think you'd want to hear from me — no, that's stupid. The point is, I felt bad.'

'What did you do after I left?'

'Finished my pint, went home, had a think.' He put his hand up to the side of my face. I could smell the crisps from his fingers. 'I want to do better. I don't want to make you feel like that again.'

'Are you going to come clean, then?'

He turned his head away, screwed up his face and said nothing for a long time. 'To be honest with you, Cate, I'm not sure I can. I'm not sure there's anything I can actually say to explain why I'm acting like this.' He looked soft and sad — showed none of the fortified urbanity I'd come to expect from him at moments like this.

I badly wanted to lean forward, take hold of his head with both hands and kiss him until our lips melded. Instead I said, 'Try.'

'I really don't want to fuck this up.'

'I'm glad to hear it. What makes you think you'll fuck it up?'

'It's . . . practically inevitable, one way or another.' He rubbed his hand across his eyes. I wished we were not locked into this conversation, could just fall silent, go into the bedroom, lie still and hold each other.

'Don't talk nonsense, Matthew,' I said, but kindly.

'No. You don't know me. Not really. You don't know how . . . '

I sighed. So this was it. I knew the next bit off by heart. The bit about being broken — not like other people, not able for the ordinary little daily achievements that keep things on an even keel. The abrogation of responsibility. I'd heard it all before. My benign feeling sped away, replaced by a twitching irritation.

'You don't know very much about my life,' Matthew went on, looking steadily at the floor.

'You haven't exactly been forthcoming.'

'True.'

'So, what is it? What's the big deal? What's the bit you're not telling me?'

He looked back at me, and in his eyes I saw real distress. I felt a surge of affection again, reached out to scratch the back of his neck. His skin was warm and smooth. I left my hand there. Again, I wanted to release us, chicken out, just go and have sex and forget about it all, let whatever twisted problems we were having take their course.

Matthew finished his hot chocolate, put the mug down and sat back. I still had almost half of mine to go, cooling now. I slid my hand out from behind his neck and looked at him. The apprehension must have shone from my face.

'I'm finding it difficult,' said Matthew. 'I'm having difficulty.'

'Yes?' I allowed myself a quizzical note.

'It's just . . . ' he went on, then faltered again. 'It's just not easy.'

'We've established that,' I reminded him.

'Oh, hell,' he said. 'Wait there. I'll be back.' He got up and headed towards the bathroom.

My stomach was full of moths' wings. I couldn't finish my drink; I put the mug down, leaned back and closed my eyes. I had to stop him from telling me. I didn't want to know. I wanted to continue swimming in my sea of ignorance, even if it meant losing him, never again undressing him in the dark, laughing with him over an old film and a bottle of wine. I'd been here before; it was survivable. I'd give him the easy way out.

I heard the toilet flush and tried to compose my face. Matthew came back in and sat down.

'Look.' I plunged straight in. 'What I think you're trying to say is that this isn't working.'

Matthew's head snapped round, and he stared at me in horror. 'No! That's precisely *not* what I'm trying to say. Oh, Cate! You don't think — are you — do *you* think it's not working?'

'Well . . . no,' I said slowly. 'Most of the time I think it's really good.'

'Really?'

Hesitantly, I nodded. 'Yeah. But then we

have these weird disagreements, and . . . dis-
connections, and now you're telling me
there's a problem . . . but you won't say what
it is.' I could barely speak against the blaze of
his confusion.

He passed his hand over his eyes. 'I know.
I'm being a total nut, aren't I?'

'Yes, you are,' I said, and suddenly we were
kissing, and his fingers were in my hair, and I
could taste the chocolate on his fresh, sweet
tongue, feel his warm breath on my face.

He drew back his head. 'You know, that's
more like it.'

I laughed, riding a surge of relief, and
Matthew laughed with me, and we kissed again.

We cuddled up together in the corner of
the sofa, my head on his chest, he stroking my
hair with a gentle rhythm that began to send
me to sleep. Time enough to find out all his
secrets when he was ready to tell me. This
was good enough for now.

'You going home, then?' I asked, but he
knew I was joking. We stretched ourselves
upright and headed for the bedroom.

★   ★   ★

It was Thursday evening, and I was packing
for Belfast: bustling around my flat, gathering
my belongings, ironing my concert dress,

ticking off my mental list of what I'd need.

It had been a good day. Paula had arrived back at work in great form from her holidays, bearing airport chocolate from Gran Canaria. Between her and George, all seemed to be forgiven.

Our last rehearsal before the trip had gone rather well. Everybody had worked hard, and Diane had been pleased with us. We'd finished with a rousing run-through of John White's 'Rocky Road to Dublin', and Diane had sent us home to get a good night's sleep.

We were catching the train to Belfast tomorrow afternoon. I'd bring my suitcase to work in the morning and leave early to go and meet the others at Connolly Station.

I had the radio on, a soothing sea of well-modulated talk in the background. Ten o'clock news. And after the reports of the latest government pronouncement, ongoing trade union unrest, the freshest economic outrage, came an item about the Belfast peace summit. Tensions were running high, it appeared. Language had become heated; the subcutaneous enmities were being unwrapped, flaunted like feather boas around old ladies' wattly necks.

And all of a sudden, I realized: this was *us*. This was *our* summit — Carmina Urbana would be singing on Saturday to these warring delegates.

I paused, iron in hand. Denise used to slag me in school for never knowing anything about what was going on in the world. 'Who's the US president?' she'd ask, and I'd say 'George . . . Washington?' to annoy her.

The reporter in Belfast was declaiming earnestly about how tight the security was around the meeting, how there had been some trouble already with protests, threats, an incident in which one of the catering staff, suspected of having connections with Republican dissidents, had had to be fired.

And I began to weave a little story about how the choir would be the perfect way for a terrorist to get in — who would suspect the entertainers, after all? Something Shakespearean in that. You would join up, attend rehearsals, go to the gig, and there you would . . . I stopped. I wasn't quite sure what you would do after that. Plant a bomb, I supposed. Or would that be just *too* last century?

I shivered a bit and looked around the dusky room. Nobody lurked in the corners.

* * *

George caught me just as I was leaving work the next day. My first thought was that he had misunderstood my request for permission to leave early, and I felt the beginnings of a leaping panic as I tried to think of ways to persuade him to let me go.

'Come in here a minute, Cate,' he said, beckoning me into his office. 'Now, you're off up to Belfast, I believe you said.' He stood with his back to the door and spoke at about half his normal volume.

'Yes, we're all going up together on the *Enterprise*.'

'I won't keep you long, so.' He paused, eyes beady. 'I want to ask you something. Are your . . . ehh, admirers still on the scene?'

I frowned at him.

'I mean the men in that car.'

'Oh!' I said, and tried to stop my eyes widening in horror. I'd never told him about the laptop.

'Are they still around?' George asked.

I'd never told him any of it — about the break-in, about my midnight escape, about Matthew going through the Bell Books company laptop with a fine-toothed comb . . .

Well, I couldn't get into it all now. There wasn't time. 'No,' I said firmly. 'I haven't seen them in a while.' Why, of all things, did it suddenly feel like I was covering for Matthew?

'Grand job,' George said. 'They must've moved on to fresh fields and pastures new.' He rubbed his chin and took a breath. 'Right, then. I want to ask you a favour. Now. Say no if it's a nuisance, but it's just, something's come up, and it would be a huge convenience to me if you could help me out. I have a friend in Belfast — Nicky Fay — he's a county councillor. He has a document for me and he doesn't want to trust it to the e-mail. He's a bit funny that way, like some others we could mention. It's . . . well. It's a document he wants me to have, as corroboration for part of the MacDevitt book, funnily enough. He thinks it'll change my mind about something. So, would you be willing to meet him and bring it back with you?'

'I . . . well . . . I don't know . . . ' I started to stumble, trying to think of a reasonable way to extricate myself. George watched me intently. 'Yeah, sure, I suppose,' I heard myself saying. 'How do I get in touch with him?'

'I have his phone number. How are you on numbers? Do you think you could learn it by heart? I'd rather not write it down, just in case.'

'Should be OK,' I said, at sea.

'All right.' He recited the number, twice.

I repeated it back to him, then hummed it in my head. Nothing I recognized, but I was fairly sure I'd remember it.

'Find a public phone, if you can at all,' George said. 'Try not to use your mobile.'

'OK.' I was well out of my depth.

* * *

When I got to Connolly Station I found the
choir assembling beside a large pile of bags. I
positioned myself with a clump of other altos
and made small talk. The train wasn't for half
an hour, and the queue hadn't yet begun to
form. Joan handed me my token for our
group ticket.

Matthew wasn't there yet. I went and
bought a coffee.

Shortly, without announcement, a queue
began to coalesce at the sign saying *Enterprise*. We finished up our drinks and headed
over to join it.

Matthew still hadn't shown up, which was
driving Diane mad, because on our group
ticket we all needed to go through the barrier
together.

'Where's your bit of trouser, Ms Houlihan?'
Here was Tom, ever tactful.

'I'll just give him a call,' I said, blushing
— but when I tried, my call went to voicemail. I left a message that I hoped sounded
jaunty rather than snappy.

Diane spoke to the guard, who said we
could all go through, and she could wait for
Matthew. He was the only one of us who
wasn't there.

By now I was a-jangle. I hadn't heard from

Matthew all day, and although I knew I was indulging my annoyance, my thoughts turned to a list of nasty, worrying things that might have happened to him. My conversation with George hadn't helped — it had brought all the sinister stuff back into the foreground. What if someone were trying to prevent Matthew from getting to the concert?

Silly. I could think of no earthly reason why that would benefit anyone.

I walked down the platform with the others, glancing every few seconds over my shoulder to where Diane still stood waiting at the ticket point. We found our carriage and piled in. Joan and Val nabbed one side of a four-seat group and nodded to me to come and join them. I put my bag up on the overhead shelf and sat down, dithering over saving the fourth seat for Matthew.

'Did you manage to contact himself?' Tom asked, leaning over from the other side of the aisle.

'No, his phone's off.' I was irritated now at my jitters. He'd show up. He wouldn't just let us go off without him. 'If he misses this train there's another one later on,' I said.

I had my coat on the empty seat. Nobody asked to sit there.

Everyone chatted about their days at work, their journeys to the train station. I didn't join in. I was still looking out the window, back along the platform, to where Diane was waiting for Matthew.

And then there they were, the two of them, Matthew loping towards the train with Diane maintaining a dignified trot beside him. She wore a big, tight smile.

They were looking in the windows of the carriages they passed, and eventually Matthew caught sight of me. He and Diane shuffled down the aisle of the carriage. Anja had saved a seat for Diane. Matthew arrived at our group of seats as the guard's whistle sounded outside, and leaned down on the table, puffing with weariness that seemed unfeigned. The train began to move.

'What happened to you?' I said, as kindly as I could.

Matthew gestured for time to catch his breath, and levered himself into his seat. Settled, he heaved a short, rasping sigh. 'I was supposed to meet my supervisor at twelve, and he never showed up,' he said. 'Then at two o'clock I get a call to say he's in his office, and I didn't feel I could say no, because we really needed to meet. So by the time I left I was dead late.' He sounded as though he'd run all the way from the bus stop.

The train began to move, and we all continued to bat a selection of standard topics back and forth. I closed my eyes and let it wash over me. I was happy to be getting out of Dublin for a couple of days. Matthew squeezed my hand under the table. I returned the pressure.

We got to talking about stage magic. Tom had an uncle who used to do children's parties. 'He did mine a few times,' said Tom, 'and there was always this older girl with gimlet eyes shouting out the secret before the trick was over.'

'It must take some nerve, though,' said Joan.

'It's a performance,' Val said. 'Like a lot of things.'

'You'd need such dexterity,' said Joan.

Matthew said, 'Well, a lot of it is just deception. Putting people off the scent.'

I looked at him, eyebrows raised. 'Speaks the expert?'

'Well, no, obviously not,' said Matthew. 'But from what I've seen, it's all about distracting people at the crucial moment. Like the three-card trick. I saw a man doing it in London a few years ago — only it was eggcups and a pea, not three cards.'

'But that is just about dexterity,' I said. 'They flick the pea under a different cup at the last second.'

Matthew shook his head. 'Not this man. I

watched him for ages.'

'I take it you weren't had,' Tom said.

'Oh no,' said Matthew. 'I was just watching. He was getting people to bet. And after I'd seen him win a few times I worked out how he did it. And it wasn't about flicking anything,' he added, turning to me. He was animated, edging forward in his seat the better to command our attention, gesturing to illustrate his story.

'OK. He starts off slowly, shows you the movements, shows you the pea, shows you how easy it all is. Then he speeds it up a bit, and you guess where the pea is, and you're right. And by this stage he's got your interest, and then he talks you into betting. Say five quid, or two if you're not so sure.

'So you agree to the bet, and he does the trick — and he moves a lot quicker this time — and then he asks you to say where the pea is. And you're pretty sure, because you haven't taken your eyes off him for a second. So you pick a cup, and he slaps a five-pound note out on the table. And of course, you think you've won. But then he gets all stroppy and asks where your money is. And he refuses to lift up the cup you've chosen until all the money's on the table.'

'Aha,' Val murmured, nodding.

'And of course, now he's winning, because

he's confused you. He's accused you of wanting to cheat him, and you feel bad, because that's what you were thinking about him. It was amazing — you could practically see it happening in people's faces. So you take out your wallet and you find a fiver and you put it on the table. And you've pretty much got to take your eyes off the cups in order to do that — and that's when he makes the switch.'

'Fiendish,' said Tom.

'Quick as lightning,' Matthew said. 'I missed it the first few times. Then when I came back the next day he recognized me and wouldn't take any bets until I'd gone. Nerves of steel, and a perfect memory for faces. I remember thinking he'd have made a brilliant spy.'

When we got to Belfast Diane insisted on personally herding everyone into taxis outside the train station. I sat in the middle of the back seat, between Joan and Matthew, and saw very little — the daylight was already gone.

The hotel was not far. Shallow steps led up to an imposing entrance in glass and chrome. The lobby was large and bright, dotted with tubs of leafy plants. Diane bustled to the reception desk to begin the process of checking us all in. The choir had commandeered a group of sofas, set in a square round a low table. Cases and rucksacks were banked at the corners. I followed Matthew and Tom over and found a seat.

'It's a lot swankier than I expected,' said Val, looking around.

'It's not the choir that is paying for this, is it?' Anja asked.

'No, not at all,' said Joan. 'The organizers are putting us all up. Gosh, you don't think Carmina Urbana would rise to this, do you?'

Diane came back with a pack of electronic key cards. She winked at me as she handed me one. 'Double,' she said, honey-voiced.

Our room was spacious and bright, with a white-tiled, windowless bathroom and a small balcony overlooking the hotel's inner court-yard. It was quiet — sounds muffled by the thick carpet and curtains. The bed was enormous. I unpacked my concert clothes and hung them up.

Matthew stepped out on to the balcony. I brushed my hair. I didn't know what to say. We were a couple in a hotel bedroom. It was too strange. I went out to the balcony, where Matthew was leaning on the railing, looking down.

'Matthew,' I said, in my best Mrs Robinson voice. 'Matthew, I want you to know that I'm available to you.'

'Shh!' said Matthew, whirling round, and

my insides crumbled. He pointed to the balcony above, and went on in a whisper, 'They'll hear you!'

I rushed back into the room, over to the other side of the bed, where I sank down to a crouch, nursing the sting. I didn't want to talk to him. I wanted to go home. He followed me in. 'Sorry,' I said.

He didn't seem to notice. 'What time is rehearsal?'

'Seven o'clock, at the Waterfront. Dinner at half five.'

He went to his bag and took out his music.

It was all wrong. We hadn't done enough to prepare. We were stumbling over our lines like the worst sort of amateurs. There wasn't time to sort this out before we had to go for dinner, either. Matthew paged through his music, the suggestion of a hum buzzing about his lips. I fished out the novel I'd brought and couldn't read it. I kept looking over at him; he kept not meeting my eye.

'What's up with you?' I asked at last, fighting the panic.

'Sorry,' he said, distractedly. 'I'm just going over this bit of the Daintree.'

He, of all people, surely didn't need extra note-learning at this stage. He must be in a mood. I left him to it, went out on to the balcony. It had started to drizzle, tiny drops

218

skimming by on the wind. The sky was dark. The uplighting in the courtyard had come on. I watched the rain racing in the dim beams.

★ ★ ★

Security at the Waterfront was tight — metal detectors and bag scanners — and we had to wait ages for our sound check. We were the last choir to have access to the auditorium, so we were stuck in a tiny, airless room until nearly quarter to eight. Diane shifted into her bright and breezy mode, which did not recommend itself to me or, as far as I could tell, to anyone else in the choir. 'Come on,' she said after a while. 'Let's make use of the time, at least.' She took us through our pieces, despite numerous mutterings that everyone knew them backwards, that singing them in this space was no use — that the purpose of this exercise was to accustom ourselves to the acoustic of the venue, to organize the logistics of walking on and off stage, to see where we'd stand.

'We can't just sit here doing nothing,' was Diane's response. I wanted to kick her.

In fact, it turned out we didn't know the music as well as we thought. The room swallowed our voices, and we couldn't keep in tune. But the singing gradually calmed me, despite everything. I was putting minimal effort in, not pushing myself in the least, and somehow the deep breathing, the control, the rising and falling phrases, made me loosen my grip on my irritation.

At last there was a knock on the door, and a suitably apologetic young man led us to the stage entrance.

It was a bigger auditorium than I'd ever sung in before. It was like a vast bowl, with seats stretching outwards and upwards in drifts and tiers. Two technicians in tight jeans and hoodies climbed impossibly high ladders to fiddle with overhead lighting and microphones. The stage was mostly occupied by the orchestra's seats and music stands, with stepped platforms behind them for the choirs. The platforms had chairs on them — apparently we'd be on stage for the entire second half, which would build up to the grand finale of our epic peace anthem. For our own individual section we'd be standing on the stage itself, right at the front. We huddled together, conscious of how few of us there were.

Diane's heels echoed smartly on the wooden surface. She was in charge. She waved us to where she wanted us, then flapped her hands at us to adjust the positioning and make sure she could see each of us properly. 'Pick a landmark, OK, so you can line yourself up tomorrow night,' she said.

We started singing again, and it went a little better. We were still making stupid errors, the sound was strained and the tuning precarious, but we were more confident than we had been in the airless room. Diane went down into the centre aisle to gauge how we sounded. 'This acoustic is super!' she announced. 'I can hear every little mistake!'

That got a laugh. My stomach began to unknot.

We started into 'Danny Boy', just the backing at first, trying to get the tuning right. Diane was frustrated, but mostly hiding it well. Eventually, she said, 'We're not going to get it any better tonight. Let's give it a bash, Matthew.'

I turned to give him a thumbs-up. He was looking white, and when he started to sing it sounded bad. There was none of the breadth of tone that he normally seemed to produce without trouble. He was pushing — trying to increase his volume by increasing the pressure. The result sounded painful and rather sharp.

I imagined what it must be like, thinking that you have to fill a hall like this with just your voice. I didn't envy him.

Diane stopped him after a few phrases.

'Relax,' she said. 'We'll be miked up. It'll be grand. Come on, shake yourself out. You're as tight as a fiddle string.'

'Sorry,' Matthew said, and even his speaking voice rasped.

'Don't be afraid of it,' Diane said. 'It sounds great. Right, from the top, with everybody.'

We started again. I felt so sorry for Matthew — he had done this with such ease in Dublin. We had thought him invincible. The rest of us were getting edgy. The tension mounted again. The mistakes returned.

There were many more hitches before we got to the end of the piece. 'We'll have another run-through of that tomorrow,' Diane said. 'You'll be fine. Don't worry about it.'

After our sound check we moved back to the choir platforms, where we were joined by everybody else. Things were chaotic for a bit, with members of all three choirs milling about and the orchestra arriving with their instruments. Both of the other choirs were significantly larger than Carmina Urbana: with the orchestra too, the stage was very crowded. I glanced round for Matthew, trying to catch his eye, but he was miles away. Diane and the other two choir conductors shouted instructions that crossed and cancelled each other.

Eventually, we all got settled. The orchestra stood to attention as — thrill of thrills

— Trevor Daintree himself took his place on the conductor's podium. He was a squat, squashy-faced man with buck-teeth and what amounted to a mullet. He looked thirty-five going on sixty. He wore a big brown jumper and mustard-coloured cords. When he began to conduct, his face assumed a manic rictus, and his head jerked in time to the beat.

Miraculously, the rehearsal went quite well. *A Song of Ireland* even began to make a mad sort of sense once the orchestra was added. The wailing of the sopranos was echoed by passages from the woodwinds, and there was a beautiful violin melody above the discordant choral crooning that had drawn such protest back in Dublin. The percussion accompaniment made the men's section sound coherent — even impressive.

We finished at ten. Most of the choir made for the bar as soon as we got back to the hotel. Matthew paused in the lobby to take a phone call, and I waited nearby. He rejoined me and said, 'Let's go to bed.'

I grinned.

He closed his eyes, shook his head. 'Sleep, I mean.'

He didn't say a word in the lift or in the corridor on the way to our room. When we got inside he walked to the window and looked silently out.

I sat on the bed. 'You'll be fine,' I said.

'Mmm. I hope so. To be honest, I feel rather as though I've bitten off more than I can chew. Foolish me.'

'You're not foolish.'

'I never should have agreed to do that solo.'

'You can do it,' I said. 'It was just nerves.'

He spun round with a sudden energy and strode back to the bed. 'Cate, I honestly don't know if I'll be able to do it.' The harshness of his tone surprised me.

'You'll get out there tomorrow night, and the audience will be there, and there'll be such a buzz — it'll be great.'

'If I get that far.'

'Oh, don't be silly.'

He shook his head. 'I wish I were being silly.'

'Come on,' I said, and I took his hand in both of mine, ran my thumbs over the knuckles. 'Let's forget about it. Sufficient unto the day be the solo thereof.'

He softened at last. 'Sweet Cate.'

★　★　★

At breakfast on Saturday morning we discussed what we'd do with our free day in Belfast. We were not due to meet until five, for a last rehearsal in the hotel. The day outside

224

looked dull but dry. Joan and some of the others were keen to visit a museum. Val wanted to go shopping. I, silently, wanted to go for a long wander with Matthew, find lunch somewhere, see what there was to see. Talk, maybe. He'd been stern and monosyllabic all morning.

Last night had been the first time we'd shared a bed without having sex. Oddly, I felt as though this had made us more intimate.

Nicky Fay's phone number nagged at the back of my mind. I'd bring Matthew along when I went to meet him. That would be fine, surely. I was only picking up a document . . . *for George*. Who wasn't exactly Anglophile. From a Belfast county councillor who didn't want to trust it to the electric mail.

All right, then, maybe not. I'd work something out.

I left the breakfast table early, and Matthew followed me into the lift. I leaned against him, clasped my hands behind his back. His body was unyielding. His arms swung slowly — almost halfheartedly — round my shoulders.

'All right?' I said.

'Hm.'

'Matthew, what's got into you? I've never seen you like this.'

'There's a lot you haven't seen.'

That stung, but for once I managed to keep

a grip. I reached up and squeezed the back of his neck. 'We're on your side,' I said.

'Yes.' He looked down at me, dark-eyed, frowning. 'I believe you are.'

Perhaps this was why he had originally been reluctant to share a room with me. Maybe he always got like this before a big performance. Why would he be in such a state about his solo, though? It wasn't even complicated — he was hardly going to fluff the notes.

I hadn't washed yet. As soon as we got back to the room I made a beeline for the shower, stood under the firm needles of water, letting them crash on to my scalp, deafen me, merge and run down my body in hot ribbons. I sang some scales, then a couple of phrases from our programme, enjoying the way my voice bounced off the tiles. I turned the heat up as high as I could bear.

When I came out of the bathroom, it took me a moment to register that Matthew was gone. I started towards the balcony, hugging the towel around me, but the glass door was closed, and I could see that there was nobody out there. I was disoriented, standing damp and barefoot at the end of the bed.

His note was on my pillow. 'Cate, I'm sorry, but I need some headspace before the gig. I'll see you later. 990'

I made the best of it. I should not take this

lunacy personally. I dressed as calmly as I could and went down to the lobby. If I met any of the others, I would defend his honour. They didn't need to know that he was being a prima donna.

★　★　★

At least this gave me the chance I'd been looking for to contact Nicky Fay. I marched out of the hotel into a bright, cold day and walked along in the approximate direction of the Waterfront until I saw a payphone. As I got closer, however, I saw that the phone had been vandalized, its receiver ripped off. The next one had chewing gum stuffed into the coin slot, and the one after that was smashed.

I decided to use my mobile. The tune I'd learned from George played back in my mind as I dialled the number.

'Nicky Fay's office, hello.' The voice was male, flat, bored. Or guarded, perhaps.

'Oh, hello,' I said, heart thumping, 'I wonder is Mr Fay available?'

'Who's speaking?'

'My name is Cate Houlihan — I work for Bell Books — '

'George Sweeney, is it?' The tone had changed completely, the pitch of the sentence swooping upwards, like song.

'That's right,' I said. There was a brief silence. 'Is that . . . Mr Fay? I'm in Belfast for the day, and George asked me . . . to meet you.' I was trying to be guarded too.

'Aye, he told me, so he did. Now, I'm tied up until four o'clock. Could you meet me at about . . . say, four-fifteen, four-twenty?'

'That sounds fine,' I said. I should have time to get back to the hotel for the rehearsal.

'How well do you know Belfast?'

I hesitated. Was this a test of some kind? 'Not at all, I'm afraid — it's my first time here,' I admitted.

'Well. Where are you now?'

I looked around. 'Em . . . ' Couldn't see a street name. 'I'm just beside the Public . . . Prosecution Service . . . ' (gosh, this is going well) 'ah . . . I can see a pub called Magennis's . . . there's a H&M up the street . . . ' I swallowed.

'Right. If you leave the Prosecution Service to your right, walk away from Magennis's, past H&M, take your one-two-three, third left, on to Victoria Square, you'll see a Starbucks. Do you think you'll be able to find your way there this afternoon?'

I was mesmerized by his accent: the slack, open vowels, the snuffed consonants. *Twayenty. Squrr.* 'That should be no problem,' I managed.

'Right. What are you wearing?'

'Excuse me?'

'What are you wearing?' he repeated, more slowly. When I didn't answer, he said, 'How will I recognize you?'

'Oh! A red coat. It's corduroy. It has . . . a big fluffy collar.'

'Good enough. I'll see you later, OK?'

'Goodbye,' I said, but he had already hung up. I tingled with embarrassment. After that first impression, it would be a wonder if he thought it worth his while to come and meet me.

I got back to the hotel just as the museum party — consisting of Joan, Tom, Linda and Donal — was assembling in the foyer. I joined them, thinking to distract myself from Matthew's absence. Joan raised a quiet eyebrow when I said he needed headspace, but asked me no further questions.

By mid-afternoon I was irritated. We had traipsed around a selection of museums and minor sights before stopping for a late, expensive, inadequate and mediocre lunch. I had no heart for the banter the others kept up so effortlessly. I wished I'd joined the shopping trip instead.

The police presence on the streets was really quite noticeable, in comparison with Dublin, and although we were fairly sure it was larger than usual on account of the summit, it made us uncomfortable. All the more so as every police officer we saw was armed. Donal was especially jumpy: he seemed to fear that each new turn would bring us slap bang into the heart of Catholic-hunting country.

I phoned Matthew a few times, but it went to voicemail. I refused to leave a message. I tried to maintain my poise, my spirit of tolerance and calm, but I got crosser and crosser as the day wore on. It was so selfish to put himself out of reach like this.

The others ran out of touristic zeal at last, and we returned to the hotel. There was still no sign of Matthew. I went upstairs to our bedroom, which was dark and deserted — and preternaturally tidy, in the manner peculiar to hotel rooms. I noted with a sinking heart that his suit bag was still hanging in the wardrobe. I rang him again and this time left a message, which I hoped wouldn't make matters worse.

It was time to meet Nicky Fay. I found Starbucks easily enough, bought a tall skinny latte and installed myself and my red coat in easy view of the main door. I was sipping away when a small man entered and caught my eye. He looked perhaps sixty, with a mane of reddish hair and the most unlikely moustache — like a section of fox-pelt glued to his upper lip. He wore a navy suit, with shirt and tie, under a scuffed brown leather jacket. He advanced towards me with a swinging gait, which I eventually read as a limp.

'Cate, is it?' The voice was unmistakable, though he spoke much more softly than he had on the phone.

'That's right,' I said, half standing up before being waved back into my seat.

'Nicky Fay,' he announced, and we shook hands across the table as he eased himself into the chair opposite. He looked sharply at me through rimless spectacles. 'Cate Sullivan?'

'No, Houlihan.'

'Houlihan, of course.'

'But my mother is Sullivan, actually.'

'Is that so?' He nodded, gathering his lips into a knowing pout, then slapped his hand on the table. 'Listen, I'll not stay. I just came to give you this.' He reached inside his jacket and withdrew a tiny package, which he slid across the table to me.

I looked at it. It was a little pellet of some kind, swathed in paper and shiny brown tape. Nothing was written on it. I hesitated.

Nicky Fay gave a throaty chuckle. 'I know — it looks a wee bit dodgy, so it does. It's one of them thumb drives. It'll not bite you.'

'Thanks,' I said.

'You'll give that straight into George's hand, won't you?'

'I will, of course. First thing on Monday.'

'And listen, next time you see Fintan Sullivan, tell him not to be worrying — this'll not cause him any more trouble.' He stood up. 'I'll be on my way. Don't lose that, all right?' He pointed a large, hairy finger at me, and his look flashed sincerity. I felt warned.

'I won't.'

'Bye, now,' he said. 'Pleasure meeting you, Cate Houlihan.'

I put the packet in my pocket and finished my coffee.

Back at the hotel room I took the thing out and looked at it. A document, George had said, connected to the MacDevitt book.

I was suddenly very thankful that Matthew had not been with me at the meeting.

Nicky Fay's face remained in my mind — the pointed look he shot me as he enjoined me not to lose this packet. I would need to keep it on me until I got back to Dublin. My concert clothes had no pockets. I'd keep it in my coat, then, or maybe my handbag. The thought of it falling out, or being taken, made me feel a little ill. It was amazing how much force Nicky Fay had packed into that one look.

It was just a memory stick, wasn't it? That's what he'd said, but I decided to make sure. Using the scissors from the hotel sewing kit I found in a drawer, I snipped at the tape that bound the packet until I was able to extract the contents. One small grey and blue memory stick, as advertised. I stuffed it deep into my handbag and headed downstairs to our rehearsal.

★   ★   ★

When I realized that Matthew was not downstairs, I was flooded with alarm and shame. Not engaging in organized fun was one thing; missing rehearsal was quite another. But how could I admit to Diane — to anyone — that my own boyfriend had left me in the dark like this? I avoided everyone's eye.

A small mercy for which to be thankful: we sang much better than last night. There was, perhaps, hope for us. After we finished we ate a buffet dinner. I sat with Donal, Linda and Mircea and made minimal contributions. As soon as I could I bolted upstairs. Surely he'd be there, with rueful explanations of whatever madcap adventures had kept him from communicating all day. Surely he wasn't going to leave us in the lurch altogether.

He was not there.

We were to walk to the Waterfront, to arrive by half past seven. I changed into my concert clothes and face, picked up my music and headed back downstairs. My heart was beating hard. Matthew knew the schedule. He should have been back long before now. I couldn't help dwelling on the fact that this was Belfast. He might have wandered into the wrong area, been set upon for speaking with the wrong accent.

I found Joan, Val, Tom and Anja in the lobby. 'We're the last,' Joan said. 'Shall we go on, or should we wait for Matthew?'

'No point in waiting,' I said. 'He'll follow us over.' I saw them noting my grim tone.

Joan fell into step with me as we got outside. 'Is everything all right? Where is Matthew, anyway?'

I took a deep breath. 'I don't know,' I said. 'I haven't been able to raise him.'

'He'll probably meet us there,' Joan said.

'Yes,' I said, 'except his music and his suit are still at the hotel.'

'Oops.'

We walked in silence for a few minutes. 'He's in a very strange mood,' I said eventually. 'I don't know what's got into him.'

'You two are getting on OK, though?'

'Yes, very well.' I thought about our recent talks. 'Mostly,' I qualified.

'He'd better show up,' Joan said.

'He will.' I hoped I was right.

We arrived just after the London choir, and

had to queue for ages at the security check. It was, if anything, tighter than last night — almost like an airport.

All three choirs waited in a large fluorescent-lit room backstage, where we wandered aimlessly or chatted in little knots. My eyes kept flicking to the door, where I was sure that at any minute Matthew would be shown in by one of the venue staff.

He was lying in a lane somewhere, bleeding and concussed, while motorists drove by, too afraid to stop and help.

He was tied to a chair in a dark basement, eyes so swollen he could barely see his captors, waiting for them to decide how to dispose of him.

Nonsense. The truth was, I was disgusted at him, his irresponsibility. Elusive he might be, but he had never been *unreliable* in this way since I'd known him, and it was depressing to discover that he had it in him.

Tension coursed up and down my body like columns of ants.

Joan caught my eye. 'No sign?'

I shook my head. 'Maybe I'd better talk to Diane.'

'Might be no harm.'

'It feels a bit strange, acting like his spokesperson.'

'Goes with the territory.'

Diane was sitting at the edge of the room, fussing over music. I took the chair next to her.

'Diane, I'm a bit worried that Matthew hasn't shown up. He's not answering his phone.'

'I'm sure he'll be along any second. Don't worry about it, OK?' She gripped my arm. 'Sure, if he doesn't turn up, we'll just do the show without him.' She was shaking her head like a teacher, eyebrows raised, voice bright.

She turned back to her music; I was dismissed.

I went over to my coat and fished my phone out of the pocket. The signal here was very weak. I stepped out into the corridor and walked along it a little way, watching the screen of the phone to see if there was any improvement. I was heading away from the stage. The corridor opened into a high windowed space, yellow lights bouncing off sheet glass. I couldn't see out at all.

The signal here was better. I dialled Matthew's number, for perhaps the fifth time since he'd left this morning, and for the first time I got a ringing tone.

After three rings, however, the sound was choked off, and the voicemail greeting cut in. *Matthew had rejected my call.* Shocked, I tried again. Again, he rejected it.

I was alone, as far as I could see, so it was

safe to let out a muffled shriek of rage and to stamp my foot, hard. Neither measure helped — indeed, my foot let me know that these were not shoes in which to pound the floor.

My phone buzzed. A text message: 'Can't talk now. Sorry for everything. See you later. Love.'

Love?

A fine time to bring *that* up.

I texted back, 'Hello? CONCERT???', and after pacing up and down a few times to regain control of myself, dry my eyes, calm my breathing, I headed back to where the others were.

Whatever Matthew had been so uptight about since we got here, it wasn't 'Danny Boy'.

* * *

Back in the rehearsal room, Joan looked at her watch. 'We're on in a few minutes.' She waved to catch the attention of Diane, who was pacing near the door, her clasped hands rising and falling in time with her steps. 'Should we be lining up?'

Diane came over. 'No, we've to wait until they send someone. What time is it?'

'Five to eight now,' said Joan. 'And' — she turned to me — 'there's still no sign of Matthew?'

I shrugged. 'He's incommunicado. I haven't seen him since this morning.'

Diane looked at the floor, took a breath, pursed her lips. 'He told me earlier that he wouldn't be at the rehearsal. He said he had to go and meet someone, that it was really important. Oh, god.' She blinked a few times, and exhaled angrily. 'I don't know what to think now.'

'But he can't just — ' Joan spluttered. 'That's outrageous!'

'I know. But, sure, what could I say? I thought it'd be OK. Listen, I'm going to have a word with . . . ' Diane hurried away towards the London and Belfast conductors who were chatting by the door.

I hardly noticed her go. There was a roaring in my ears and shock waves running through me. Somehow, despite everything, I had not expected to catch Matthew in an outright falsehood. I felt sick.

'Are you all right?' Joan's head was tilted, her eyes sympathetically gathering at the corners.

'No,' I said, teeth clenched.

'He never said anything to you about having to meet someone, did he?'

'He did not. *Bastard*.' Bastards, the whole bloody lot of them.

Flashes of thought were arcing through the

mess in my brain. A Matthew retrospective.

Here is a man who styles himself a historian but who can deftly probe the inner workings of a computer.

Here is a man who styles himself a full-time student but who can afford to pay for two on evenings out.

Here is a man who styles himself my boyfriend but who tells me as little as he can about his personal life, who doesn't invite me into his flat until it's an emergency.

Here is a man, I am beginning to think, with something ugly to hide.

Diane came towards us again, clapping her hands and waving for attention. 'Carmina Urbana, I want to do some warm-ups.'

We shuffled into a rough formation and followed her lead. The stuffy, carpeted room soaked up all we had to offer. 'Whatever we do on stage,' Diane pointed out, 'we'll sound better than this.' She took a deep breath. 'Now, I want to run through 'Danny Boy'. Anja, will you sing the melody for us?'

Anja, confused, looked round. 'Is Matthew not — '

'Well, it doesn't look like it, at this stage,' Diane said briskly. 'Will you be OK, do you think?'

Anja was speechless.

'Come on, we'll try it,' Diane said. She

plucked her tuning fork from her jacket pocket and gave the notes. We started too slowly, and the breathing was hard for Anja. She cracked on the top note, and finished the last phrase in little more than a breathy whisper. There was a smattering of applause from the other choirs.

'Now,' said Diane. 'You'll be fine. We'll take it faster than that.' Nobody said anything.

There had to be something I could *do* about all this. The powerlessness was unbearable. I was fretting about that memory stick again, too. I couldn't get Nicky Fay's parting injunction out of my head. My concert clothes had no pockets, but maybe I could bring it on stage. I hurried over to my bag and fished it out. It was chunky enough: I didn't want to carry it in my hand in case I dropped it. On impulse, I stuck it into my bra, pushed it right in under my left breast. I felt the plastic warm up as I took my place in the line again.

* * *

It was after eight now, and every second seemed to drip away in slow motion. Our formation had grown uneven before the door opened at last, and the apologetic young man from last night entered the room. He raised

240

his voice, and the murmur of chat died away. 'Hello, everyone? Hello. The audience has been seated, so if Carmina Urbana would like to follow me . . . '

We trooped after him down echoless corridors towards the stage. The backstage area was a mess, full of cables and screens and bits of wood. The steps up to the stage itself looked a little rickety. We stood in a double row, trying not to fidget. We could hear ourselves being announced, the cadence of the woman's speech unmistakably Northern Irish.

The applause began, and Diane windmilled her hands at Tom, who was leading. The men filed onstage, followed by the women. I stumbled as I mounted the steps, caught the hem of my skirt in a shoe buckle, then had to hurry after Val so as not to leave too large a gap. I was hot and cold and miserable — and still seething with rage.

Diane's name was announced, and she strode out on to the stage, head held high. She had taken off her jacket to reveal an expanse of glittering blouse. The blaze of the footlights swallowed everything else. I tried not to squint. My mouth and throat were dry.

As Diane situated herself in front of us I took a look out at the audience. I wondered what it might be like to be attending such a meeting, as the representative of your country. The psychological armour you'd have to wear. The necessity of presenting only the pre-arranged and approved face to your counterparts from other countries.

Perhaps it wasn't like that at all. Diane gave us our notes and raised her hands.

The first chords of 'Danny Boy' suffused the auditorium, and I knew it was going to go well. Something had clicked into place between five minutes ago and now. We were attuned to each other, moving together as deftly as a shoal of fish. Anja acquitted herself honourably in the first verse, and the rest of us began to croon our way through the bridge.

And then there was a crash, and I looked round to see two uniformed police officers come pounding up the steps on to the stage. Our lush harmonies tumbled into ragged silence. The officers wore high-visibility vests. One made for the lectern at the side of the stage, while the other went straight to Diane and began to speak urgently to her.

'I'm sorry, ladies and gentlemen,' said the officer at the lectern. 'This is an emergency, and we're going to have to cut short this evening's performance. This is not a drill. Please proceed calmly to your nearest exit. Leave the building as quickly as you can, and assemble on the plaza opposite. You'll be shown the way.'

On stage, we were milling around in confusion. 'What's going on?' Anja demanded of me. I shrugged at her, indicated the police officer, who was again talking to Diane. The officer was young — not much older than me, with dark hair scraped back from her face in a pony tail.

Diane raised her voice. 'All right, listen,' she called, above the murmur of questions. 'We can't go back to the room. We have to go across the stage, out the side exit and round.'

The police officer began to herd us towards the opposite side of the stage from where we'd come on; we formed a more or less orderly queue.

'What's wrong?' I heard Anja ask.

The officer hesitated. 'We've had a warning,' she said. Her voice was scratchy, as though she had grit in her throat.

'A warning?'

'A bomb warning.'

That shut Anja up. I found myself wanting to giggle. I was probably in mild shock. I felt remarkably unafraid.

And then I remembered Matthew.

He could be *anywhere*, I told myself. He could be miles away, doing something completely different.

It didn't help, this attempt at mental discipline. He could be trying to contact me right now, and my phone was in my coat pocket in that room, along with my handbag. At least I had Nicky Fay's memory stick.

We had crossed the stage and were hurrying along an anonymous corridor, indistinguishable from the ones on the other side. My shoes, not built for haste, were really beginning to hurt me. I could not erase from my mind the idea that my phone was ringing, ringing, Matthew trying to get in touch, to tell me what was going on. Explain.

Love, he'd said.

I was grasping at straws. Not even. Raindrops, maybe. I stumbled along with the others, hearing the hiss and crackle of the police officer's walkie-talkie, her answering description of our location and trajectory.

Matthew wouldn't be phoning me, would he? There was a bomb scare, and he wasn't here. And he'd been on edge ever since we'd reached Belfast. He must have known about this in advance.

In another layer of my mind I was still strangely calm. I found myself wondering about the statistics. How many bomb warnings resulted in explosions? Of those, what proportion caused injury or death? How many emergencies had this particular police officer had to deal with in her career to date? She seemed practised — almost blasé.

She's thinking, bomb scare, schmomb scare, same old story — why can't they be a wee bit original for a change?

At a peace summit, too. How ironic. I laughed out loud without meaning to. Lost my balance, shouldered into the wall. Used it to hold me up for a few steps. I couldn't stop laughing. Some of the others were turning to look. Diane frowned. Joan hurried over, picked me off the wall and hooked an arm under my shoulders. 'Thanks,' I whispered, tears in my eyes. We stumbled on together.

At last we reached the outside, through a squeaky glazed door beside a roaring vent. Our guide directed us to the right, along the side of the building. The cold air woke me up, and I was able to relinquish Joan's support. I squeezed her arm in thanks, and she moved back to walk with Val. We all hurried after our police officer, who was making fast for the front of the building. Without coats, in our delicate evening wear, the sopranos and altos were soon shivering.

The plaza was black with people. Officials shouted blurred instructions through loudspeakers, and there was a general movement away from the building and along the street. The way was punctuated by uniformed figures in fluorescent bibs, gesturing with torches. Parked police vehicles still had their roof lights flashing, head — and tail-lights ablaze. My breath glowed red, white, blue.

Carmina Urbana quickly lost its momentum and its group integrity, and became just some more of the hundreds of people hurrying towards the assembly point. I was afraid of falling behind, so I tried to keep Diane's blouse in sight, and Tom's wayward curls. I felt panicky now — fell victim to a grim procession of thoughts about all the things that could go wrong.

Such as the building beside us blowing up, for a start. We were far too close to it. I fought the urge to barge into the crowd, lay about me with fists and feet until I'd carved a path to safety.

Joan looked back to catch my eye and give me a thumbs-up. Beyond her I could see the police officer who had led us out, turning to come back our way. She asked Joan and Val a question and leaned in to hear their answer.

I'd come to a bottleneck and had to pause. I looked back at the building we'd left — the foyer still warmly lit, with people milling about inside.

Among them, a familiar figure. My heart stopped. Surely I'd imagined it. Then he turned round, and I saw him clearly.

It was Matthew.

'Sorry,' I said, automatically, as I turned and pushed my way back through the stream of people.

Some of them probably tried to stop me. I paid them no attention. I didn't understand what they were saying.

He'd got delayed, innocently, and had hurried to the concert hall hoping to be in time to join us on stage, had arrived just as the building began to be evacuated.

No, that didn't fit. He had said 'sorry', and 'love'. There was something bigger going on.

I was panting his name, in soft little screeches almost under my breath. I reached the door, where a large man in a fluorescent jacket turned to bar my way. More people were coming out every second, shouldering their way past him.

'I have to!' I said.

'Madam, will you please go to the assembly point.' He stood across the entrance, blocking even my view. I craned to see inside.

'I have to get in!' I was openly crying now: fat, hot tears rushing down my cheeks, cooling quickly in the night air.

'I'm sorry, everyone has to get out.' He folded his arms, looking genuinely apologetic.

I couldn't see Matthew. People were coming out another door. I patted the man on the arm, to reassure him that it was going to be all right, and made for the other door.

Saw him in the crowd on the plaza.

I was crossing the current now, which was even more difficult. I dodged between people, desperate to keep Matthew's head in view. For a few agonizing seconds I lost him, then spotted him again, moving diagonally across the plaza, away from me.

There was a clear patch between us. I ran for it.

He tensed like a wrestler when I flung my arms round him, threw me off and spun round, his face stretched into a grimace of rage and determination.

When he saw me, he froze. 'Cate!' His voice was a wheeze of shock.

All the things I wanted to say came crowding to the front of my mind, jostling and howling and clamouring to be spoken first. I stood there, silent, crying.

'Oh, Cate. I'm so sorry,' Matthew said. He raised a hand to his forehead.

'Where *were* you?' I was hating my weakness, my descent into snivelling incoherence. My teeth chattered violently.

'Come here,' he said, opening his arms for me.

Gratefully, I sank towards him. He folded himself and his coat around me like a blanket, hugged tight. I reached in under his arms, slipped my hands up his back, between the smooth lining of his coat and his cotton shirt. Laid my head against his chest; smelt his wholesome, forthright smell.

Felt the alien shape under his arm. Something hard, heavy. I drew back, brushing my bare arm deliberately against it. Metal, warm from his body, encased in strong fabric.

A gun in a holster?

He realized. He tensed again, his arms like hawsers clutching me. My head cranking back to stare at him, mouth opening to take breath in, to yell.

And then his mouth closed over mine, before I could think, before I could say a word, and he was kissing me harshly, urgently, with colliding teeth and rigid muscles.

It was only a few seconds. We drew back, his arms still clasped hard round me, our breaths dampening each other's faces. I was breathing hoarsely, a geyser of outrage building inside me, just about ready to burst forth.

'How *dare* you . . . ' I whispered.

'Cate, please trust me,' he said — calmly, as though my assent were a formality.

There was a steady authority in his eyes. He glanced behind me, scanning, scanning with such assurance that it had to be reflex. Years of practice. For my part, I was barely hearing what was going on around me, let alone seeing it. I was aware that we were perhaps the only ones not moving, a pair of standing stones around which the stream of people parted.

There might be a bomb in the building to my right. I remembered that much.

'I don't know what to do,' I heard myself say, again hating the whininess of my voice, the thought that even after all this I was still prepared to turn to him. I drew in breath again to cry out.

He leaned right in over me so that his lips brushed my ear. 'Don't blow my cover,' he murmured. And my heart thumped hard in my chest. My eyes widened in shock as he withdrew his head and I met his earnest blue gaze. I couldn't speak. My throat throbbed as though I had been choked, my mouth was as dry as old leaves, and my vision swam with little dots.

'We'll go together,' Matthew continued, 'but don't say anything until we're on our own.'

I began to shake my head, wanting to say *no*, no to all of this — to erase everything that had happened since we'd arrived in Belfast — or maybe earlier. Clean slate. Start again.

I gave a crooked nod, and Matthew turned us and began to walk the two of us towards the assembly point, one arm locked tight round my shoulders, fingers gripping my upper arm.

We were among the last to leave the plaza.

We trailed along after the river of people converging on the crowd up the road.

I couldn't speak. Tears ran down my face and I felt bruised, as though I'd been knocked down and kicked. If Matthew hadn't been holding on to me I might have sunk to the ground.

I paid no attention when Matthew spied the rest of the choir, far off towards the front of the crowd, and began to steer us towards them. For reasons unfathomable I preferred to lean my face into his coat and pretend that the danger lay beyond the two of us. I was shuddering now as much from shock as from the cold. Matthew held on to me, a squeeze of my shoulder every few steps being in equal parts comforting and terrifying.

Matthew has a gun. Matthew has a gun. Matthew has a gun.

Guns are for killing. This beautiful man, this man I thought I had a real connection with, was carrying a gun. Some ideal he held, some set of principles, had made him believe that it might sometimes be all right to take a person's life.

I couldn't look at him, the whole interminable time we took to cross the gusty street and worm our way up to the others. I let the tears run down my cheeks unchecked, their salt tracks tightening in the breeze.

★ ★ ★

We were almost there. I could see Donal and Linda with their arms round each other, Joan standing with Val. Diane was talking to a police officer with a clipboard.

I felt as though Matthew and I were on the far side of an uncrossable gulf. We couldn't reach that happy space, where things were normal and safe, you could trust your friends, and all you had to do to get out of an unpleasant situation was walk away. Walk away.

The officer who had led us off stage loomed without warning in front of me. 'Caitlín Houlihan?' she said. *Catchleen*. It stuck in her gritty throat.

I stopped walking, resisting Matthew's pull. 'Yes?' My own voice rasped like an ill-fitting door. 'That's me.' Out of the corner of my eye I saw the other officer look up from his clipboard and make his way towards us.

'You're a member of the Carmina Urbana choir?'

'That's right.'

'What's the matter?' Matthew asked, and he packed so many layers of hostility and distrust into the question that I turned and looked at him at last. His face was like stone, and his hand on my shoulder was no less rigid.

I saw Diane looking over at us, shocked and wordless.

'Miss Houlihan, we need to ask you some questions,' said the female officer. She nodded briefly at her colleague as he joined us. 'My name is Sergeant Hall,' she continued. 'You've stopped at my request, and I must now search you. Please step this way.' Her tone was personal — almost intimate.

'Oh, you are joking!' Matthew exclaimed. 'This is . . . no. Seriously, you do *not* want to do this.'

Hall regarded him coolly, then turned back to me. 'Step this way, Miss Houlihan.'

Stunned and confused, I moved slightly towards her, but before I'd taken a step, Matthew gripped my shoulder harder — hard enough to hurt. 'What's this about?' His voice was close to a growl. A bolt of panic shot through me. This was not safe. Not at all.

'It's just routine,' said Hall, blinking at him. She seemed entirely calm, in control of the situation.

I could just tell her, I realized suddenly. I could lean forward and say, *he has a gun*, and he'd be arrested on the spot, wouldn't he? I glanced at him again, his beautiful mouth, the hair curling around his ear.

'Well, she doesn't consent,' said Matthew.

I gasped. '*You* don't get to say what *I*

consent to!' I wrenched free of him and took a few steps forward. I wondered what she thought I might be hiding under my thin, close-fitting concert dress.

Then I remembered the memory stick, and sweat beaded out all over my body. It was all I could do to stand still. Tears were streaming down my cheeks again. Dimly, I heard Hall inform me that she'd be using the backs of her hands on my breasts, buttocks and inner thighs. I was so numb from cold that I could barely feel her touch, but as she approached where the memory stick was hidden I lost my nerve and shied away.

Hall spoke softly. 'Is there something in your bra?'

I nodded.

'Is it a weapon?'

I shook my head.

'Please take it out and hand it to me.'

I dug out the memory stick, my own fingers chill against my private flesh.

Hall reached to take it from me. Before she got hold of it, though, her colleague dropped his clipboard and shouted 'Stop!' We both turned sharply to see him dive into the crowd, walkie-talkie at his lips.

The reason for his behaviour was immediately apparent: Matthew had disappeared.

Hall took the memory stick from me, and

her other hand landed heavily on my shoulder. 'Caitlín Houlihan,' she said, 'I'm arresting you under Section 41 of the Terrorism Act. You don't have to say anything, but it may harm your defence if you do not mention when questioned something which you later rely on in court. Anything you say may be given in evidence.'

I heard my voice as though from far away. 'OK,' it said.

Sergeant Hall led me to a police car and guided me into the back seat. I clicked my seatbelt into place and settled myself, almost as though I were meant to be there. All this new knowledge boiled in my brain and burned away at the flesh under my ribs. The two officers in the front of the car communicated by radio with the station, but all I could make out was a babble of syllables. My eyes were stinging now, but tearless. My hands and feet prickled as they began to recover from the cold.

What had I done? How could I *possibly* be sitting in the back of a Belfast squad car, under arrest? Why hadn't I left that stupid memory stick in my bag? This — the police getting hold of it — was exactly what Nicky Fay had been trying to avoid, presumably. What a monumental fuck-up I'd made of George's assignment. He might fire me.

That's if I even came through this mess without going to prison. That thought made me retch. It dripped through my head like some sort of corrosive slime. I couldn't go near it.

What on earth did they think I'd done? 'Terrorism Act', Sergeant Hall had said. Well, that was ludicrous. I wasn't a terrorist.

If my mind refused to dwell on these subjects, I couldn't think about the choir either. Diane and some of the others must have seen me being searched, taken away. How could I ever look them in the face again?

All this without even mentioning Matthew. Whatever about anything else, how had *that* happened? I'd risked my safety and joined up with a man who'd bring a gun to a bomb scare and run away from the police.

The journey seemed to take a week, but at last we stopped outside a big bunker of a building, and I was led inside. After the booking procedure, which would have been mind-numbing if I'd had any mind left to numb, I was brought to a smallish, windowless room lit by a glaring fluorescent oblong. Someone would see me 'shortly'. The door closed with a loud click behind me.

And there I stayed. The room was bare apart from a table and two chairs. I sat gingerly on the dirty plastic seat of the chair nearest me and rested my elbows on the cold surface of the table. My feet screamed their thanks for the reprieve. Without my phone I had no notion what the time might be. It must be around nine, I guessed. I was still shivering, but from what mixture of cold and emotion I couldn't tell. Scanning round the room I noticed the camera lens in the corner by the ceiling. I resisted the temptation to wave.

So, they'd be interviewing me soon. Questioning me. Here I was, *assisting the police with their enquiries*. I'd waived my right to a solicitor, not seeing a viable alternative. I wondered if there was anything I could do to prepare myself. How could I make them believe that I wasn't a terrorist? I wished I knew more about body language. I wished I knew more, full stop.

What if they asked me about Matthew? Despite the gun, despite everything, I still found a tiny flicker of loyalty to him, somewhere deep down. In one little puddle of clarity I knew that, despite everything, if he was going to get in trouble I didn't want it to be greater because of me.

Cate, there was a fucking *bomb scare*. People could have been *killed*.

I remembered the warmth of his hand on my shoulder, the reassuring solidity of it.

I'd stay as calm as I could, and I'd answer their questions truthfully. But I wouldn't give them more than they were asking for.

It was none too warm in the room, but eventually I thawed. Then there were just the jitters of stress to contend with. I stood up and paced the short distance back and forth across the room, feeling like a cliché. Next, perhaps, I'd carve those bristly day-counting marks into the wall with my hairclip.

Maybe I could escape — maybe if I tried hard enough, I could turn myself into mist or smoke, snake under the door, waft through the building, curl around the officers' heads and hands as they went about their business unaware, disperse out through vents and windows to resolidify in the street outside. And why stop there, indeed? Life as an evanescent fog held a certain appeal just now.

Why was I in this room on my own? Were they going to leave me here all night? When would something happen?

Nothing did, not until I had given up hope that it would, had given up pacing and stretching and had sat in that horrible chair until my buttocks froze.

I had just stood up to try and get my blood circulating again when the door opened. I turned to see Sergeant Hall coming in with a tray on which there was a jug of water and two plastic beakers. Following her was another officer, a man, who carried a leather briefcase.

I stood as tall as I could, fighting off my feebleness.

The male officer went to the other side of the table and put his bag down on the floor. He reached across to shake my hand. 'Miss Houlihan?' Some eddy in the air as he leaned forward gave me a noseful of worthy-smelling soap.

'That's right,' I said, aiming recklessly for a tone of serene entitlement, as though I did not have a tear-streaked face, goose-pimpled arms and a blister forming on the ball of my right foot. I was in freefall. This was totally unreal.

'Sergeant Phillips is my name.' He gestured for me to sit down, and sat opposite me. The chair creaked as it took his weight. Sergeant Hall placed her tray on the table and went to stand at the door; she didn't catch my eye when I looked over.

Phillips spoke. 'Just some questions, if you don't mind, Miss Houlihan.' He took from the briefcase a slightly dog-eared notepad and a pen. No mention of how long I'd been waiting, or why I was here at all.

So this was it. In a flood of certainty I realized I'd tell them everything. Matthew could look after himself.

Phillips looked straight at me. 'Who is David Cornwell?'

The room whirled.

I sat and breathed, riding this latest billow of shock. *David Cornwell?* The name meant nothing to me. Slowly, I gathered my lips to form *What?* — but Phillips went on before my throat made any sound.

'How do you know Noel, Eric and Frank?'

I managed to shake my head. This was weird — something had gone badly askew. I was in the wrong room of the wrong police station on the wrong night. I coughed, and found my voice. 'I don't know anyone called Noel. Or Frank. I was in primary school with an Eric . . . '

Phillips was writing. 'Eric what?'

'I don't remember.' I was doing my best, trying to give Phillips what he was looking for. He was grey-haired and soft-spoken, with a deeply lined face and big, pendulous ear-lobes. 'O'Connor?' I ventured. I was shaking again now, worse than earlier.

'Eric O'Connor. And where was that?'

'Queen of Angels, Ardee. County Louth. In the . . . Republic . . . ' I faltered.

Phillips scrutinized me for a second or two, then wrote again.

I said, 'Sorry, what's this about?' I felt

weak, empty, dreamlike, floored by astonishment.

Phillips gave the tiniest smile. 'You know what this is about.' He nodded, looking straight at me again, brown eyes set close together under thick brows.

'I honestly don't,' I said, offering him my open palms as though to prove my point.

'Come on, Miss Houlihan. Use your brain.' He leaned back in his chair. 'Who gave you the thumb drive?'

'Nicky Fay!' I exclaimed, feeling bizarrely relieved that I was able to tell him something relevant.

Phillips nodded as he wrote. 'That's right,' he said. 'Nicky Fay, in the Starbucks café, earlier today.' The rhyming was deliberate. There was an air almost of celebration in the room.

I wanted to say, *If you knew, then why ask me?* But that would not be wise. Instead, I said, 'May I have some water?'

Phillips poured out some and handed it to me. I sipped gratefully, feeling the cold liquid proceed down my oesophagus.

'What's on the thumb drive, Miss Houlihan?' Phillips looked straight at me again, face serious.

'I think it's a file . . . ' I began, and he tilted his head very slightly to one side, as if to tell

261

me to get on with it. 'It's a document that my boss needs for a book.'

Phillips was writing again. 'Who do you work for, Miss Houlihan?' Such an ordinary question, so quietly delivered, but in this context, so sinister.

I paused, thinking of George, his matted jumpers and ready laugh, his robust stance on printer errors . . . his political sympathies. *Our side. Or theirs*. Where did the Police Service of Northern Ireland fit into that schema?

'I work for a small publisher in Dublin called Bell Books,' I said.

'And your boss's name?'

'George Sweeney.' My voice was very small.

Phillips repeated, 'George Sweeney. And what's in this document that George Sweeney needs?'

'I don't know,' I said. I was on auto-pilot. My mind was shutting down, refusing to co-operate with me.

Phillips waited.

I went on. 'He didn't tell me what it was. He just said it was corroboration for a book we're publishing in the spring.'

'And that's what you believe is the case?'

'Yes, of course.'

'Tell me about this book.'

Again I hesitated, recalling the obsessive

elusiveness of Eddie MacDevitt, the trouble his book had already brought upon my beloved uncle, and not least, the searing look Nicky Fay had given me as he left Starbucks. I was in deep waters here, and I didn't know enough to keep safe. 'It's just a memoir,' I said. 'It's by a guy called Eddie MacDevitt. He's not famous or anything.'

'And what has Nicky Fay got to contribute to this memoir?'

'I don't know. George asked me to collect the document for him while I was here for the concert. That's all.'

Phillips sighed. 'And if I put you on the spot and told you to make an educated guess? Hmm?' He looked at me, eyebrows raised and mouth bunched in a sceptical expression.

I was unable to hold his gaze; I dropped my eyes. I licked my lips and took a breath. 'I'd guess that maybe Nicky Fay and Eddie MacDevitt might have a connection through Republican circles?'

Phillips feigned astonishment. 'You don't say!' He wrote laboriously. 'Republican. Circles.'

I shrugged.

'I'll tell you what I think, Miss Houlihan,' said Phillips, serious again. 'I think you know more than you're telling. You and your nimble-footed companion. What's his name, by the way?'

A bitter marble of unease now, rolling around in the pit of my stomach. Had they arrested Matthew too? Was he maybe in another room in this very building, being questioned about me?

'Matthew Taylor,' I said, feeling like a traitor.

Phillips made a note, then leaned towards me and spoke even more quietly than before. 'What *else* did Nicky Fay give you?'

I blinked. 'What do you mean?'

'What do I mean? Well, you tell *me*. Was it information? A message for someone, maybe?'

I was hollow with fear. Whatever about Matthew, I couldn't give them Uncle Fintan. I shook my head and lied. 'No. He just gave me the memory stick and told me to give it to George on Monday.'

'Monday,' said Phillips. He stopped writing, sat back and folded his arms, gazing calmly at me. Neither of us said anything for a long time.

At last Phillips spoke again. 'Now, if you'll please have a look over my notes and sign at the bottom if you feel they are an accurate record of what you said.' He passed over a single page, covered in cramped, clear writing.

'I — what? Are we finished?'

'I'm afraid not. We'll be back in a wee while

to check one or two details.' He put his pen and pad back into his briefcase and waited for me to read the notes. Notwithstanding my near-inability to make sense of anything at this point, they seemed perfectly clear and fair to me. Phillips stood up then, and he and Hall went outside, shutting the door behind them.

I sat in a welter of nerves, wondering if this was a strategic move on their part. Did they disbelieve me? Were they trying to catch me out? It made no sense. I poured myself some more water and sipped it slowly. When would they come back? The silence in the room was thick and heavy. More than anything else now, I wanted my bed.

Time passed. How much, I had no way of knowing. The next time the door opened it was not Phillips but another male officer, accompanied by a woman who introduced herself as Inspector Nolan. She called me Cate, and wanted to know how long I'd been working at Bell Books and how I'd got the job. Her niece worked in publishing too, she said, in London.

Nolan also took notes by hand. Just as I began to relax, she turned the conversation back to Nicky Fay. She wanted to know everything about our meeting this morning. I told her what I could remember.

'What else did he say to you, Cate?' she asked, echoing Phillips. 'Who else did you talk about?'

'Nothing,' I insisted again. 'Nobody.' I felt sick.

Nolan paused. 'And so he gave you a memory stick with some documents on it?'

'Yes. Or maybe just one document.'

'Did you open it?'

'No.'

'Why did you take it with you when you went on stage tonight?'

'I don't really know,' I said. 'He told me not to lose it. I felt safer bringing it with me.'

'Now, the man you were with when you were stopped by Sergeant Hall,' said Nolan, and looked at me with eyes harder than before. 'What's his name again?'

My breath caught. 'Matthew Taylor.'

'Boyfriend?'

'Ex-boyfriend,' I said, because that seemed inevitable now.

'And what was he doing at the Waterfront tonight?'

I looked down at my hands, wondering if I was going to break down and sob. All I could think of was the warmth of Matthew's skin in the darkness. 'He's in the same choir as me,' I said.

'Carmina Urbana.'

'That's right.'

'And do you know why he ran away while you were being arrested?'

I shook my head.

'Would you care to speculate?'

He had a *gun*. I looked up at her. 'I suppose he must have had something to hide.'

Nolan finished writing with a decisive full stop and passed me over three pages of notes. 'Please sign the bottom of each page.'

'When will we be finished?' I asked her. I felt impossibly small and weak.

She smiled and shook her head. 'Oh, we've a way to go yet, so we do.'

My eyes widened. How long could they keep me here, anyway? I had absolutely no idea.

Nolan collected her things and left with her silent colleague, and I was alone again. This time, though, I had not long to wait. After just a few minutes, the door opened again, and Phillips and Nolan came back in together. This time, it was a double act, with Nolan taking the notes and the two of them pelting me with questions. Over again we went through all I had told them before. For good measure they asked me to repeat the details of my meeting with Nicky Fay *backwards*. I had no notion what good that would do them, but I gave it a try.

I was close to the end of my endurance. There was nothing left to squeeze out of my exhausted brain. I moaned at the two of them to stop, but they went on. There was so little to tell. At the end of the day, no matter how many times they repeated their questions, I still couldn't tell them who David Cornwell was or how he might relate to Noel or Eric or Frank. At last they seemed to come to the same conclusion. They handed me yet more pages to sign and left.

As the door shut behind them I stood up and began to pace, favouring my stinging foot. I was fully awake now, scared and impatient. There must be some sort of limit to how long this could go on. Why did I have to be such an ignoramus? I let out a long, loud sigh, and something about it put me in mind of a scale, so I sang some. Up and down, humming and trilling as though I were warming up for a performance. I opened right up into the top of my range, let every cavity in my head vibrate, didn't care how much noise I made . . . until I recalled the camera in the corner of the room and stopped abruptly.

The silence that fell then was thicker and heavier than ever. I tried leaning against the wall for the sake of variety, but it didn't help much. I considered lying on the floor, but I changed my mind when I took a closer look at it. I sprawled across the table for a while, which was not as comfortable as one might have thought.

★   ★   ★

I was, regrettably, still prone on the table when there was a tap at the door and Sergeant Hall came in. I scrambled to my feet.

The police officer was looking more pleasant than I'd seen her thus far. 'Miss Houlihan, you've been extremely helpful tonight. Thank you for that.'

'OK . . . ' I said.

'That's it,' she said. 'You're free to go.'

An avalanche of relief poured down my slopes, engulfing all in its path.

Hall showed me out. Phillips met us in the corridor and handed me back Nicky Fay's memory stick.

'Goodnight,' I said to the two of them, aware of how inappropriate it sounded. I stepped out into the icy air, feeling cautiously cheerful. I understood none of what had happened, but I was free. I started walking as best I could in what I hoped was a likely direction.

Every atom of cheer drained precipitously away when I saw Matthew standing under a streetlamp a short distance down the road. I was empty, barren of fortitude or firmness of purpose to bring to bear on this situation. I simply kept walking towards him. Past him. He fell into step beside me. We walked in silence, with just a little more space between us than there might naturally have been.

'Um, hello,' Matthew said after a while.

'I don't think I can talk to you.'

'Please, Cate.' He touched my arm. I shrugged him off.

I was looking for landmarks, hoping I was heading in towards the centre of the city, somewhere I might recognize. I felt utterly lost.

Matthew began again. 'Look, I know you've had a difficult evening — '

'You brought a gun to our concert.' I spoke barely above a whisper.

'That's right, I did.'

I stopped walking. 'So, who were you going to assassinate?'

'Oh, no.' He shook his head. 'You've got the wrong idea.'

'Look — ' Anger rose in me.

He reached out a hand and touched my arm briefly. 'Cate, it's all right.'

'It's bloody not, you know.' I started walking again. It was better than hitting him.

'I wasn't going to assassinate anyone, OK?'

'Yeah.' I kept looking straight ahead. Some part of me was enjoying the moment. He'd spoken almost petulantly. He didn't like me treating this as though it were something I had a right to know about. But he was the one who'd said *love*. 'You weren't planning to use the gun, then?'

'I wasn't!'

'Who was the target? Which of the delegates?'

'Oh, for goodness' sake, Cate. I'm not a bloody terrorist.'

I wasn't even particularly interested in the answer to my question, I realized. It was all the same. 'You'd call it *freedom fighter*, would you?'

'No!' He darted round to intercept me and stood blocking my way, reaching both arms to me now, moving to touch me but stopping short. 'Cate. Please. I've told you. You've got the wrong idea.'

I looked at him, his face earnest and strained in the streetlight, his eyes full of distress. Everything went very still. A monstrous thought was taking ghastly shape. 'Well, what are you, then? Some kind of . . . undercover agent?'

He said nothing, but blinked his assent.

I gasped and took a step back. 'You mean . . . like . . . MI5?' I managed.

He gave me a distorted little smile. 'Six, actually. Overseas work.'

'Oh, my god,' I whispered. I whirled past

him and set off along the street, walking as fast as I could. He kept pace, saying nothing. I could see his worried face out of the corner of my eye, but I wouldn't look at him. I couldn't think of anything more to say.

There was a fire in my mind. This was unbearable. I had spent fevered hours absorbing the revelation that Matthew was a gunman, a terrorist, intent on causing harm in the name of some political ideal. A man on the run from justice. And now even that unsavoury picture was shattered. This man, the man I had thought of as rational and kind — maybe even one who might provide an antidote to past hurts — this man who had delighted me, who had held me in his arms in the dark, was not a terrorist. Not an assassin. Not a wrong-headed ideologue with romantic notions of armed struggle and blood sacrifice. Just a spy. A fucking British spy.

This was the twenty-first century. Surely things had moved on.

I was frozen. I kept walking.

'Cate, please — just try to understand — it's not what you imagine — '

'How the fuck would you know what I imagine?'

'Cate, this is me. I haven't turned into a different person. I helped you, Cate.'

'You *helped* me, did you?'

'Yes, I fucking helped you! You'd still be in police custody if I hadn't intervened. I took a big risk for you. A *big* risk. The least you could do is thank me.'

'I should *thank* you, now? Oh, that's fucking rich!'

I sped up. Matthew snorted in frustration and kept pace.

'Look, Cate, slow down. I'm trying to talk to you. Stop!' He reached out an arm to bar my progress.

'No fucking way!' I growled. I barged past him and was off down the street, running, stumbling, limping away as fast as I could. My heart thudded, and I kicked off my shoes before they twisted my ankle for me. I could hear him behind me, calling my name. Coming closer. How could I have let him touch me? How could I ever have thought that he would keep me safe?

I heard his breath, his feet on the pavement, felt his hand on my arm. 'Get off me, you sick fuck!' I shook his hand away, kept running.

'Cate! Please! Listen!' He grabbed at me again.

I spun round to face him. 'How dare you! How fucking dare you lay a hand on me! How dare you even speak to me when you're a . . . you're a — '

'*Shut up*, you stupid woman! You'll land us both in even deeper trouble!' His voice was a fractured whisper.

'Are you OK, pet?' A woman was leaning out of a car window. 'D'you need a lift somewhere?'

I looked at her, dumb. She was blonde, petite, the passenger in a car driven by an older man. She was gesturing at the car door behind hers.

'I . . . ' What was the right thing to do? Was it more foolish to take a lift from total strangers or to stay here with Matthew? A few long seconds passed. 'I'm all right, thanks very much,' I said.

'Are you sure, now?'

'Yes, thanks,' I said, and the car moved on.

Matthew was staring at me. Again, he took my arm.

I ripped his hand off me, twisting out of his grasp, and I was running again. Running. When I did not hear him follow, I looked over my shoulder to see him walking slowly back the way we had come.

★ ★ ★

I paused to recover my breath, bowing all the way over to ease the pain in my side. My tights were shreds, my right foot bleeding where the blister had burst. I stood up and looked around. Miraculously, there was the Starbucks where I'd met Nicky Fay. So at least I knew the way back to the hotel.

Without money or phone, I had nowhere else to go.

One step at a time, I made my way there. As I approached the glass façade I saw for a split second the doors exploding out towards me, cruel shards plunging into my flesh, piercing and slicing me.

Nothing of the sort, of course. The lobby was its own bright, plush self. The thick carpet felt heavenly.

I went to the desk and requested a new key card. The receptionist listened to my story, asked me a few questions about the choir, and to my immense relief, consented to give me a new card.

The lift doors closed on me, and I shut my eyes. My throat and head hurt. I shivered violently. I felt strung out, grazed, disconnected. Skinned. Ice crystals forming in my heart.

Thankfully, I encountered nobody in the corridor.

I stumbled into my room — our room — and shut the door, leaning against it for support. Again, I wanted to run — run to the station, get on a train, go home. I escaped into the shower instead, undressing slowly, feeling as though I were peeling my bones clean. The water was like an assault — I was so cold — but gradually I thawed and began to enjoy the warming prickle in my fingers and toes.

I couldn't think about Matthew at all.

He was standing by the window when I came out into the room again. He turned as he heard the bathroom door.

I roared.

'It's OK,' he said.

I stared at him. The world rushed in at me from all sides, crashing and heaving and resolving to one absurd circumstance: he was holding my shoes. My strappy, pinchy, sparkly evening shoes, splattered with mud, dangled from his hand.

'You went back for those?'

'Thought you might miss them.'

I stood paralysed for a long time. Eventually mustered a whisper. 'Thank you.'

We were silent as statues, staring at each other from either side of the wide bed.

He was still in his coat. My heart thumped.

'Do you have . . . ' I couldn't say it. I took a deep breath and gestured instead.

He gave a heavy sigh. 'Yes, I do.'

I glared at him, and at last my voice returned. 'Tell you what. I'll go back into the bathroom and get dressed, and when I come out, there will be no . . . *gun* . . . in evidence. Capeesh?' I moved to my suitcase and fished out some clothes, hugging the bundle to my chest as I went back into the bathroom.

I dressed and came out again. Matthew was in shirtsleeves, sitting on the armchair by the window. I hitched myself up on to the bed and looked at him.

'Where is it?'

He indicated his rucksack.

'Did you bring it with you from Dublin?' My eyes were burning now, but my head was clear. Droplets of cooling water escaped from my hair, down past the collar of my shirt.

Matthew shook his head. 'It was issued this afternoon.' He looked away.

I sighed. As usual, the minimal answer to my question. Now it had an entirely different significance. One little piece of information had changed everything. I had the sudden sensation of *missing* Matthew, mourning him, as though he were not sitting here, four feet away from me. And perhaps it was as simple as that: perhaps the pain I was feeling came down to the banal fact that I'd been sleeping with a stranger all this time.

I did my best. 'So . . . you were working today?'

He nodded. 'They only told me yesterday.'

'That explains a lot.' I looked at him. This was a man I knew, after all. A man with whom I had felt more at ease than with most people. A man I had begun to trust, a little — to love, perhaps, a little. I breathed. I waited.

He said, 'Cate.' He stopped. 'I can't tell you any more. I'm sorry. I can't. I shouldn't have told you as much as I have.'

A blankness in my mind. A grey hole, expanding, almost blurring my vision. We sat motionless in the gratingly dim light from the bedside lamps. I was cold and tired, and my damp hair was starting an ache in my shoulders. More than anything else I needed a long walk, in daylight, on my own. Time to think, to draw towards each other the edges of this awful grey hole and see how they might fit back together.

'I'm sorry,' Matthew said again, and I heard his voice as if from far away. He reached across the bed to touch my arm.

I did not respond. Dispassionately, I noted the crack in his voice.

When Matthew's phone buzzed in his pocket I almost yelped. The sound was an attack.

'Hello . . . No, I'm back at my hotel . . . I'm here with Cate Houlihan . . . Look, it's not a — oh . . . OK, then.'

He ended the call and sighed deeply. To the

wall, he said, 'I have to go out.'

To the wall, I nodded once.

As he furtively retrieved the gun from his rucksack and strapped the holster around himself, then put on his coat, I gathered together the energy I needed. 'Matthew.' There was nothing left over to animate my voice. 'Will you do one thing for me, please?'

'Anything I can.'

'Take your stuff with you. Find somewhere else to sleep tonight.'

★   ★   ★

Next morning I left the ruins of the night behind and struggled downstairs, where I joined Donal, Linda and Anja at a breakfast table, eating silently and barely listening to their conversation. They did not ask me where Matthew was.

Diane and Joan moved from table to table, letting people know that the expedition to retrieve the choir's belongings from the Waterfront would start from the lobby at ten o'clock.

As we sat waiting for the stragglers, it became clear that a good night had been had by many. Although most of the women had found themselves in the same position as me — bereft of money and phones after the evacuation — several of the men had had the luck to carry their things in their suit pockets, and they had bankrolled the rest. Drink had been taken. Eyes were bloodshot, heads sore. Debts were argued over in a good-natured way; ribald remarks were passed on the subject of payment in kind. The atmosphere resembled the rowdier sort of school trip. My attention washed in and out, and I was very grateful that nobody was trying to engage me in conversation.

At last we set out for the Waterfront. I succeeded in walking alone most of the way; the rest of the time I was with a group of basses who did not feel the need to include me in their talk. Without my coat, I was soon shivering. On arrival, we were ushered to the back of a long queue, which snaked round the entrance area and almost spilled out on to the plaza. I recognized some people from the other choirs.

'How are you?' Joan's voice made me jump. She and Val were behind me.

'Oh, fine,' I said. I nodded, biting my lips together. 'I mean. Not remotely fine. So, yeah.'

'Did Matthew show up in the end?' Val asked.

'He did, yeah. And then I told him to go away again.'

'Oh, dear,' said Joan. She lowered her voice. 'Are you all right, Cate? I mean, do you need any help? You know you can come to us any time.'

'Thanks.' I sighed. 'It's all a bit of a mess, really.' I looked at the two of them. They were on the other side of that gulf, and I had no way of reaching them.

Val said, 'You know, it only just occurred to me there, as we arrived, that we never even got to sing that bloody peace anthem.'

'I know,' Joan said. 'After all that.'

'I was even beginning to like it,' said Val. 'OK. Slightly. What? Sue me!'

When Carmina Urbana finally reached the head of the queue, Diane stood with two police officers, vouching for each member of the choir. Once we were all identified, another officer escorted us to the backstage room.

It was strange to see it looking just the same as it had before. I felt as though it ought to be different, as I was. My coat and bag were where I'd left them.

As we walked back to the hotel I fished out my phone and looked at it. Seven missed calls. Tingle of misery. I'd check them later.

I fled to my room the minute I could and sat for ages before I deemed myself ready to face the phone again.

Eventually I took it out and looked at it. Froze.

Seven missed calls, but not from Matthew. Four from Ardee. Three from a private number.

I dialled and waited impatiently for the messages to begin. Mum's voice, with an unaccustomed note of urgency. She had left the three voicemails last night, the third one well after midnight. Nothing of substance, just a plea that I phone home as soon as I could.

My fingers shook as I found the number. The phone rang, rang, rang. No answer. No answering machine — I'd grumbled to them about this, and so had Mícheál, but they insisted they didn't need one.

I listened to Mum's voicemails again, in case I'd missed something. My breathing felt constricted, and the sobs came on hard. I threw myself on to the bed, and lay face down, tears trickling. It's just Mum's way, I told myself. She's so useless on the phone. She gets panicked and can't tell the right thing to do.

Such as let her daughter know what the fuck is going on that has her in such a state.

Had something happened to Mícheál or Dad? Something shameful? Mícheál got someone pregnant? Dad embezzled the club funds? Or had somebody died? Surely if somebody had died, Mum would have found the guts to say it, even to a machine.

I tried Mícheál's mobile. Switched off. I didn't leave a message. His voicemail greeting was too jaunty, too offhand, to invite such a sombre query. I didn't have the language to address him in that way.

I would just have to wait.

The rest of the day was a terrible jumble of hefting bags and milling in lobbies and shuffling in queues and edging along the train aisle and jolting through the improbably green countryside. There was no sign of Matthew at the station, and nobody mentioned him to me. At last we were piling off the train and saying our goodbyes. I took my leave of the others and escaped down the quays.

As I walked from the bus stop to my house, I discovered that I'd missed yet another call. There was a message — and at last a hint of what was going on. Mum said, 'We're all over in Swords with your Auntie Rosemary — you won't get us at home.' She sounded calmer.

Back at the flat, I spared seconds to tear off my coat before sinking on to the sofa and phoning Uncle Fintan's house.

The phone rang eight times before it was picked up. 'Hello?'

'Hello, is that . . . Mum?' I was momentarily disoriented — it was so unlike her to answer the phone in someone else's house.

'Caitlín! Oh, thank goodness!'

'Hi, Mum, yeah, I'm just back from Belfast.'

'Belfast? Oh, your choir. Of course. I'd forgotten. Listen, did you get the messages I left you?'

'Yes, I did. What's going on? Is everyone OK?'

'Well, yes. Everything's going to be all right.' Mum heaved a deep sigh. She sounded exhausted. 'There's no need to worry. We had a scare. Fintan is in hospital.'

'Oh, my god — what happened?'

'He had a heart attack yesterday.'

'Oh, no! Is he all right? Was it serious?'

'Well, it was quite serious, yes.' Mum's breath whispered; her voice shook. 'He's still in intensive care, but he's stable, thank god. They're going to give him a pacemaker. We drove Rosemary home — she's asleep at the moment. I'm making us something to eat.'

Mum released a series of disorganized data that eventually enabled me to piece together the story.

It turned out that Uncle Fintan had been staying in Mum and Dad's house when it happened; Mum didn't quite explain why. He'd been reading the paper in the sitting room with Dad and Mícheál, while Mum cooked dinner, when he had suddenly listed over in his chair. They'd called an ambulance, and he'd reached Our Lady of Lourdes Hospital inside half an hour, unconscious, with about an even chance of making it through the night.

Mum had phoned Auntie Rosemary, who had cut short an evening with her friends and hastened to her husband's side. The night had been a long, horrible ordeal. Uncle Fintan had suffered two further heart attacks in the small hours. Then towards dawn he had stabilized, and by the time the doctor had seen him on Sunday morning he'd been conscious and coherent, and with a reasonable shot at recovery.

Mum didn't say it in so many words, but she had been phoning to give me the chance to come and say goodbye.

After we hung up, I sat still for a long time. Dusk had been gathering its forces as I'd arrived home; now it had taken hold and was deepening into darkness. I would have to get up soon, go out, drive for an hour or so to the hospital — I'd promised Mum I'd go this evening. My eyes stung, and I had not an ounce of strength in my limbs.

The screen of my phone flashed rudely into the shadowy room.

Text message.

Matthew Taylor. (Who?)

'In Belfast about to get on a train. Can we talk when I get back to Dublin?'

Delete.

Part Four

The Living

I sat at George's desk and plugged in the memory stick as he watched. It contained just one item, not a text document at all, but a sound file. As I clicked to copy it across, George said, 'You're as white as a sheet.'

'Well,' I said, 'I had a bit of an intense weekend.' My stomach gave a lurch. How much did I need to tell him? The whole story was an enormous tangle, and I had not the faintest idea of where my little thread fitted in.

'So I read in the papers,' said George. 'Well, did you get to sing your songs, at least?'

'No. We were just starting when everything went pear-shaped.'

The file finished copying. 'Is that it?' George asked.

'I think so,' I said. I set it playing before he could tell me not to. I wanted to hear what had so intrigued the PSNI.

A lot of rustling, to start with. Then, slightly muffled, a man said, 'David Cornwell.' He sounded English.

'Pleased to meet you, David. You can call me Noel,' said another voice, much closer to the microphone, and a third man, further away again, said, 'Eric.' There was a soft cough, and then, 'Oh, I'm Frank, very pleased to.'

'Well, gentlemen,' said David Cornwell, 'I want to start by emphasizing that I'm here in an unofficial capacity. This is strictly an exploratory meeting, and it may lead to nothing.'

'Turn it off, there, Cate. That's it, all right.'

Reluctantly, I clicked Pause. I sat for a moment, taking in what I'd heard. I looked at George. 'That was actually Nicky Fay, wasn't it?'

George tipped his head back and lidded his eyes in grudging assent. 'In his younger days.' He chuckled. 'Noel,' he said, in a Belfast accent broader even than the one on the recording. 'That was a pocket tape recorder, you know. Seemed like magic back then. I bet it never even crossed your man's mind.'

'And Frank was Uncle Fintan. And Eric? Was that Eddie MacDevitt?'

George nodded.

Light dawned. 'This was the Blackpool meeting, wasn't it?'

George looked sharply at me for a moment. 'All right, young Cate, you've a head on your shoulders.'

'George,' I said, 'you should probably tell Mr Fay that the police know about that file. They questioned me after the bomb scare. I think they thought I was involved somehow.'

'Oh, lord god. What happened?'

I gave him a summary, skirting around the parts about Matthew, which made for a deformed little tale.

'Well,' he said when I'd finished, 'if I'd known I was sending you into the lions' den like that I never would have asked you.' He paused, looking at his clasped hands. 'Thank you, Cate — thank you.'

'You're welcome,' I said, and I meant it.

'And listen to me. You were lucky with the PSNI.' He pronounced it *piznee*.

'I was, I think.'

'You were very bloody lucky. That shower can keep hold of you for days without giving any reason.'

I stood up and let him have his chair back, then headed towards the outer office. But there was still one thing more. I turned back. 'Uncle Fintan asked me to let you know he's in hospital.'

George's face fell. 'Oh, no. What's wrong with him?'

'He had a heart attack on Saturday night. And . . . he said not to visit without phoning first. Because Rosemary . . .'

George nodded. 'Yes, that's right. We're not supposed to be in touch.' He shook his head once and sucked his teeth. 'Sure, we're all getting older, I suppose.'

★   ★   ★

Text message. Matthew Taylor. 'Cate, please can we talk?'
Delete.

★   ★   ★

I hurried along the corridor, rubbing foul-smelling alcohol gel into my hands. I was still learning my way to Uncle Fintan's room.

It took me a second to recognize George out of context. He was walking towards me, side by side with Paula.

'Hello!' I said, and they both nodded their greetings. 'I'm just . . . You've just seen . . . ' I stood looking at them.

'He's in good enough form,' said George. 'He's on the mend, I'd say.' Paula said nothing.

I edged past them. 'I'd better . . . '

'On you go,' said George. 'We'll see you tomorrow, bright and early.'

'Bye-bye.'

Uncle Fintan lifted his hand in greeting and gave me a weak smile. He was very tired, the nurses had explained — he used an oxygen mask to conserve his strength. 'Cate,' he said, his voice blurred by the mask. He let his head tilt back on to the pillows, but his eyes were open and alert.

'I brought you some more grapes,' I said.

'Oh, lovely.' His speech was mostly vowels.

I didn't mention George and Paula straight away. He asked about Sheila and Aidan from the downstairs flat. I'd barely spoken to them since they'd got back from China. 'Sheila's doing her tax exams soon,' said Uncle Fintan, managing the consonants a little better now. 'Tell her good luck.'

He had a music player on the bedside locker, and a big set of headphones. I told him about the music Carmina Urbana was rehearsing for the Christmas concert — Bernstein, Mendelssohn, Mahler, Copland. 'All the Jews,' he said. I was delighted that he was so on the ball.

After a bit I said, 'Hey, Uncle F, you never told me you knew Paula.'

He looked out the window. It was starting to rain. 'Oh, yes,' he said. 'We were going to get married, once, long ago.'

I absorbed this in silence. Uncle Fintan seemed on the point of going to sleep.

There was something I needed to tell him. I'd been putting it off. 'Uncle Fintan, I met Nicky Fay when I was in Belfast.'

With effort, he turned his head and opened his eyes.

'He told me to tell you . . . He gave me a recording for George — it was that meeting in Blackpool — and he said to tell you it wouldn't cause you any more trouble.'

Uncle Fintan mumbled into his mask. 'Closing the stable door.' I wasn't sure I'd heard him right.

A little while later I stood to go. As I bent to kiss him goodbye he grasped my hand. 'Cate!' he whispered. He scrabbled at the oxygen mask and pulled it away from his face. 'It was coming for a long time. If it hadn't been Eddie's book she would have found some other reason.'

I nodded. 'OK. Goodbye, Uncle Fintan — I love you.'

★   ★   ★

Diane clapped her hands for silence. 'Now, we have *three* more rehearsals before the Christmas concert, all right? Some of you have work to do between now and then. You know who you are. Tenors, Matthew will not be joining us for this concert after all, so sing up.'

The rehearsal went well — the Bernstein, in particular, was starting to sound pretty good.

At break time, Joan clapped her hands to get everyone's attention, and announced that she and Val proposed to make honest women of each other in the spring. They would, of course, be needing a choir for the occasion.

Text message. Matthew Taylor. 'Cate, I know you're upset. You're right, and I'm so, so sorry about everything. But please don't leave it like this. Please talk to me. (990)'
Delete.

★ ★ ★

'I was in with Fintan yesterday, Caitlín, and he says you visit him all the time.'

I looked in vain for the unspoken reproach. 'I go when I can,' I said. 'He's bored rigid in that place.'

'Well, I'm very glad to hear you're making the effort. He appreciates it, you know.' Mum's tone was warm and uncomplicated, and I felt a rush of affection for her, for all of them. I turned my attention back to my dessert.

I didn't mention that my work on Eddie MacDevitt's memoir had given me a rich vein of conversation to explore with Uncle Fintan, who was recovering nicely and eager to talk about his old friend's book. He wanted to hear all about my meeting with Nicky Fay, and I told him, although I omitted the part about my arrest. He was amused to hear about the memory stick — said that Nicky had always loved having the latest gadget. He was planning to ask George for a copy of the recording, for old times' sake.

During another visit, he told me with rare animation about how he'd collected Eddie's manuscript when he and Auntie Rosemary were on holiday in Spain, sneaking out of the apartment while she was having a siesta.

When I recounted one of the book's more dramatic anecdotes, he said, 'Ah, Eddie's an exaggerator, Cate, he's always. I hope George is reining him in a bit. Don't believe more than half. It wasn't nearly as exciting as he seems to . . . ' He turned to look out the window, then continued almost to himself, 'I'll tell you, if I wrote my memoirs, nobody would publish them, because most of the time I was up to nothing at all.'

★ ★ ★

Dad placed his knife and fork carefully together on his picked-clean plate. 'That was splendid!' he announced. He raised his glass and beamed round the table. 'To Nora and Rosemary!' The family dutifully followed suit.

Christmas in Ardee was always elaborate, but this year Mum and Auntie Rosemary had pulled out all the stops. It was clear that this was mainly for Uncle Fintan's benefit. He was out, and home, and still slightly bewildered at the reprieve his wife had granted him. He had been silent through most of the meal, but apparently out of contentment, rather than fear.

I sat at the table feeling empty and brittle, like a seaworn shell, despite being stuffed full. I was two people: one the festive Christmas daughter, the other in a state of explosion, spattered around the walls.

Mum had asked, as we set out smoked salmon in the kitchen earlier, 'Would your boyfriend like to come for a meal some time before the New Year?'

I took care to breathe evenly. 'Actually, we broke up.'

'Oh, dear, I'm sorry, love,' said Mum, trying to hide her good cheer. 'Still, chin up, eh? It's not the end of the world.'

Now Auntie Rosemary was calling for attention. 'It's important to remember at this time of year all those people we loved who are no longer with us.' She raised her glass. 'To absent friends!'

★   ★   ★

Denise's New Year's Eve party was as much a fixture as Christmas itself. I was exhausted and despondent all day, but as the evening approached I ground into gear and forced myself into party clothes, if not mood. I had a vile head-cold, and I'd almost certainly have to interact with Denise's rat of a cousin. A hard, mirror-like bonhomie would surely get me through.

I put off my arrival until after ten, by which time there were enough people there that I did not have to make more than superficial conversation with any of them. There was dancing, in which I participated gratefully, and there were lots of foreigners, for some reason, to whom I held forth at length about the joys of living in Dublin.

The college gang were there, and at one point we all happened to congregate by the kitchen door.

'So, is your Brit still on the scene?' Fenian Mick asked, leaning in to give me a nudge.

'Nope!' I forced a grin . . . managed not to double over with the pain. 'Didn't last.' There was no way I could possibly explain to them what had really happened. That gulf again. I was marooned.

'Ah well,' Noreen said. 'Plenty more fish in the sea.'

'Yeah, but the problem is, fish are terrible in bed.'

I got a laugh.

A couple of hot whiskeys cleared my stuffed-up head a bit, but all the same, by the time the bouncing, roaring countdown arrived I was aching for my bed.

'Happy New Year!' I shouted, over and over, grudgingly allowing that it was good, once again, to spend this moment with old friends.

Five past midnight. Text message. I hastened to open it. 'Happy New Year!'

It was from Joan.

Oh.

★ ★ ★

Uncle Fintan's heart stopped as he sat reading in his favourite armchair on the afternoon of New Year's Day. His new pacemaker couldn't keep up. Auntie Rosemary came into the sitting room with a tray of tea and biscuits to find him slumped there, the newspaper sliding off his knee.

Auntie Rosemary phoned an ambulance first, then phoned Mum. Mum phoned me, and the family converged on Swords. I arrived as the ambulance was pulling out of the driveway. I parked on the street, behind Dad's car. Mum answered the door and explained that Uncle Fintan's body had been taken to the mortuary. An undertaker was due in the morning.

Auntie Rosemary was sitting in the kitchen without her glasses on, drinking sherry, looking lost and white. She barely acknowledged my arrival. I kissed her cold cheek and set about making myself useful.

The next few days passed in the sort of blur I'd heard about, but never experienced until now. I slept at home with my family, going with them to Swords each morning, participating in discussions with the undertaker, making pot after pot of tea. Mum, Dad and Auntie Rosemary seemed to respond to the shock by slowing down, spending hours over every decision, eating little, speaking in monotones.

I couldn't bear them. I was all action, finding comfort in efficiency and speed. I organized the funeral notices, spoke to the florist, made endless lists. It was like that for Mícheál, as well. To my utter astonishment he began producing plain but tasty and nourishing food for us — and snapping at us like Mum if we didn't eat it all up.

Conversations were filled with long silences. On the second day after Uncle Fintan's death, as we were drinking tea round the kitchen table before getting ready for the removal, Auntie Rosemary announced suddenly that she would be selling the house in Terenure. 'The probate will take a little while,' she told me, 'and I'm not in any rush. But I wanted you to know so you could keep an eye out for a new place.'

'Thanks,' I said. I added this to my

unwieldy heap of things to deal with.

Uncle Fintan, it turned out, had left instructions about funeral music: Bach and Fauré, Ó Riada's 'Ár n-Athair' and an uilleann-piper to play at the end. The choir rallied round with grace and generosity, and after some dithering over whether it would be all right to have a Protestant organist, I contacted Tom's partner, Steve, who was willing.

George gave me the week off work and told me more than once that he'd do everything he could to help. He appreciated that he was not welcome in Swords, but he would see me at the church.

★ ★ ★

Text message. Matthew Taylor. 'Heard the sad news about your uncle. I'm so very sorry. Hope you're doing OK. M. xx'

I kept that one for two days before deleting it.

★ ★ ★

At the removal, I sat in the front row, between Auntie Rosemary and Mum, and stood up to receive condolences when the ceremony was over. Most of the people I didn't recognize, but of course there were lots of relatives, and neighbours with familiar faces. Aidan and Sheila were there, and it was odd to shake hands with them, knowing — as they did not — that they would soon have to move house.

When George and Paula came past they nodded wordlessly at Auntie Rosemary, who nodded back, eyes full of grief. They didn't shake hands.

The church was full, and before half the mourners had filed past — each one clasping or hugging and nodding and saying 'sorry, sorry, I'm so sorry' — my face ached from the awkward smiling, and the fingers of my right hand felt numb and useless. The church was too bright. Four white glass globes, suspended above the altar, glared at me. My feet were cold, my head hot, my heart heavy.

Towards the end of the apparently endless line, there came a group of four men who seemed to stand our from the crowd. It might have been the way they held themselves, heads hunching forward in earnest solemnity, or it might have been their lined faces, skewed noses, shrewd and watchful eyes. I felt Auntie Rosemary stiffen as the first of them approached and took her hand.

'Patrick Spillane,' he murmured. His voice was low, and crackled with phlegm. 'I knew your husband well.'

'I know,' Auntie Rosemary said. 'Thank you for coming.' When she let go of his hand she drew hers back towards herself as though it were hurt.

Spillane moved on to shake my hand, with 'sorry for your trouble', and Auntie Rosemary said, 'thank you, thank you,' and did not relax until all four had passed by.

When we finally left the bright space of the church and emerged into the barbarous evening, we found that it had started to snow. 'The forecast was right,' Dad said, looking up at the flakes tumbling in silhouette against the streetlight. 'They're saying it'll be country-wide.'

'Snow was general,' I whispered faintly to myself.

Spillane and his three friends were among the few mourners still standing around in front of the porch. They huddled in dark overcoats, in a group on their own, collars turned up against the softly falling snow. Auntie Rosemary gripped my arm when she saw them. 'Don't go anywhere, please,' she muttered. I laid my hand over hers and left it there, like a promise.

'We wanted a word,' Spillane said, turning, his eyes beady, the eyebrows a single bushy line. He advanced on Auntie Rosemary, who failed to stop herself from recoiling.

Dad did a little sliding step on the tarmac, placing himself between the family and the four men. 'Now, lookit. This isn't the time or the place,' he said, and I heard in his voice the rising intonation that meant he was about to lose his temper.

The group swung their attention to him, a gesture not without a hint of violence. Dad paused, took in a big shuddering breath and squared his shoulders.

And suddenly there was George Sweeney, inserting himself neatly into the group and saying, with his easy smile, 'Ah, Packie Spillane, for goodness' sake, is it yourself? God, it's been years, hasn't it? You haven't changed a bit! Pity to meet on such a sad occasion. Oh — were you in the middle of? I'm sorry . . . '

'No, no, no,' Dad said, ceding gratefully. 'We need to be getting back: there'll be people arriving at the house.' He stretched out his arm like a harbour and manoeuvred Auntie Rosemary and me back towards Mum and Mícheál. We headed for the car, the black-coated driver holding open the door.

As we drove away I looked out the window and saw my old friends from the Special Branch swing out of a parking space across the road. I felt almost kindly towards them.

The Swords house was full of talk and laughter and the clatter of forks and plates, and even Auntie Rosemary seemed to have relaxed a little. The doorbell rang as I came through the hall, and I opened it as I'd been doing all evening.

George stood in the porch. He had a package in his hands, wrapped in brown paper, held slightly away from his body, almost reverently.

'I'm sorry,' he said. 'I won't come in.'

'Hi.'

'If I could have a word with your mother?'

'Sure,' I said, and trailed off. I held the door wide open.

'I'm not coming in,' George repeated.

'Oh, grand, yeah. Sorry. I'll get her.'

I found Mum in the sitting room, and my whispered message sent her hurrying to the hall. A few minutes later she came back, carrying the brown paper package, to ask where Dad was. I pointed her to where he was holding court in the dining room. My attention was claimed then by Denise's parents, who were determined to express to me the full extent of their sympathy, and I forgot about George until later, when all the guests had gone.

'Paddy?' said Mum, as we sat in the kitchen

having one for the road. She looked utterly worn.

Dad visibly gathered his strength and began, 'Rosemary? There was a deputation.'

'What?' Auntie Rosemary's eyes were glassy, her face like a rubber mask.

I saw Dad hesitate, trying to pick out a safe route across the mire. 'George Sweeney called to the door earlier. He didn't want to come in.'

Auntie Rosemary's expression was for a moment transformed, eyes blazing, mouth set in an unforgiving line. Then her lips parted, and she blinked slowly and let out a tiny sigh. 'What did he come for, then?'

'Fintan's . . . old friends,' Dad said, feeling his way. 'George talked to them outside the church after we left. They were hoping.' He stopped, squeezing his eyes shut and passing the back of his hand over his forehead. 'Ah. As a mark of respect.'

'What respect?' Auntie Rosemary said, pausing dangerously on the consonants. 'What do they want?'

Dad put both hands on the table and leaned forward. 'They have a tricolour for the coffin,' he said softly. 'George brought it round.'

Auntie Rosemary said nothing for a long time. Eventually she drew a breath that sounded as though it came from several miles beneath us. 'No guns,' she said.

Dad said, 'Ah, no, Rosemary, that was all over years ago.'

★　★　★

The snow didn't stick. The next morning a stinging sleet swiped at us as we scurried from the funeral car into the church. We were early, of course, but the place was half-full already. Mum was driving me mad with her fussing over shoes and hair and flowers — more like a mother of the bride than a sister of the dear departed. I bit the insides of my cheeks and reminded myself that there are many ways of coping with grief. Just some are more tolerable than others.

Diane had asked me if I wanted to join the choir, but I'd declined. They sang beautifully without me, bringing a sweet salve to the bitterness of the day. I sang the psalm myself, alone at the lectern, looking down at the coffin, with its burnished fittings, its coating of fine water droplets, and trying not to think about how much I'd miss the man inside it.

After the ceremony the sleet had abated enough to allow the grand old tradition of standing around outside the church to proceed without undue discomfort. We huddled in little groups that dissolved and reformed in a ceaseless dance. The choir came and queued up to hug me, and I thanked them with brimming eyes.

Near the church gates I encountered George and Paula talking to a bulky man I recognized. 'You remember John Lawless, Cate?' George said, putting a hand on my arm.

Matthew's supervisor. I concealed my wince well enough, I thought. 'Yes, we met last summer at the Bell Books office.'

'That's right,' confirmed Lawless. He enveloped my hand in both of his. 'I'm sorry for your loss. Your uncle was a fine man.'

'Thank you,' I said. 'We'll all miss him.'

It was time to go to the cemetery. I drifted back towards my family at the car.

'Hey,' said Mícheál as I reached them. He was looking over my shoulder. 'Isn't that your boyfriend over there?'

A painful shiver spread rapidly from my neck to my toes. I forced myself to turn and look where Mícheál was pointing.

He was dead right. Over by the railings stood Matthew, by himself, apparently reading something on his phone. What the fuck did he think he was doing here? As I spotted him he looked up and saw me. I bit down hard on my tongue, stiffened my face and managed to keep hold of myself.

Mícheál said, 'Are you not going over?'

I shook my head.

'You have time, sure. Mam, Cate's boyfriend is here.'

No. Idiot.

Mum had her arm round Auntie Rosemary. She looked over her shoulder at us. 'What's that?'

'We're not going this second, are we?' Mícheál persisted.

'We are, yes, why?'

'Cate's boyfriend is here.'

'He's not . . . ' I said. My throat was sudden agony. 'I'm not talking to him. We don't have time.'

Mum scanned the crowd with narrowed eyes.

'Look, he's over there by the railings,' Mícheál said. 'Oh, no, he's gone.'

'Come on, we're going,' I said. Without waiting for the undertaker's man, I wrenched open the door of the car and flung myself inside. After a few moments the others followed.

Mum was livid, I could see. She sat in beside me and murmured, with barely moving lips, 'That was hardly appropriate, now, to use the funeral as an excuse to try and see you.'

'I don't think that's what it was, Mum,' I whispered. I wasn't capable of speaking aloud.

'Well, why else? Did he know Fintan? Had he any personal connection? Because the Brits don't go to funerals the way we do. It's not the done thing.'

I locked my jaw and looked away. My thoughts were spiralling into dark places. Because either Mum was right, and Matthew *had* come to see me . . . or he had come for other reasons, which I couldn't countenance at all.

We arrived at the cemetery, and the coffin was hefted by four sombre professionals. Dad, his face a mixture of reverence and sheepishness, shook out the tricolour and laid it across the top.

Walking to the grave, I fell back a little from the rest of the family. My fingers shook as I fished my phone out of my coat pocket.

Text message to Matthew Taylor. 'Please just leave me alone.'

Send.

I didn't know how I was going to get through this awful day.

★ ★ ★

January unfolded like a stained, ash-strewn carpet: the aftermath of the excesses of December and the surreal week of Uncle Fintan's death. In my grief, I took pleasure in the return to austerity and silence, calm greyness after the relentless green and red and gold, welcome banality after the taut and solemn procedures of the funeral.

The filth of my flat, however, was getting to me. It was weeks since I'd done any kind of regular housework. I couldn't even walk around without shoes on, for fear of what I might feel underfoot.

I attacked it one Saturday, scrubbing the bathroom first from top to bottom, then tackling the kitchen. When both gleamed, I began to tidy my bedroom, which was silted up with dirty laundry, unfiled papers and plain old rubbish.

I found my concert clothes from Belfast still stuffed in a green supermarket bag, forgotten in a corner. I picked out the black dress, and underneath it I found my pinchy, sparkly shoes, still muddy — the shoes that Matthew had gone back to retrieve for me, even though I'd been running from him, even though he'd been the gunman, the spy, the betrayer of my trust and of my heart.

I cried, then, for what seemed like hours, kneeling on my bedroom floor, body draped over my bed.

When I'd finished crying, and before I could change my mind, I went and found my phone.

'OK, if you still want to talk, let's talk.'
Send.

★ ★ ★

We met the next day at the Papal Cross in the Phoenix Park — Matthew's suggestion. He said he'd gone there when he'd first arrived in Dublin. I'd said, 'Let's go somewhere we can walk.'

The wind whipped at us as we stood at the foot of the cross, craning our heads back to watch it fall towards us through the clouds. Matthew had a new coat, long, dark grey, with a broad collar. The ends of his hair brushed at the material in a way that made me ache.

'You're looking well,' he said, after our initial greeting.

I glared at my feet, willing this treacherous wave of pleasure to pass.

We left the mound and walked slowly away from the cross, down the long flight of concrete steps to level ground. I was aware of every breath, struggling to keep myself on course, floundering. We said nothing as we made our descent.

At the bottom, I decided that enough was enough. I stopped dead and rounded on Matthew.

'So are we going to talk, then?' I spoke like steel.

'That's the idea,' he said.

'Are you going to tell me the truth?'

'I'll tell you everything I can.' He looked straight at me, and I realized — suddenly, startlingly — that he was being entirely open with me. Maybe for the first time since I'd known him, the barriers were nowhere to be discerned.

And suddenly, that cut no ice with me. It was too late. This whole thing was a bad idea. I was overcome by a wash of fury. 'Is *Matthew Taylor* even your real fucking name, by the way?'

'Yes, it is,' he said, and despite myself, I believed him.

'Are you armed?' I sneered.

'No!'

'And what about the day you turned up at my uncle's funeral?' I put as much spitting and clawing into my words as they'd take.

He bent his head, brow furrowed. 'Cate, I'm sorry, I know, that was stupid. I wasn't thinking rationally. It was completely insensitive. I shouldn't have gone.'

'No kidding,' I said, and started walking again towards a likely-looking path. I had no route in mind. Ravens croaked in the old grey trees. I stuck my hands far down into my coat pockets, searching for a bit of warmth.

'I missed you,' Matthew said.

'Yeah, well, I bloody missed you too, that day in Belfast.'

'I know.'

'What the hell were you doing, anyway?'

'I was drafted in at the last moment to . . .' He heaved a sigh. 'Look, there was a lot of sensitive stuff going on in Belfast that day. I was there on the ground, and I had an assignment. It's not important now.'

I bit back my exasperation. 'So why did you run away from the police when they were busy arresting me? Weren't you meant to be on their side, or something?'

'It was complicated. I wasn't strictly meant to be at the Waterfront at all, you see.'

'Why not?'

'I'd . . . well, it was all a bit of a mess at that point. And you see, I couldn't allow myself to be searched, because they'd have found the gun, and then all hell would've broken loose. And most likely I wouldn't have been in such a good position to help you. So I made a risky decision, I suppose.'

I noticed how he hadn't actually answered my question. Old habits die hard. Still, he was clearly making some kind of an effort. 'What did you do?' I asked.

'Melted into the crowd.' He made a melty

gesture with his fingers. 'Got the hell out of
there. I rejoined . . . I went back to where I
was meant to be. But I had secured one
crucial piece of data.'

'Oh?'

'Sergeant Hall's badge number.'

'And?'

'Well, that allowed me to find out where
they'd taken you. I went there as soon as I
could — after my assignment finished. They'd
got their knickers in a monumental twist
about that recording Nicky Fay had given
you, but I was able to tell them what it was.'

I turned my head slightly to frown at him.
He was looking terribly pleased with himself.

He went on, 'I also had the privilege of
seeing their faces when you started singing
scales. I assured them that no terrorist . . . '
He trailed off as I stopped walking.

So he had watched me on CCTV. I could
think of nothing to say. I stood there, gasping
for breath.

'What?' he said. 'Too soon?'

'Too fucking right!' I got moving again.

There was a track leading up a bank beside
the path; I took it. It was narrow, so that
Matthew had to drop behind me. I felt a
furious sort of affirmation as I reached the
top, panting, and kept going, skirting a large
playing field on which half a dozen

weather-hardened boys were wielding hurleys, and making for some young woodland. I was not crying, though the wind was drawing water from my eyes.

Matthew caught up easily once we were on level ground again, his long legs scissoring along beside me. The path through the trees was wide enough for both of us. 'Cate,' he said. He was out of breath, I was pleased to hear.

I twitched a shoulder at him.

'Cate — oh, come on.'

'Fuck off.'

'Cate, please don't do this.'

'I don't want to talk to you.'

'Cate, be reasonable.'

I stopped dead, swung round. 'You patronizing bastard.' I spoke calmly, the words wrenched from my stinging, breath-starved lungs.

'Look, I'm just trying to — ' A sharp exhalation, and when he spoke again it was softer. 'I'm just trying to explain. You have to believe me. I've said I'm sorry. I am sorry. Cate.'

'Noted.' Gritted teeth.

'Look, I really want to work this out.' There was a rasp in his voice. 'Can't you understand how hard this is for me?'

'Oh, for fuck's sake! Are you completely

stupid?' I ignored his raised eyebrows and pressed on. 'Does it actually come as a surprise to you that I'm upset about this? You *watched* me in that room! You've been lying to me ever since we met! In what universe would my reaction be unreasonable? You're a fucking *spy*, Matthew.'

His face hardened, and he turned from me. 'Well, I suppose I thought it might be safe to assume you'd be relieved that I was an intelligence agent rather than a terrorist.' His voice was full of controlled anger.

I kept quiet.

'But then again, this is Ireland.' Muttered, just loud enough to make sure I heard.

I rose to it, too. Didn't even pause. 'How dare you! How fucking *dare* you! You arrogant prick! You swallow whatever ridiculous propaganda they feed baby spies over there in your poncey, over-funded London Spy A-fucking-cademy, and then you come over here and assume you can make sweeping statements about the way things are. You don't have a clue.' I was clawing and spitting even more than before.

'Oh, and you know the way things are, do you?'

'I know how arrogant and blinkered and fucking *ridiculous* it is for a British bastard to say that Ireland is pro-terrorist.'

He sprayed laughter in my face. 'Oh, don't come over all moral high ground now, Cate Houlihan. You're the one with a fucking gun-runner for an uncle.'

I tripped over my reply, as what Matthew had just said trickled through to my brain. Our eyes met. Mine, treacherous, began to brim with tears. 'What did you say?'

'My god, Cate, do stop pretending to be so naïve.'

'What? My uncle? What?'

He sighed, his expression disbelieving. 'Your uncle the suspected bank robber? Your uncle the convicted arms smuggler? Your *uncle*, Cate — Fintan Sullivan, RI-fucking-P. For crying out loud, wake up!'

There was a long silence. I had no words.

'Oh, my god,' said Matthew, in an entirely different tone. 'You didn't know?'

The boil was lanced. Loops of deflated tension hung from the trees like opera-house swags. We couldn't look at each other. I cried silently. Matthew stood with his face in his hands.

Eventually, I took a step towards him. He looked up. 'I didn't know,' I said.

But here was the thing I realized as I spoke: I did know. I'd known all my life. I'd simply kept it secret from myself until now.

I knew, in the way you know your address

or your granny's birthday, that Uncle Fintan had been involved in some questionable activities in his youth. But somehow, I'd managed to assume that it was no more than what most people were doing at the time. My own law-abiding father, after all, had gone so far as to throw a half-brick at a window of the British Embassy after the Bloody Sunday massacre in 1972. Uncle Fintan had been a tearaway, was the impression I'd grown up with, who might have done one or two things to blush about, all forgiven and forgotten now.

But gun-running? Bank robbery? I tried to reconcile these notions with the man I'd known. The mild, smiling uncle, whose sentences never quite, who had always tended, unlike other adults, to engage me in conversation, enjoying and encouraging our shared interests. The man who helped me out when the constraints of home life grew too great to be borne.

The man whose old associates made his widow flinch. Whose friendships, in life, were enough to rock his marriage. Whose sister . . . Why was I thinking about Mum now? I recalled her vehemence, all through my childhood — 'This is about *blood*.'

But anyway! Everyone agreed that partition was a dreadful burden on Ireland — North and South — and that those who took up the armed struggle, while not exactly to be applauded, were nonetheless doing something that a compassionate person couldn't whole-heartedly condemn.

Except . . . of course . . . *not* everyone agreed, as I'd eventually discovered at university. Truth be told, I no longer agreed myself. And yet, it turned out, the ancient assumptions of my childhood had not caught up.

A memory from Irish college sprang to mind — the whole lot of us, singing the college song at one of the daily flag cere-monies. Declaring ourselves in *aghaidh gaill sa tír seo* — 'against foreigners in this country' — belting out with muscular enthusiasm those rolling phrases full of cheerful xenopho-bia and vague exhortations to readiness. We'd sung it with such fierce, uncomplicated pride, and followed it up with the national anthem, including the extra verse that felt like a shared secret. At fourteen, I'd swallowed it whole, along with all the other rhetoric.

It was a generational thing, I suddenly realized, this attempt to pass on beliefs and attitudes to a fresh cohort. But without the experience to underpin them, no matter how heartfelt, beliefs and attitudes ring hollow. Our parents' conclusions do not fit us: if we try to adopt them wholesale, we warp ourselves.

God, the sooner Mícheál got out of there, the better.

★ ★ ★

The light was beginning to fade, the tree trunks to turn blacker. A fine mist was contemplating turning into rain. Matthew spoke at last. 'Cate, I'm so sorry. I shouldn't have lost my temper.'

'It's OK,' I heard myself say.

'Should I go?'

Should he go? The question seemed absurd, an irrelevant speck in this awful lump of knowledge I was chewing. 'No, I want you to stay,' I said.

'Do you think we could go somewhere warmer?'

'My car is parked back by the Papal Cross.' We turned, oriented ourselves, and set off.

We did not speak on the way back to the car. My mind was boiling. Had Matthew really been sent to spy on me because my uncle was once involved in Republican activities? If so, it just showed how blinkered and small-minded these people were. Some *intelligence* service. I thought hard, and could not identify a single thing I'd done that might suggest my sympathies tended in an unsavoury, let alone an illegal, direction.

He'd lost his temper. He must have been caught in the heat of argument. Exaggerating for effect — making me think all that nonsense about my lovely uncle, who was barely cold in his grave. Bastard. I felt a roar building in my chest, and balled my fists in my pockets to steady myself.

Think, Cate. *Be reasonable*, as the man said.

We reached the car; I opened it and got in. I watched Matthew fold himself into his seat and nearly started crying again. I wanted so much to clamber over the handbrake and hug him. He was a liar and a traitor. He was a spy. He had spoken ill of the dead.

I tried not to look at him. My face burned.

'Cate, are you all right?' His voice was once again soft. Spoke to the centre of me. I did my best to push him out. But even as I tried to collect my thoughts to deliver the cutting arguments that would make Matthew take back what he had said about Uncle Fintan, I felt my anger dissipate.

He sat perfectly still, waiting. I started the engine and backed slowly out of my space, then rolled towards the car-park exit.

'Not really,' I said. 'Are you?'

'Far from it.' We were silent for another few

minutes, and then he said, 'There is one thing you should know.'

'What's that?'

'I'm not — I'm not with the intelligence services any more. I resigned.'

We had joined a small queue to turn on to the main road. I looked at him. 'Wow.' I moved out and headed downhill, towards the quays.

'Well . . . to be totally honest, they offered me the option. I wasn't really cut out for it. I'd known that, even before. That life — it wasn't for me. But, well. Things got a bit more complicated after Belfast. I was pretty seriously out of line.'

'Hey, you did a great job of making sure I didn't blow the place up, didn't you?' I couldn't keep the bitterness out of my voice.

'Oh, Cate, don't be like that.' Tired and pleading, no longer angry.

'Sorry, Matthew, but you're the one who was sent over here to spy on me.'

'Ah,' he said. 'No. I'm sorry. I haven't been clear, have I?'

'What do you mean?'

'My being sent here didn't have anything to do with you.'

'But you said — '

'No, I originally came over because of John.'

'John Lawless?'

'Yes. Leading expert on Irish Republicanism, and apparently a little too cosy with
various breakaway groups. My mission was to
worm my way into his confidence.'

I gaped at him. 'And what did this
. . . *staunch nationalist with dissident Republican connections* make of an inquisitive Brit
showing up to learn his secrets?'

Matthew smiled, and something in me
crumbled. 'Well, I've studied the subject quite
extensively — I do know my stuff, so that
helped. Also, it didn't hurt that my research
was trying to prove duplicity on the part of
the British. And I played up the Antrim
connection.'

'Your cousins that you used to visit?'

'Indeed. But you're right. I hadn't got very
far.'

We had hit the eternal crawl of cars along
the river. I was still mired in confusion. 'How
did you know all that stuff about Uncle
Fintan?' I took a deep breath and hoped I
wasn't going to find out something irrepa-
rable. 'Did he — in Belfast — was he
. . . involved?'

Matthew shook his head. 'No. He'd been in
retirement for decades. The things I mentioned, I learned when I was investigating
Eddie MacDevitt's book.'

Oh, of course. That book was at the bottom

of practically everything, it seemed.

'The government got wind of one of the claims MacDevitt was making.'

'Which government? The British?'

'Yes, the British. Though of course the Irish were fairly interested as well — as your friends in the car with the musical number plate will attest. Anyway, they wanted to find out what he was basing this one particular claim on, and whether it was likely to cause the British government any real trouble, and as I was in Dublin anyway, they asked me to look into it.'

'Ha,' I said. 'Not only were you in Dublin, you also happened to be in a choir with the unlikely linchpin of Bell Books, yes?'

He spoke very quietly. 'I'm sorry, no. I joined the choir later on.'

'Because I was in it?'

'I'm afraid so.'

I set that aside for later consideration, and scrolled through what I could recall of Eddie's book, trying to pick out any assertion that might have alarmed the British government. Trying now to see it from a totally different perspective. I could think of a few things in there that would embarrass our own politicians — or should, if they had any compunction — but the British? I could think of nothing. 'So, what was the claim, then?'

Matthew took a breath and held it for a long moment. 'Cate, I need you to know that I'm trusting you. I should categorically not be telling you any of this.'

'Oh,' I said. 'Well, you know, I'm not going to . . . I won't blow your cover.'

'OK.' He closed his eyes and went on. 'Eddie claimed that in 1974 he'd taken a huge personal risk and informed an MI5 agent that the IRA were planning to bomb Birmingham. He said that the British did nothing about it.'

'But why would that cause trouble now, when it happened in 1974?' As soon as I'd spoken I realized how stupid I sounded. All my life I'd been hearing about *Birmingham* — that savage injustice done by the British to six innocent men, whose eventual exoneration epitomized 'too little, too late'. But before the injustice, and separate from it, there had been a crime. People had died.

Matthew said, 'Seriously? You don't think British people would be a tiny bit put out if they thought the government knew in advance about the IRA's plans and did nothing?'

A small spark of outrage. 'The British government did plenty, Matthew. They weren't exactly on their best behaviour after Birmingham, were they?'

'Well, no. But that was afterwards. And the

326

British public has magnanimously forgiven them for that little justice wobble.'

I frowned, confused. 'But that still doesn't make sense. Eddie's book is only at proof stage now. How did the British government find out about it so early?'

'Martin Bright saw the first draft. He ran it past his lawyer, as a matter of routine, and the lawyer showed it to someone at the Foreign Office.'

Now, who was Martin Bright again? 'Oh,' I said. 'The London co-publisher . . . But hang on, I don't remember that part at all.' Was I so naïve, to use Matthew's word, that I'd missed it?

'Ah. Well. Actually, as it happens, that particular claim didn't make it into the final version.'

'Why not?'

'Pressure from the Foreign Office. The lawyer warned Bright that he'd be in hot water if he published the claim. Bright made George delete it. George did as he was told, despite Nicky Fay's attempt to change his mind, because he needed the rights money. And I . . . checked to make sure it had gone.' He sniffed. 'Thanks again for that.'

'Mmm.' I asked the obvious next question: 'Was it true?'

'I couldn't possibly comment.'

This was too much. 'You're awful smug, you know, for a man who's being driven down the north quays by the woman he's been lying to for months. I should probably throw you out of the car.'

He seemed not quite sure I was joking. I wasn't either.

We fell silent, rolling slowly along.

OK. If I wanted to see this thing through, I was going to have to keep asking the hard questions.

'What really happened in Belfast? What were you doing?'

'I'm sorry. I can't go into the details. It was a surveillance job.'

'They gave you a gun.'

'Yes, well. The people I was watching weren't very nice. I knew I'd miss the rehearsal — that couldn't be helped, and I'd told Diane — but I was still hoping to make it to the Waterfront in time for the performance.' He shifted uncomfortably in his seat, angling himself away from me, turning to look out the window. His fingers came up to pinch the tip of his nose.

I waited for him to go on, and when he didn't I turned to look at him. His eyes were dark with emotion.

Eventually he said, 'I got a phone call at around half past seven from one of my colleagues, who was in a real state over a security breach at the Waterfront. At first I couldn't work out why he'd phoned me, but eventually I realized . . . it was you.'

The hairs on the backs of my hands actually stood on end. I felt the skin buzzing.

Matthew said again, 'You were the security breach.' His tone was gentle, ruminative, otherworldly.

I listened to the blood rushing in my ears . . . 'What? How on earth? I don't get it.'

'I know. I argued with them. I said there was no way you were a risk. It was a nightmare.'

'So, what . . . did they think I was somebody else?'

'No.' He hesitated. 'They knew who you were, all right.'

'They knew? But that means . . . ' That meant . . . *that meant* that the British government considered me a threat of some kind. Panic began to rise, and, twining through it, fury. I gripped the steering wheel. 'OK, so, they have, like, a file on me, or something?'

'You're in the database, yeah.' He was trying to speak casually.

The road here was completely choked up. We were going nowhere fast. I turned my head and looked him straight in the eye. 'Why's that, Matthew? Why am I in the fucking database? Did you put me in there?'

'No! You've been there for years, as far as I know. It was nothing to do with me.'

'Years? Really?' I raised my eyebrows and waited.

He met my challenge. 'OK, then, let's see. You come from an actively Republican family, more than one member of which has been tried for terrorism-related crimes.'

More than one? Matthew raised a hand as though to say, 'Bear with me.' I let it pass.

'You've attended meetings of Sinn Féin Republican Youth, and you're the author of 'Thirty-two Counties: An Honourable Goal', published in *Trinity News* as part of a series of political opinion pieces.'

'But that was years ago!' I felt sick.

'Five years ago, yes.'

'I was in first year! I don't think that way any more.'

'Well, what do you want me to say? I'm not trying to defend them, I'm just telling you what was there to see. So. You live in a flat owned by Fintan Sullivan, who for all his excellent qualities . . . and I'm not saying he wasn't a fantastic uncle . . . was known to have ongoing social connections with Republican terrorists, active and retired. You pay a rent that can only be described as nominal to a man who isn't exactly rolling in cash. Your downstairs neighbours pay four times what you do.'

I blinked at this, but said nothing.

'Then you take a job with George 'Mad' Sweeney — founder member of Laochra na Saoirse — and you act as a messenger between him and Sullivan. It's not all that odd that we might have wanted to keep tabs on you.'

'Now, hang on,' I said, grasping at a passing straw. 'What has George got to do with any of this? Laochra na Saoirse is completely defunct. I mean . . . I know Eddie's book will ruffle a few feathers — but it's not a crime to tell the truth.'

'Certainly not, but when you try to tell uncomfortable truths about powerful people you tend to run into difficulty.'

'OK, I'll grant you that.'

'Though to be fair, George is pretty good at what he does. He's thorough. I like that in a publisher.'

Another thought struck me. 'Wait a minute. If I'm in your precious database, why was Carmina Urbana allowed anywhere near Belfast? Why not just cancel us? Find another choir? Or tell Diane she'd have to let them prune out the bad wood?'

'Well, first of all, it was sensitive. You'll recall Diane's history?'

'Oh! The Jennifer Mallon thing.'

'Yes. Bit of a tender spot for the government. Plus you've got the whole Daintree business. Hot young composer from a mixed background. Massed voices of the two islands singing as one, and so forth. Highly symbolic. It would have been rather difficult for the British to suggest that Carmina Urbana wasn't on the level.'

'But we *are* on the level!'

'Yes, I know. And fortunately, it didn't come to that, because . . . well, because, to be perfectly frank, nobody put two and two together.'

'What do you mean?'

'Human error. Nobody cross-checked. The MacDevitt book and the Belfast summit were being handled by different people. And they'd have to have been doing a specific search to spot the connections, anyway, because the database has about four different spellings of your name.'

'What?'

'Yeah.' The air lightened as he ticked off the variations on his fingers: 'Cate-with-a-C, Kate-with-a-K, Caitlín, Houlihan, Ní Uallacháin — we're basically no match for you Irish and your devious naming ways.'

He was humouring me. British intelligence must be well up on the instability of Irish names. Surely.

He went on. 'But then of course you met Nicky Fay that day. Not a good move if you want to avoid attention.'

'What, we met for two minutes. If that.'

'Yes, and he gave you a package,' he said gently. 'Fay was under active surveillance, so they kept an eye on you for the rest of the afternoon. They nearly dropped dead when they saw you march into the Waterfront.'

'Why didn't they stop me there and then?'

'They needed to find out who you were. And they reckoned they had a little bit of time, because the security on the door was good and tight, and the delegates weren't in the building yet. So that's when they went back and did those specific searches. And contacted me.'

My fury flickered again. 'See, what we're avoiding discussing here is the fact that you were *spying* on me.'

'Yes,' he said heavily, his enjoyment snuffed out. He squeezed his eyes shut.

Why did everything have to be so complicated? 'So you believed I might be a terrorist?'

'No. I didn't.'

'What — not cagey enough? Insufficiently glamorous?'

'I just had a feeling I could trust you,' he said miserably.

'Yes, I thought I could fucking trust you, too, until you turned up at the Waterfront with a gun.'

'I know.'

'So . . . you were sent to shoot *me*? Was that it?'

'No. No, I told you. I wasn't supposed to be there. I argued with them, Cate. I tried to tell them you weren't a risk, but they were just looking at the data in front of them. I was afraid you were going to get hurt. So I went to the Waterfront to try and find you. But by the time I arrived the evacuation was already in full swing.'

Much to my surprise, I found that I was driving us to my flat. I wondered if I could bear to let him in there again. I wondered if he realized.

'Ha,' I said. 'And here was I thinking the only vaguely suspicious thing I ever did was my heroic rooftop escape.'

'Indeed. You might like to know, incidentally, I neglected to mention that in my report at the time.'

'Oh,' I said. 'Thanks. I still don't really understand why I did it.' I remembered the night, how I'd been so frightened, how phoning the Gardaí had seemed such an impossibility. 'I suppose I was brought up to distrust the police.'

'You know,' Matthew said, 'I hate to say it, but that tallies pretty closely with the stereotype we have in Britain about the Irish.'

'Of course it does,' I said. 'That doesn't mean it's the whole story.'

'I used to think that if I knew all the facts I'd know the whole story,' said Matthew.

'More fool you.'

We were moving more smoothly now, trundling down Patrick Street towards the canal. I sighed, bone-tired. 'Go back to the bit about resigning from your job. What are you going to do now? In fact, why are you back in Dublin at all?'

He was silent for a long time, looking out his side window. 'Two reasons,' he said at last. 'One, I am in fact genuinely writing that PhD.'

'Oh!' This hadn't remotely occurred to me. 'Even though your supervisor is a Republican dissident?'

'Yes, oddly enough. Although, to be honest, I'm not totally convinced that he is. Meanwhile, by the way, I'm enormously grateful to you for getting that recording from Nicky Fay. I very much doubt I'd have got hold of it otherwise, and it's quite important to my research.'

'Yes, because it shows your civil servant was at that meeting in Blackpool.'

'That's right. You've heard it, then?'

'Just the first few seconds. George wouldn't let me listen to the rest.'

'I'll e-mail it to you if you like. It was also apparently the basis for MacDevitt's claim that he'd warned MI5 about Birmingham.'

'Oh, of course. And does it support the claim?'

'Not really, to be honest. The language is all pretty oblique. I don't know if they actually thought David Cornwell was an agent, or if MacDevitt was just embroidering.'

'Eddie's an exaggerator,' I said, echoing my mild, dead uncle.

I felt sad now, imagining what Uncle Fintan might have said if he'd seen me chatting away to Matthew like this. Not to mention what Mum might say in real life, if things went the way I apparently wanted them to.

I asked, 'What was the second reason?'

Matthew took a breath, and when he spoke it was as though I was hearing his real voice for the first time. 'Cate, I'd like to go out with you properly. No big lie getting in the way.'

'Go on.'

'I want you to be part of my life. I want to be able to tell you what I'm doing, what I'm thinking, who was on the other end of the phone. I know it's a tall order, but do you think we could possibly start again?'

'From the beginning?'

'Da capo.'

We were stopped at a red light. I reached across and took his hand, turned to meet his glistening eyes. The rope of meaning tautened. His hand was warm — real. We smiled at each other, carefully.

I said, 'I'm glad you joined the choir. I'm glad I know you.'

The light turned green; I moved forward. We were nearly home.

Acknowledgements

Thanks to my agent, Zoë Waldie, for being the first industry professional to tell me that my book was worth publishing, for showing what needed to be done to improve it, and for guiding it surefootedly along its path. Thanks to my editor, Margaret Stead, for seeing past my ungainly draft to the novel I'd been hoping to write, and for holding me in the editorial crucible until the one had been transmuted into the other. Thanks to my copyeditor, Tamsin Shelton, for giving the text such thorough attention and for smoothing dozens of rough patches on which an unsuspecting reader might have snagged. (Copyeditors work to make themselves invisible. They should have their praises sung.)

Thanks to Anne Enright. You taught me, back in the last millennium, to grab the guts of a story and kick against cliché. More recently, you offered support both moral and practical (and always kind).

Thanks to Cormac Ó Cuilleanáin and Phyllis Gaffney, first for bringing me up to assume that I could tackle any creative project, and later for all your help with this one — not least that epic title-brainstorming session. (There were other parts in between. Thanks for those too.)

Thanks to Kay Murphy, for always being ready to discuss Irish history and identity, and for those afternoons you spent absorbing the children's energy while I wrestled and raged away at my desk.

Thanks to everyone who read a draft for me — Órla Ní Chuilleanáin, Fionnuala Dillane, Helen Finch, Deirdre Ní Fhloinn and Barry McCrea (twice; you deserve a medal). Thanks to Iseult Fitzgerald and Gillian O'Brien for telling me about political and diplomatic logistics, to Aaron Gray for helping with some Belfast details and to Eoin Ó Cuilleanáin for a conversation about the Gaelic Athletic Association in County Louth. Thanks to the Mornington Singers — all of you, past and present — for inspiration, beauty, harmony and hilarity, and for allowing me to be a mole in your midst all these years. Thanks to the many, many people who weighed in on the internet when I had idiom queries. You are brilliant.

Thanks to Niall Murphy for your poet's eye on my drafts, your bloodyminded belief in my ability to finish this thing, and your agreement (ongoing) to share with me the joyful freedom of true partnership.

Thanks to Oisín Ó Cuilleanáin and Fiachra Murphy for ensuring that *The Living* was not completed until I'd grown up all the way.

We do hope that you have enjoyed reading this large print book.

Did you know that all of our titles are available for purchase?

We publish a wide range of high quality large print books including:
Romances, Mysteries, Classics
General Fiction
Non Fiction and Westerns

Special interest titles available in large print are:
The Little Oxford Dictionary
Music Book
Song Book
Hymn Book
Service Book

Also available from us courtesy of Oxford University Press:
Young Readers' Dictionary
(large print edition)
Young Readers' Thesaurus
(large print edition)

For further information or a free brochure, please contact us at:
Ulverscroft Large Print Books Ltd.,
The Green, Bradgate Road, Anstey,
Leicester, LE7 7FU, England.
Tel: (00 44) 0116 236 4325
Fax: (00 44) 0116 234 0205

THE MIRROR

Richard Skinner

Venice, 1511. Oliva is about to take the veil and become the bride of Christ. When her world is shaken, first by an earthquake and then spiritually, she begins to question her faith and her future. And when she agrees to sit for a renowned portrait painter she discovers how dangerous her reflection can be . . . Erik Satie — composer, dandy, eccentric — is dead. Told he must select a single memory to take with him to the afterlife, he finds himself in limbo. Friendships with his great contemporaries? Nights with his lover? His musical triumphs? How will he choose his own legacy?

SEASON TO TASTE

Natalie Young

Meet Lizzie Prain. Ordinary housewife. Fifty-something. Lives in a cottage in the woods, with her dog Rita. Likes cooking, avoids the neighbours. No one has seen Lizzie's husband, Jacob, for a few days. That's because last Monday, on impulse, Lizzie caved in the back of his head with a spade. And if she's going to embark on the new life she feels she deserves after thirty years in Jacob's shadow, she needs to dispose of his body. Her method appeals to all her practical instincts, though it's not for the faint-hearted. Will Lizzie have the strength to follow it through?

A LIFE LESS LONELY

Jill Barry

A quiet English town is home to Dr Andrea Palmer, the young widow of a military hero and mum to little Josh. Focused upon her son and vulnerable mother, she has no thoughts of finding romance. Events conspire to change that, but she wonders how many times a broken heart can mend . . . Keir is the self-styled bad boy of the consultants' dining room. He dislikes his eligible bachelor tag and anticipates meeting Andrea only because her qualifications perfectly equip her to co-present his findings. When Andrea and Keir meet, each feels a frisson. But flirtatious nurse Moira has other ideas, and is determined to have Keir for herself . . .